More Praise for *LABYRINTH*

This fast paced story of intrigue and bioterror is all too plausible, and it is a page turner. What makes this fascinating reading is the crucial role of scientists and epidemiologists in place of the usual sleuths in unraveling the who-done-it; there are only a few people in the world who have Richard Wenzel's deep insight and expertise in this area, and fewer still who could have brought forth a compelling novel out of that knowledge.

—Abraham Verghese, author of *Cutting for Stone*

At the hands of author Richard Wenzel, today's fears become tomorrow's headlines. When antibiotic-resistant pathogens strike a London hospital, researchers suspect the worst: a microbial hacker has manipulated staph cells into a bio-weapon of terrifying potential. American epidemiologist Jake Evans and MI5's Elizabeth Foster pursue their quarry at a fevered pace, racing like the pulse of one of the infected victims but always a plot twist behind. This is a tale of cross-border intrigue told by a storyteller who knows from the inside the frightening world of infectious diseases and their threat to our society.

—Nelson D. Lankford, author of *Richmond Burning* and *Cry Havoc!*

Labyrinth of Terror, Richard Wenzel's suspenseful new medical thriller, deals with a threat as real as today's headlines. The action is nonstop as bioterror and politics collide to produce a rogue designer bacterium, drug-resistant and set to spread.

Microbiologist Chris Rose and Epidemiologist Jake Evans must use all their medical expertise, exploiting cutting-edge technology to trace and understand the illness. But meanwhile, the bacterium's developers remain at large, preparing to release a pandemic.

Then intelligence officer Elizabeth Foster, whose mission is to find the terrorists and disrupt their plans, enlists the doctors' help. The three join forces for a heart-stopping chase across two continents, a chase during which Jake falls for the beautiful Elizabeth—hard.

Labyrinth of Terror is a thrilling medical procedural, and so much more, as Wenzel, an internationally recognized epidemiologist, shares his knowledge of how researchers track and contain communicable diseases. Wenzel weaves a riveting medical mystery that takes us right into the lives and minds of today's microbe-hunters—and also into their hearts.

—Dierdra McAfee, member, National Book Critics Circle

In this gripping tale author Richard Wenzel has crafted a frighteningly plausible tale of germs gone wild. Based on his own experience as one of the world's most respected infectious disease detectives, his story exposes the consequences of what could happen if the microbial survival tactics designed by nature were combined and exploited by human terrorists. Beware—this is not a science fiction novel. It is a sobering reminder of what is possible today.

—Julie L. Gerberding, former director, The Centers for Disease Control and Prevention

LABYRINTH OF TERROR

1   NOVEMBER 2010

With best regards

Dick Wen,

LABYRINTH OF TERROR

By Richard P. Wenzel

Brandylane Publishers, Inc.

ISBN 978-1-883911-39-3
Library of Congress Control Number: 2010934024

Brandylane Publishers, Inc.
brandylanepublishers.com

This work is fictional, and any resemblance to people living is completely coincidental. Of reference to the Palestinian-Israeli conflict, the following books were especially helpful: *Blood Brothers*, by Elias Chacour; *Understanding the Palestinian-Israeli Conflict* by Phyllis Bennis; *How Long, O Lord? Christian, Jewish, and Muslim Voices from the Ground and Visions for the Future*, edited by Maurine and Robert Tobin; and *Tinderbox: U.S. and Middle East Policy and the Roots of Terrorism*, by Stephen Zunes.

Author photo by James A. Stygar, Stygar Group, Inc.

To Jo Gail,
Amy, Richard and Eric
Josie, Jonah and Jude

who provide meaning for life's narrative,
adding wonder, adventure and love

And in this labyrinth
Where night is blind
The Phantom of the Opera
Is here
Inside my mind

-Andrew Lloyd Weber

ACKNOWLEDGEMENTS

I wish to acknowledge the efforts that my wife Jo Gail and daughter Amy made in reading early and late versions of the book with a keen eye for verisimilitude. Thanks to free-lance editors Kenny Marotta and Larry Mazzeno for careful critique and encouragement. Special insights about Palestine were provided by close friends: Doris Abboud and the late, great surgeon Shukri Khuri, M.D.

PROLOGUE

The flickering candles on either side of the four-poster, mahogany bed illuminated the couple's glistening skin as they lay exhausted after lovemaking. She remained rapt in the afterglow of sex, excited with this man who had playfully refused to enter her until her first orgasm was reached from continual arousal of her engorged clitoral nub with his exploring fingers. Most of the neighbors in this posh section of Hampstead Heath were asleep at the midnight hour, but just in case anyone cared about the doctor's guest, Jeffrey had earlier pulled the black curtains tight.

The cotton sheets rested just below her navel, and she thought the material was the softest she had ever felt next to her body. She fondled the edge of the top sheet where it met her skin, delighting in the soothing texture of the fine fabric he'd brought back from a business trip to Egypt. "I feel wonderful, Jeffrey."

He leaned over, holding both of her flanks, sucking her left nipple and admiring her glowing, bronze skin. Intrigued by her beauty, he traced the contours of her soft body with the fine dexterity of a skilled surgeon. His admiration for her was an aesthetic feeling, not just sexual arousal. This woman brought him into an emotional zone where he not only experienced great comfort, but also a sense of curiosity and fascination.

Though they had known each other for years, they'd only begun speaking frequently at teatime in the last ten months, and five months ago they became lovers. Yet Jeffrey still felt he knew nothing about this lovely woman. Only a perceived goodness, an intense quest for professional excellence, and a quiet mystery were obvious to him. He imagined a time when he would know her dreams and secrets.

She responded by clutching gently at his back and then, with both hands, tugging his head firmly to her breasts. It was the second time in a week that they had made love, and she was safe and comfortable in his arms.

He is bold, but gentle, she thought; sensitive and caring. Lately he had told her that one day they would be more open about their romance, but he cautioned that it was too soon after his divorce and too complicated currently since they worked so closely in the same department.

In recent weeks he had invited her to stay over, but tonight she demurred in deference to his obvious sensibility for a degree of privacy in the neighborhood. Instead, she would take a brief shower in his luxurious tile-lined bathroom and race home.

This time he decided not to argue with her, realizing that an earlier headache had not abated after taking two aspirin tablets, and both temples were now throbbing. Some stress from work, he conjectured, but he also sensed a mild chill, very likely the onset of a viral infection. What a nuisance, he thought, that productive people have to be slowed down intermittently by invisible life forms.

Pulling on a maroon silk robe, he leaned against the wall leading to the bathroom, listening to the hissing sounds of water pulsing from the two shower heads. Usually they shared the shower, soaping each other's bodies and shampooing each other's hair. But it was late, and she was in a hurry. He imagined her beautiful body encased in thousands of tiny droplets sliding over the slopes of her body, falling to her moist pubis, and skidding down over her thighs. As she exited the shower, he held up a large white towel with a soft, thick, and absorbent surface, ready to dry her skin.

She dressed, kissed him briefly, and held his hand as he escorted her out of the kitchen door to her car parked in the back of the house. He was effusive in his thanks for a special meal once again – hummus and pita, kibbi, brown olives, tabouli, falafel, and homemade baklava. When she was safely locked in her car, he returned to the house and went directly upstairs, hoping he could inhale the scent of her perfume, her hair, and her body on the sheets. Her presence was magical, and when they were together, she removed all sense of the loneliness that occasionally enveloped him. She gave him a sense of purpose outside of his profession. He felt a strong need to reclaim those thoughts.

He paused briefly in the hallway to his bedroom to look at a framed representation of Daedalus, a mysterious gift she had presented to him two weeks earlier. Wondering why the architect of the Labyrinth in Crete was significant, he had softly inquired of her interest in Greek mythology. Saying only, "You are my Daedalus," she had very much hoped he would understand someday. Jeffrey rubbed his eyes and continued on to his bed.

At 1:15 a.m., when she opened the door to her flat, another woman was waiting up for her, appearing angry and tense. With pursed lips and the scornful look of a teacher who has surprised a tardy student sneaking into class, she spoke nervously. "You... you are a ri-risk ta-taker." Both women knew that she had a slight stutter only when she was extremely distressed. To her good fortune, few acquaintances were ever aware of it.

"I'm sorry you waited up for me and were concerned. I admire that man intensely and like spending time with him. He is a genuinely good man, humble and kind, and a wonderful, considerate lover." Both women knew that he was also professionally accomplished and sensitive to the fates of downtrodden people throughout the world. "And he is important to us."

"You... you need to keep fo-focused. Besides, you have to be scrub-scrubbed by 7:00 a.m."

"I'll be bright and available in the morning, dear. I know that you have always worried about me, and I love you." The women embraced, holding each other closely for a few seconds.

Jeffrey tossed restlessly throughout the early morning hours, the result of nagging muscle pains, the continuously dull aches that defied any repositioning. A new pain emerged – more of a sensation of muscle contractions grasping the back of his neck – and by 5:00 a.m. he was experiencing chills.

Reaching over the bedside table and pushing the candlesticks aside, he fetched the phone and rang up the operating theatre, cancelling his cases that day "for the safety of my patients." He needed to call the families later that morning, but asked the nursing director to ring up the rest of his team, some of whom might not need to report to work as a result of his absence.

He would soak in a warm bath and ask the housekeeper when she arrived at 8:00 a.m. to prepare some tea for him and attend to the main floor before taking her leave. The living room would need to be neat and clean, as he anticipated a visit after dinner from a long-time research colleague. Over a glass of Fonseca Port they would discuss a brief proposal for a new study. If by chance he still felt ill, perhaps his colleague would take him for consultation at the hospital.

For now he sensed a slight shortness of breath and tightness in his chest, really more fatigue than either air hunger or chest pain. Surely after a full day's rest he would feel much improved. Fortunately, the chills ceased, and he was immediately more optimistic about a quick return to well-being. A visit from a trusted colleague was always uplifting, and new research ideas could be so exciting. So much work required for so many deserving patients, and so little time.

I

In his laboratory on the second floor of King's College Hospital, Professor Christopher Rose hovered motionless over a teaching microscope at the center of a long table. The microscope, equipped with two sets of binocular lenses, allowed instructors and students to examine specimens together. The table stood at the end of several rows of workbenches. Each bench held electronic machines that helped the small team of laboratory technologists identify unknown bacteria. There was a rubbery smell of agar growth media in the lab as two nearby techs repetitively examined tiny bacterial colonies growing on the gels.

Chris's sparse, wavy hair, aquiline nose, and thin, slightly stooped frame gave him the impression of dour studiousness. But his bright, green eyes, easy smile, and vigorous gestures quickly told the truth about his energetic and engaging character. And all of London's young and aspiring medical microbiologists now imitated his trademark attire: grey slacks, a blue shirt, and a forest green bow tie.

Chris peered intensely though the lenses, scrutinizing the grape-like clusters of bacteria, stained blue with the one of the two Gram stains. He still found Hans Christian Gram's discovery infinitely marvelous. The creative nineteenth-century Danish physician devised a series of stains that differentiated bacteria by their shape (spheres or rods) and color, by whether they take up a red (negative) or blue (positive) stain. Gram's system, the foundation of microbiology, was as useful a tool in the twenty-first century as it had been since scientists began exploring microbes.

Chris easily recognized these Gram positive cocci as *Staphylococci*, surely *Staph aureus*. He nodded his head. Something most strange and serious was afoot. This specimen, like the others Chris had looked at, was cultured from the blood of surgical patients after their operations. Four cases of staph and two deaths had occurred in the last two days alone. The original patient had gotten infected twenty days ago and, since then, two others had come down with the illness. Seven cases and four deaths altogether. Chris had been on holiday recently. His lab partners hadn't suspected anything unusual with the original three cases, possibly because they had been diagnosed at different times and on different wards. But he had spotted a pattern besides the usual microbiological background. All seven patients should have been in and out of hospital quickly after relatively benign procedures. Not only had some died, they'd suffered rapidly advancing deaths, another disturbing feature. They'd gone into shock – septic shock – within twenty-four hours of surgery. And nothing had helped: antibiotics, vasopressors, intravenous steroids, and huge volumes of IV fluids failed in each case. Chris pushed away from the scope and reached for the stack of clinical summaries.

Ms. Janet Woolsey, a 32-year-old, white female librarian from London's South End, with a right breast mass, presented for surgery for a biopsy-proven carcinoma. There were no underlying diseases, although Ms. Woolsey smoked a half-pack of cigarettes daily. She had never before been hospitalized. She had no known allergies.

Surgical removal of the tumor and excision of the sentinal node went uneventfully. The vital signs were stable throughout the operation. Patient was returned to her room 70 minutes after the incision was sutured. She was awake, had lunch, was voiding urine normally, and felt well at 12:30 p.m. Her temperature was normal at 37 degrees centigrade. Specifically, she had no pain in the breast beneath the sutures.

At 4:30 a.m. the following day, Ms. Woolsey complained of sudden fever, a "blinding" headache, and dizziness. Her incision site was extremely painful. She complained of muscle tenderness, particularly in the proximal legs and arms, and was noted to have a single red patch – an elevated rash, 1 by 2 centimeters – over the skin of her right thigh.

When examined by the senior Registrar, she was sweating profusely. Her blood pressure was low at 78/40 millimeters of mercury, her pulse was elevated at 130 per minute, and her respiratory rate was rapid (32 breaths per minute). She was quite febrile, with an elevated temperature of 40 degrees centigrade, and was shivering uncontrollably.

An examination of her chest revealed signs of respiratory distress with fluid in her lungs, as heard on auscultation, and she was immediately transferred to critical care. The Sister assisting the clinician recorded that Ms. Woolsey, who could not speak in full sentences because of shortness of breath, had a morbid sense of impending doom.

The patient received four liters of intravenous fluid over the next two hours, plus dobutamine to maintain her systolic blood pressure over 90 millimeters of mercury, and additional doses of IV steroids. Appearing desperate, she repeatedly asked clinicians what was happening. Intensely thirsty, she drank continually from a half-liter container of ice water.

One hour after arriving in critical care, she was gasping for air and required mechanical ventilation to support her breathing, even when receiving 100% oxygen. Despite all interventions, her blood pressure fell precipitously. Her heart went into asystole at 6:14 a.m., and all efforts to regain a rhythm failed. She was pronounced dead at 6:42 a.m.

To see if this outbreak resulted from the same strain of staph, Chris had used pulse-field electrophoresis for molecular typing. He began by adding enzymes, the molecular scissors that cut genes from each of the staph bacteria into pieces at prescribed locations. He placed each set of pieces on a rectangular agar gel. He then exposed the DNA slices to an electric current to see how they distributed themselves as bands along the rectangular gel.

The distribution of lines in the gel, like a special bar code, defined the bacterium's molecular fingerprint. A computer-supported electronic camera compared the bar codes of all tested DNA samples for matches.

Chris was dismayed to find that all the specimens matched. This meant a deadly epidemic was spreading at King's College Hospital!

Rosemary Keyes, Chris's chief lab tech, interrupted. "Professor Rose," she said, "I do have some bad news about the organisms' antibiograms," referring to the resistance pattern an organism shows when exposed to a series of antibiotics. Rosemary, who had worked with Chris for five years now, was small and slight, no more than five foot two. She had the oval face of a porcelain doll, brown hair pulled tightly behind in a bun, but her bright brown eyes were always on high alert for anything unusual.

"They're all *Staphylococcus aureus*, all right," she continued. "But all are resistant to methicillin." For the past two years Chris had insisted that his staff routinely test all suspicious organisms for resistance to vancomycin, the most widely prescribed drug for treating Staphylococcal infections. "One of my new techs did the test. The organisms I isolated appeared to be vancomycin-resistant *Staph aureus*. Initially I thought it was a lab error, but after we retested the isolates we know they *are* vancomycin-resistant – the first I've ever seen." The normally serene Rosemary was clearly upset.

Chris, too, was shocked. This would not only be England's first instance of fully vancomycin-resistant *Staphylococcus*, it would be Europe's first as well. The U.S. was the only place in the world where such isolates had been recovered, and in eight years there had been only eleven cases. Cases which, luckily, involved no transmission to other patients and had not occurred in clusters.

"The tabloids will have a bloody field day with this story if it gets out!" Chris muttered. "And distorted or creative reporting will sell a lot of newspapers." Chris and Rosemary were well aware of the politicians' criticism of U.K. hospitals because of past outbreaks of methicillin-resistant *Staph aureus* – MRSA. But what he had on his plate now was a far more frightening problem. Vancomycin still cured MRSA almost everywhere in the world. A vancomycin-resistant staph wasn't just bad medical news; it was dreadful political news as well. "The front page headlines and the politicians could crucify King's," Chris went on.

"Even the threat of an inquiry would certainly make headlines. Let's keep this confidential for now."

They were interrupted by a call from the admitting physician in Casualty, who was cross-covering on the wards. "We have five new cases of sepsis in post-surgical patients, two in septic shock. It's chaos here, Chris. We're barely keeping our heads above water. We'll send you a series of blood and surgical site specimens for stains and cultures *stat.*"

The call amplified Chris's fears. He hung up the phone and asked Rosemary about the microbiological workup of the strains of staph analyzed thus far. "They are all strains of *U.S.A. 300*, not typical hospital strains as I would have suspected, but more like the community-acquired MRSA seen in the States. And one more thing: I also completed the tox testing, including *PVL*. Finished the tests late last night. Four of the eight isolates are positive."

The PVL toxin, Panton Valentine Leukocidin, was what made the aggressive *community-acquired* strains of MRSA so deadly. The leukocidins killed white blood cells, piercing holes in their membranes chemically. In addition, PVL-positive strains quickly killed all nearby tissues, often in hours.

The epidemic's cause was a unique strain of the organism that had one gene for resistance to the stalwart antibiotic – vancomycin – *and* a second gene set providing the power to invade and destroy tissue, often leading to premature death in otherwise healthy people.

But why did only some of these strains have PVL? Why, if they were clones, didn't all of them have PVL? The probability of two major genetic changes occurring at once was overwhelmingly low. Winning the lottery was more likely. Furthermore, why did this, the first epidemic with this strain in the world, seem to be so easily communicable?

Why would the organism do that naturally? What selective advantage in the early twenty-first century did such a change as this one provide? Like all molecular biologists, Chris knew that what microbiology often reveals is a random code mistake, a minor gene mutation followed by a failure of genetic proofreading. He paced the lab, pondering the situation, and the more he walked, the more certain he became that this was *too much* of a coincidence.

"Rosemary, here in London we've never seen vancomycin-resistant staph, and PVL is rare in our hospital-acquired MRSA. But now we have not just a new strain but a new *outbreak* in hospital of a unique antibiotic-resistant staph plus PVL in the same isolate. The odds are incalculably against it happening randomly."

He resumed his seat at the microscope, leaning on both elbows. He put his hands over his eyes, and his voice grew grave. "All that I know about molecular biology says we should keep an open mind and consider the possibility that someone tampered with this organism. It might seem melodramatic, but I can't ignore the possibility."

Chris thought that his team had to factor in the dark chance that a molecular hacker might be loose. "The phenotype is unique and totally consistent," he said. "We should examine the genetics. We have to find out exactly what DNA pieces are coding for this organism's strange profile."

Chris lifted his head up from his hands. "Nonetheless, because of my unshakable concerns, I think we should take a pre-emptive step and alert MI-5 sooner rather than later, at least as a precaution." Chris thought it would be wise to alert the nation's security agency at once; admittedly, his concerns were radical and as yet unproven, and could be simply a result of his inability to explain all the improbabilities. But he didn't want to be in on of those situations in which an outbreak has occurred and a medical-legal inquiry, instigated by a group of angry barristers, is continually asking, *"What did you know and when did you know it?"*

Thinking out loud, he continued, "I'll tell the Head of Hospital tomorrow morning about the news. It will be quite disturbing to Cecil Barnes – probably his worst nightmare. At least I'll have some good news to tell him; Professor Jake Evans, my close friend and colleague from America, arrives tomorrow for a conference." Evans, a professor at Stanford University, was an epidemiologist recognized internationally for his work in the field of infectious diseases. *As soon as he lands,* Chris thought, *I'll solicit his help in identifying the causes of the outbreak.*

Another anxious call from the physician receiving patients in Casualty gave Chris a chill: "The Professor of Surgery, Jeffrey Allen, was just admitted with a high fever and disorientation. He's in septic shock and looks terrible. Worse than that, he just developed *status epilepticus* with uncontrolled seizures and bizarre posturing. A CT report of his brain showed multiple abscesses! Chris, I don't know if he'll make it."

An hour later, the lifeless body of England's leading breast surgeon was being wheeled slowly to the autopsy room in the lower reaches of the hospital.

II

The sign over the door read simply *Administrator*, and the window filling most of the top half of the door had its tan shade pulled down.

A closed view – and probably the sign of a closed mind, thought Chris skeptically as he knocked on the door.

Chris dreaded his interactions with Cecil Barnes. The annual cuts to his laboratory's budget in the last two years had cost him the loss of two experienced microbiology techs and a delay in instituting some new, rapid-testing systems for investigating the viral etiologies of community-acquired pneumonia. He could hardly stand the administrator's boring monologues, offering excuses for the hospital's need to have an ever-increasing bottom line. In brief, they had nothing in common; Cecil knew nothing of science or the value of an excellent microbiology team, and he abhorred free discussion and debate. In any conversation about the shortcomings of management, the administrator placed the blame on the professional staff, refusing to accept the slightest critique. In Chris's view, Cecil was an industrial-strength narcissist.

"Come in, please," Barnes replied to Chris's knocking.

Chris entered the room, a place familiar to him as the scene of many unpleasant meetings. Rows of file cabinets lined one side of the large office with three windows on the far end facing the tree-lined street outside. There was the smell of recently applied furniture wax. No rugs lay on the old wooden floors, their random-width strips slightly warped, and no art work hung on the walls, which were painted stark white. In perfect symmetry and exact spacing from each other were Barnes' black, wood-framed diplomas on the office wall opposite the file cabinets, along with four certificates of awards or honors for administration. Cecil Barnes had graduated from the University in Birmingham and subsequently received his Master's degree in economics with an area of focus in hospital administration from the University of London fourteen years earlier.

The staff at King's had learned quickly that the administrator enjoyed recounting the story of his life to anyone, in social or professional gatherings, elaborating the details in a way that was apparently therapeutic for him. He had grown up near the town of Buxton, approximately twenty-seven miles from Manchester and 170 miles northwest of London, and was the son of a dairy farmer whose alcoholism had led to an intermittent, verbally abusive relationship between the two.

Chris could not help but notice that despite all the paperwork that surely crossed the office of a busy hospital director, the large maple desk of the administrator looked essentially untouched. There were only a few thin manila folders – each one labeled on the upper right corner – off to one side. *His expertise at moving paper is magical,* thought Chris.

Cecil Barnes was fifty-one years old with a balding crown surrounded by a rim of black hair at the lower edge of his scalp. He never wore a sport coat while in his office but always wore starched white shirts and striped ties. He remained standing behind his desk as Chris approached, and he pointed to one of two wooden chairs facing his desk, as though commanding Chris to sit there. "What is so urgent that you needed to meet with me first thing on a Monday?"

Chris ignored the abrupt and dismissive tone of Barnes's question, instead getting right to the point.

"We have an infection control problem at King's, and it's important for you to know that by any measure, the cluster of *Staphylococcal* infections is serious. Previously healthy individuals, our patients, have died unexpectedly.

"I've done a preliminary investigation already. This is no simple *Staph aureus*. The organism appears to have a distinctively rare antibiogram – it's resistant to vancomycin, the drug used to treat difficult species of staph. The Americans have the only experience with strains of vancomycin-resistant *Staphylococcus aureus*, and they've recovered only eleven apparently unrelated isolates. Their first case occurred in 2002 and the eleventh case in 2010. Now it looks as if we have the world's first *epidemic* with vancomycin-resistant staph. That's why I will request the assistance of a friend, a world-class expert in infection control – who is fortuitously attending an international infection control meeting in London – in helping me complete the epidemiological work-up."

Barnes opened his mouth as if to speak, but Chris continued before he could say anything.

"It has a surprisingly high mortality rate, especially unusual in low-risk patients. As a result, I explored the genetics of why it kills so readily. It possesses special characteristics that make it unique. Not only is it difficult to treat because it has the ability to resist vancomycin, but some strains I've studied contain a gene coding for virulence, the ability to destroy tissues.

"The organism expressed the worst of its intensive repertoire in the infection of our colleague, Professor Jeffrey Allen, who died rapidly. Such a loss! We're still investigating his death along with the others."

Although Chris was sure Barnes knew of Allen's death, it was clear this was the first time the administrator was getting an explanation for the professor of surgery's demise. Barnes had an alarmed expression on his face, and he appeared to be holding his breath. Then suddenly he exploded in a tirade. "Hold on a second, Professor! Are you saying that here at King's, one of the leading academic institutions in Europe, we are contaminated with a transmissible and deadly bacterium that has rare resistance traits?"

Chris felt himself beginning to brace for another bitter encounter. *First, I'll have to deal with denial*, he thought.

"I regret to say that it's so. It's incredibly bad luck to have an improbable series of events resulting from changes in the genetics of an organism. But improbable events do occur in nature. However, now I need you to hold on to your seat. An alternative hypothesis is also possible – although improbable – but that's why I'm meeting with you here and why I'm so concerned. At least hear me out. Some clever but sadistic microbial hacker may have purposefully tinkered with the genes of the staph."

Displaying a crooked smile, the administrator responded somewhat sarcastically, "Isn't that a bit far-fetched, Rose? A bit histrionic of you to think that someone would deliberately try to hurt or kill patients at King's with a terrifying microbe? You've been reading too many sci-fi books." Raising his eyebrows as though to say "I got you!" Barnes folded his arms across his chest.

Ignoring the cynicism of his CEO, Chris responded, "It's not totally out of the question, however, and I may know for sure after I do some confirmatory studies in the lab. Nevertheless, just as we've seen hackers in the computer world create unimaginable viruses and worms that destroy information technology programs, the possibility exists that a microbe hacker has created a superbug with programmed characteristics never seen before – with lethal consequences. The question for science is what is more probable – two or three extremely rare and simultaneous natural mutations, or one destructive personality purposefully altering the genetic makeup of a bacterium."

Barnes looked as if he remained unconvinced.

"Surely you know the principle of Occam's Razor," Chris continued, "that unnecessary variables should be shaved off to create the most simple or parsimonious hypothesis." Chris knew there were numerous – maybe unlimited – possibilities to explain so many rare genetic aberrations. He was not yet certain the idea of a biohacker should be considered as number one. However, logically and scientifically, it explained all of the observations, had scientific parsimony, and had to be included in the top few probabilities.

"Of course not everything simple is correct, and often our world is found to be complex when we understand more," said Chris. "What I *am* telling you is that the principle of Occam's Razor should be the starting point, and that we can still maintain an open mind."

What Chris didn't say was that if Barnes insisted on the alternative theory – a sudden appearance of a combination of incredibly rare mutations – he would be putting forward a much more complicated and unlikely model to explain the laboratory findings.

At this point Barnes looked exasperated. He could hardly tolerate the idea that someone who reported to him would be lecturing him on logic. In an irritated tone, he exclaimed, "So you are saying that some son of a bitch may have manipulated a staph and dumped a killer organism on my hospital, creating bedlam? Is that what you're proposing?"

"I'm just reporting the observations and my restless, late-night deductions."

"Well, you must have some bloody idea! After all, you have a PhD in microbiology."

Chris could feel his pulse quicken and a wave of anger begin to warm his face, but he was resolved to maintain his composure and contain his emotions. "My doctoral degree of course means that I know a great deal about the mechanisms governing the biology of bacteria, but nothing about the criminal mind capable of creating a monster pathogen."

Just then the phone rang, and Barnes's secretary announced that the gross pathology on the brain of Professor Allen had just come back and that the pathologist, Dr. Thomas Quesenberry, was on the line for Dr. Rose. Barnes said he would put Quesenberry on the speaker phone so both of them could hear the results.

"Chris, this is Tom. We just examined the gross cross sections of the brain, and I counted over a hundred abscesses – something I've never seen before! This confirms the finding of the brain CT. There's more. We found a large fungating lesion on the mitral valve loaded with Gram-positive cocci. Surely the abscesses in the brain were seeded from the bacterial growth on the heart valve. I've seen many cases of endocarditis before, Chris, but never one showering a brain with a hundred small abscesses. No part of the brain was spared, from the frontal lobes to the midbrain to the cerebellum. No area was free of the infection."

Rose immediately translated the information to Barnes, explaining that a heaped-up and crumbled infection on the heart valve continually flipped off tiny fragments infecting various segments of the brain.

"Thanks for the update, Tom," Chris said to his caller. "I appreciate your rapid response in checking this out. I'm explaining the epidemic to Mr. Barnes and updating him on the lab findings. Let me know if you have any further insights."

"Sure, Chris. The only other thing we found were superficial scratches on both shoulders – nothing significant. Goodbye." Cecil Barnes slapped the button disconnecting the speaker phone.

"Rose, this is terrible! We've lost one of the finest surgeons in the world. His death will demoralize our entire staff and terrify our patients if word gets out. How did this happen at my hospital?" In his mind he was wondering, *Why would someone choose us? Would this be the work of some disgruntled laboratory person here? Is a psychopath trying to hurt the staff? Could this be targeting laboratory personnel? Am I in any personal danger?* Cecil Barnes briefly put his hands over his eyes and said nothing for a few moments.

Chris decided not to answer immediately. He could feel the tension.

"What in hell do we do now, Rose?" The words came out as though Cecil were gargling them.

Finally, Chris said, "We know that we need to move in three areas. I will ask my friend Dr. Jake Evans, a world-class expert in infection control, to assist me in the epidemiological work-up. He's attending an international infection control meeting in London this week. Professor Evans will lead the epidemiological investigation. I'll pursue my studies of the organism's biology to try and understand how it does what it does. But we have some very serious administrative issues, too, which is why I'm here."

"What bleeding administrative issues are you talking about?"

"First, even though it may be premature, we need to notify the national law enforcement, specifically MI-5. This may be a security issue that goes well beyond King's Hospital. If we're right, they will have had all the advance warning we can give them, we will not have sat on a threatening issue, and we may avert a worse crisis. If we're wrong, then we will have taken little time from MI-5, and I doubt if they will criticize us too severely for being cautious, especially after the American experience on 9/11 and our own recent experience in the summer of 2005." Rose knew the reference to the bombings in the Underground and on buses would not be lost on the administrator.

"Second, we need to inform our own staff that we are doing everything we can about the cluster of infections. Professor Evans will help us by advising on infection control procedures. Most importantly, his epidemiological studies may also pinpoint clues to the cause of this cluster of infections. Specifically, he may identify some practice in the operating theatre that caused the infections."

Chris paused, waiting for Barnes to say something – specifically, to state what he would have to do in his role as administrator. But when he said nothing, Chris continued with what almost amounted to a directive.

"And *you* need to decide when and how you want to deal with the press."

Barnes stood up from his chair abruptly. "You've lost your crackers! I don't want any press on this. Bloody hell, do you realize what this will do to our reputation? You just solve this goddamn issue and give me updates every twelve hours. No press! Just get to work on this. But one more thing I need to ask you bluntly: Can we trust the American expert to avoid speaking with the press?"

Barnes's questioning of Jake's loyalty to Chris and the hospital seemed to point a finger at Chris, which irritated him.

"My American colleague is discreet. Let me remind you that his expertise will cost us nothing, and he's internationally recognized in his field. As for the press, if you're proposing some type of cover-up, I want no part of it. More importantly, it won't work, and the results

14

will be worse for King's and for you – its CEO – in the long run. Sooner or later the general public will hear about the outbreak and deaths. We should manage this issue immediately. Simply stated, there's no alternative. If we confirm a genetically strange organism, we should quickly decide how to relate this to the press. Finally, when MI-5 gets involved, we'll have a PR decision: when and what to announce to the public. And the reason to invite MI-5 early? In my mind, although a microbial hacker seems unthinkable, it is still a plausible explanation, and we can't afford to stand by, can we? After we discuss this with MI-5, we could also ask their advice about the press."

Cecil Barnes began to look not just agitated but also frightened. His voice became more strident and began to quiver slightly. Beads of sweat began to surface on his forehead, which was now accented by a serpiginous, dilated vein traversing towards the right temple. "Let's review this again," he said somewhat more softly, "and I want to go through each step carefully and explain the position of the hospital. Rose, I'm really angry with you." His tone was now harsher and louder. "No, in fact I'm pissed off! How could you let this happen to King's? As I recall, Professor Rose, your five-year review is coming up in a few months. Now, if you can't solve this fucking problem quickly, I need to get a professor of microbiology who can. Am I being clear?"

Chris looked directly into Barnes' eyes and responded firmly, "You are quite clear, Mr. Barnes. But you're threatening the messenger, not the creator of the organism. If you care about solutions, and I am sure that you do, you'll support giving my colleague immediate access to all the charts, and all the help he can. You'll also need to support my expanded studies in the laboratory, which will surely exceed the budget I presented last spring. At this point I don't give a good bloody goddamn about my five-year review! I'm also suggesting that at some time in the next few days you may be inundated with the press, and you need to be prepared."

He delivered his admonition in crescendo fashion, initially soft but peaking in pitch to his final point. "I *will* call MI-5 to get their oversight, with or without your approval. The families of thirteen victims will want answers, and our faculty and staff can't expect to be calm and quiet. Now, have I communicated anything vague, anything unclear?" By this time Chris was pointing his right index finger at Barnes's chest.

Sensing Chris's fury, Cecil Barnes tried to regain his self-control, to calm the situation and dial down his level of anger. Taking a handkerchief from his pocket, he wiped his brow. "Rose, you keep me informed. Hourly if necessary! Work with one of my junior administrators to secure the charts and other administrative help. I'm upset, but don't mean to blame you. You understand the possible ramifications of this, I'm sure! I'm the one in the hot seat – not you in your lab. When shit hits the fan, you'll be safely protected behind your sterile lab benches, and I'll be facing a harsh public. Now you go and get this worked out as quickly as possible!"

Still bristling from the confrontation, Chris got up from the chair and turned to leave, forsaking any handshake or farewell comments. He left the door open wide as he strode away from the office. Cecil Barnes followed him half-way down the hallway to issue some final instructions. Raising his right hand into a fist, he now implored him, "Prepare a first draft of a press release, one that would shed the best light on a grim situation. I want this as fast as possible, before the editors of the *Guardian* and *Times* descend on my hospital!"

Hearing Cecil's emphasis on "my hospital," Chris Rose shook his head and mumbled under his breath, "What an arrogant bastard!" Still, he responded in his usual calm-but-firm, self-assured manner, turning his head only ninety degrees to the right. "I need to tell you that I plan to approach this issue as a scientist, following the logic and data from my lab's testing of the organisms. What I learn from direct observation of the facts will guide my response. The rest will fall squarely on your shoulders: how you deal with the facts, the politics, the publicity and the reality of the deaths of four of the first seven infected patients and a prominent surgeon. Now we have five more victims. I wish you luck!"

He started to leave once more but stopped. He turned to the pursuing administrator, again looking directly into his eyes, and added pointedly, "If you think I would withhold any important observation, you're out of your mind – bloody mistaken. Furthermore, if you think there is a way to sugarcoat a colossal tragedy in the making, you're blind to reality. Right now you *need* me and my American colleague to perform at our best. And if you truly care, you'll move quickly and carefully to manage the truth, as unsavory and uncomfortable as it is."

III

Jake Evans found the rumbling, underground ride from Heathrow Airport to central London exhilarating, reminding him of his sabbatical at the London School of Hygiene and Tropical Medicine ten years earlier. No interrupting calls, no inane academic meetings, no administrative reports due for those twelve months. New friends, new colleagues, and time to think and write – all luxuries that vanished when he returned to California. The excitement of watching his family react to new situations had been memorable. A resounding success – except when Deb discovered his indiscretion with a dark-skinned microbiologist from Florence. It all started innocently. He was attending a professional dinner where the speaker was horribly boring. Catching the eye of a microbiologist who was also bored beyond belief, he made a motion to the door. Their mutual escape led to the hotel bar and unusually generous volumes of Brunello by the glass. After a night filled with sex and fantasy, both rationalized that it should be a one-time event. However, Deb found a series of coquettish e-mails that led her to confront Jake about the tryst. In Jake's mind, the affair was almost worth the grief he suffered at Deb's hand, but he wished he had been more discreet. He wondered what Maria had been doing since he last saw her, and if by chance she might attend the London meeting. These thoughts filled his mind as he watched the brick homes and verdant English landscape race by the window of the Tube.

After his fellowship training in infectious diseases, the then thirty-two-year-old physician had taken a year abroad to work at one of the leading institutions in the world to learn the nuances of epidemiology, the study of disease and health in populations. A decade later, still appearing young, although now a professor at Stanford University, he had been invited to give one of four keynote addresses at the First Global Congress on Healthcare-Associated Infections. Organized by the World Health Organization in Geneva, the Centers for Disease Control and Prevention in Atlanta, and the Communicable Disease Centre in Colindale, the meeting promised to be a big deal. After all, the Conference would be hosting the combined talents of 900 clinicians, microbiologists, epidemiologists, and hospital safety engineers under one roof.

Stations along the color-coded network of underground tracks defined all travel in London. Jake would take the dark blue Piccadilly line to Piccadilly Circus and change to the brown Bakerloo line. At the Oxford Circus tube stop, Jake emerged to a drizzly, dank day. *Typical of the city in August,* he thought. Pushing through the silver-gray mist, he dragged the handle of his black canvas suitcase on wheels piled high with his carry-on bag for the six block walk to the John Snow Hotel. On the way, he passed a Malaysian restaurant, an A&W Store, Fortnam and Mason's, a florist, a tourist agency, an outlet for Port Meiron pottery, and several small antiquarian bookstores.

He paused briefly to pick up a copy of the *Times* and briefly noted the three headlines: *15 Homes of Palestinians Bulldozed by Israeli Army – Prime Minister to visit Mid-East; Parliament to Address Aging Casualty Departments – Need to Respond to Modern Emergencies; Queen Mother to Address Global Relationships.*

He waved to the greengrocer who barely acknowledged his presence with a brief upward nod of his chin. Jake ignored the reserved response, for this was exotic London, packed with small businesses focused on a single product usually led by the expertise of its owner, a deeply focused specialist, not a superficial generalist.

Jake chose the small hotel because it honored the name of the ingenious physician who resolved the 1854 epidemic of cholera in London and ended it abruptly by removing the handle from the Broad

Street pump. An anesthesiologist with keen epidemiological skills, Dr. Snow meticulously mapped the cases of cholera to the subscribers of London's two water companies. Most cases clustered around the distribution of one company, the Southwick and Vauxhall, which drew its water from the lower Thames where it had become contaminated with the city's sewage. In contrast, the Lambeth Company drew its water from the upper Thames, for the most part avoiding exposure to the billions of curved, rod-shaped bacteria causing the deadly diarrheal illness.

Jake thought of himself as fairly confident, but at some level he wondered if he had the intellectual courage, the guts of a great physician like Snow. Would he, if he were in that situation, have been able to face a skeptical-yet-panicked assembly of local administrators, exhorting them to take the handle off the Broad Street pump to end the epidemic based on epidemiological data alone? Yet Snow did it, thirty years before the germ theory of disease became generally accepted. To Jake and most medical epidemiologists interested in infectious diseases, John Snow was brilliant, legendary, and heroic.

There were two male guests conversing quietly on one side of the black-and-white, marble-floored hotel lobby as Jake approached the clerk, who was standing stiffly behind a small counter framed by wide panels of dark oak wood. The clerk was a tall, gaunt man, about fifty years old with pale skin and thinning gray hair, and was dressed in a dark brown suit, light yellow shirt, and red and black striped tie. He observed the American and smiled widely, exposing a mouth full of slightly crooked teeth. "Good morning. May I help you, sir?" he articulated in a basso tone reminiscent of a refined butler.

"Yes, the name is Evans, and I have a reservation," said Jake, dabbing the moisture on his forehead with a white handkerchief.

"Oh, Professor Evans. Right, we are indeed expecting you. Kindly sign the bottom line on the card and initial the rates. Your room is already prepared, number 320, and here is your key. Ah, let me see – here it is – you have already received a note, dropped off only two hours ago. Yes, here is the envelope, sir. Please enjoy your stay," he said, pointing to the right side of the lobby.

Jake grasped the envelope and started to place it in the pocket of his black sport coat, but it fell to the floor. He picked it up and held it in his left hand, along with his briefcase handle, reaching for his luggage with his right hand.

The open lift rose slowly to the fourth level – the Brits don't count the first floor until the one above the reception, Jake recalled – and its iron-gated frame rattled as though shivering uncomfortably all the way through its ascent. Though noisy, to Jake it was charming, reminiscent of a bygone period, always erroneously assumed by people to have been less hectic than their own era.

Four doors to the left was number 320 – the room was spartan, clean, and small, the bed occupying two-thirds of the floor space. The increased intensity of the day's early downpour was announced by the staccato drumming of raindrops on the window panes overlooking the main entrance to the hotel. A fading print of the Queen Mother elegantly dressed in regal red colors, the only framed picture in the room, hung over the headboard, her narrow eyes peering downward as though critically inspecting the guest who had just arrived. Jake nodded deferentially to her and turned to the bathroom – or loo – which was tiny, yet functional. It had a bath with a shower head connected to a movable cable, quite common in small European hotels. A triangular-shaped nightlight with a pale green shield in front of the bulb was plugged into the wall opposite the bathroom mirror.

Now to unpacking, Jake thought, *a hot shower and a brief restorative nap after reading the note, no doubt a formal welcome from the Congress Organizing Committee.*

But the note was not from the Organizing Committee.

Dear Jake, Please meet me in my lab at King's College Hospital as soon as you arrive. We have a dire problem here and request your prompt assistance. Anticipating your kind help. Yours sincerely, Chris.

A note from Chris Rose would always be serious, thought Jake. *Was he ill? Did he need help with his family or a colleague? Was he in some administrative or political trouble?* Chris was always bold, direct, and occasionally impolitic. Jake, of course, would not hesitate. There was time only to drop the bags and catch a cab to King's.

London's famous black cabs were luxuriously spacious, he recalled, compared to the cramped taxis in Palo Alto. Jake could stretch his legs out as far as possible, and this was especially pleasing with his six-foot-three-inch frame supporting a 225-pound body. He had a great sense of freedom in this city, an unusual invitation to speak at a special symposium, the opportunity to see his foreign colleagues, no frenetic series of obligations. But first he would see what his friend needed.

The driver, a round-faced man with a ruddy complexion, was clean-shaven and dressed in a perfectly ironed white shirt. Wearing a dark jacket and tie, with his cap squarely on, he appeared recently scrubbed and starched. With a demeanor that was immediately cordial but formal, he quickly demonstrated that he knew the city's history and could navigate its streets. Jake moved to the middle of the back seat, placing both arms comfortably out, and commented, "You can't imagine what luxury it is to ride in such spacious cabs." He felt exhausted from the sleepless flight over the Atlantic.

As the cabbie made an abrupt U-turn, Jake was also amazed at the agility of the distinctive black automobile with its famous twenty-five-foot turning radius – mandated by the Public Carriage Office of London since the early 1900s. In his sabbatical year he had learned that London is a city of traditions.

As conversation quickly lagged, Jake began musing about the first time he and Chris Rose met at the London School. Chris, now the Professor of the Clinical Laboratory Department at King's College of Medicine, had been in the master's degree course in microbiology when Jake had entered the master's degree program in epidemiology and biostatistics. Chris subsequently earned his PhD from the University of London where he specialized in molecular biology, concentrating on the mechanisms by which cells transmit information.

Chris, Jake, and ten to twelve male classmates would meet at the Dog and Duck Pub late on Friday afternoons and discuss world problems, the politics of each person's country, and the attractive women in their respective classes. Both friends were married, but the international assembly of female graduate students from all over the world prompted critical discussions of the perfect sexual partner. After weeks of light-hearted exchanges about libido, athletic prowess, striking beauty, and anatomic preferences of breasts, thighs, calves, and hips, the conversation lifted more sublimely towards the elements of mystery, energy, surprise, dedication, intensity, and a luminescent quality on first sighting. Medicine, science, philosophy, art, and theatre were also occasional topics in these animated conversations, but the crowning achievement of the year's meetings was the classmates' definition of sexual perfection in a woman.

The cab pulled up outside King's College of Medicine. Jake exited, handing the driver the fare and a handsome tip. Walking up the rain-covered outer stairway, Jake eagerly anticipated catching up with his friend and colleague. He wanted to tell him about his nomination for the International Award at Stanford, his need to deliver an electrifying address, and his upcoming wedding anniversary. He would also confide in Chris about his invitation to compete for a professorship and funded chair at Harvard.

Jake made his way to Chris's office and opened the door without knocking.

"Chris, how are you, and what exactly is the dire issue?"

Surprised but delighted, Chris immediately rose from his laboratory stool, enthusiastically wrapping his arms around his friend. "Oh Jake, I had sent you an email with a few details, but realized later you were in flight. Sorry for the brief note at the hotel. At any rate, it's fantastic to see you! Thanks so much for coming directly. How was your flight over? How are you?"

"The flight was uneventful, thus perfect." He suddenly realized that his BlackBerry was still in the locked mode in his carry-on bag. "I, on the other hand, am now permanently chilled by the cold rain you always have at this time of year, and since I don't have a hat, my hair has apparently trapped all the moisture of London's skies."

"Bracing!" responded Chris. "You Americans always make too much of the weather. We Londoners can't be so absorbed by the elements. Besides, it changes quickly. How are Deb and the children?"

"Outstanding. And they all said to give Mary and your two girls their best," said Jake.

"Brilliant!" replied Chris. "And Mary looks forward to catching up."

Chris's tone became more serious. "Sit down, please," he said. "I have much to tell you. We do indeed have a dire situation here." Chris proceeded to give Jake an account of the unique *Staphylococcal* outbreak, letting him know they would soon be accompanied by a member of MI-5, who had just arrived in the library conference room.

Jake focused on Chris's words intensely. Staph was an emotional subject for Jake because of a terrible incident that occured while he was attending medical school in Boston. A classmate was admitted to the ICU during Jake's clinical rotation, having suffered three days with fever and muscle aches from influenza, which became complicated by bacterial pneumonia. He, his resident, and the attending physician treated the student for infection caused by pneumococcus, because the patient was so ill. Sixteen hours later, however, the blood cultures were read as *Staphylococci.* The antibiotics were changed to those targeting the antibiotic-resistant strain of staph, but it was too late to save his twenty-three-year-old classmate. Even though Jake had been a student when that happened, he retained a sense of guilt. That was the turning point when Jake decided to enter the field of infectious diseases. He never again wanted to miss a staph infection.

It was clear from Chris's description that a cluster of life-threatening staph infections showing up in healthy people suggested an especially aggressive strain. He now understood what Chris meant by *dire.*

Jake's brain went into overdrive, planning a logical way to begin looking at the situation. He loved a good challenge and assisting Chris would be a pleasure.

"Chris, I'd be very curious to see the clinical profiles of all the patients. Can you get me the medical charts so that I can prepare a line list of the cases?" asked Jake. He was referring to the initial step in the investigation of an epidemic in which the cases are listed by name on a wide spreadsheet, top to bottom, with details about each patient listed from left to right. The latter include the patient's age, gender, date of admission, the dates of specific procedures such as surgery or the insertion of a vascular catheter for intravenous fluids. Details also identified all medications, diagnostic tests performed, and the names of principal health care providers with whom they had contact, including physicians who attended to them, nurses, technologists, and medical and nursing students.

Chris escorted Jake into the next room, which held eight-foot-wide blackboards on both sides, a cherry wood bookcase filled with molecular biology and genetics texts on the end near the entrance, and three windows on the east end of the room, facing the street. Standing behind one of six leather chairs around a dark, oak conference table across from Jake was MI-5 inspector Elizabeth Foster.

Dressed in a navy pinstriped suit with her skirt falling just above the knees, and a ribbed, starched white blouse with a high collar, she had the formal appearance of a business CEO. In Jake's quick estimate, she was easily five-foot-ten, with swept-back chestnut hair. The glimmer of nascent sunlight reflected off the small, triangular, silver earrings she was wearing. Standing erect, she had broad shoulders and an athlete's physique. She must weigh about a hundred and thirty-five pounds, thought Jake, whose clinical eyes examined the muscular architectures of her well-defined calves and concluded that she worked out routinely. Her pleasant but cautious smile was framed by the subdued cinnamon color of her lipstick. Her eyes seemed to peer right through the person at whom she was looking. Her high cheek bones and alabaster skin gave her a classical look, reminiscent of a sculpture in a Greek temple.

Chris introduced Jake to Ms. Foster, who he indicated was a twenty-year veteran of MI-5. Her almond eyes were fixed on Jake Evans across the table, as he explained to her that he had just arrived in London, was an epidemiologist, and was available to assist his friend. She removed her laptop computer from its black canvas case, sat down across from him, and began typing notes.

Chris summarized the clinical presentations of the victims and reviewed the postmortem findings on Professor Allen – heart and brain abscesses and minor scratches on both shoulders.

Elizabeth turned her attention to Chris. "Professor Rose, you suspect this isn't a common organism, but something unusual. What can you tell me?"

There was a hint of skepticism in the way Elizabeth asked the question. She felt she had reason to be cautious. Perhaps in the post 9/11 era, some physicians remained edgy about terror in general. On the other hand, she thought, if there was merit in the doctor's worry, this could be a great assignment for her. It had not been easy for a woman in the man's world at MI-5. She had to do even more than her male colleagues – the extra assignments, the late hours. The little-mentioned sacrifices that allowed her to succeed at the office had created tension at home. A big case might offer her an opportunity to pierce what appeared to be a bullet-proof glass ceiling at MI-5.

"I hope you're up on your biology, Ms. Foster. Stop me if you need an explanation of any of the technical terms."

"I will – and please, call me Elizabeth," she replied. "But I must say, I'm not yet sure why MI-5 should become involved in this matter."

Chris began an update of his laboratory findings. "What I can tell you so far is that I have never seen a staph organism like this. The key points about this organism are the following: one, it's resistant to almost every antibiotic available in the world; two, it's unusually aggressive, in part because it possesses enzymes – toxins – that destroy the body's tissue in a rapid way; and three, it has killed people as part of an epidemic."

Chris added that the organism appeared resistant to vancomycin. "The antibiotic," he noted, "has been a time-honored, last-resort drug for treating staph, a safety-net antibiotic."

"However," he continued, "these organisms can grow in liquid media even when the concentration of vancomycin is very high. Unlike the eleven American strains resistant to vancomycin, it's not susceptible to many older and some relatively new antibiotics. Our organism is only susceptible to trimethoprim-sulfamethoxazole, one of the older drugs that many clinicians would not consider as first-line therapy. And if this older antibiotic is not administered early, we may not be able to save the patient.

"And last, there is something else that is unique: some isolates make a toxin, which we call *PVL*, a marker of their ability to cause tissue damage, including abscesses in skin and soft tissue, lungs, heart, and brain. When I lined up the strains over time, I noticed that, while the first four didn't have the PVL toxin, the last four, among the most recent patients, did. This is a toxin that essentially punches holes in patients' white blood cells, as though trying to disable a part of the immune system."

"Why would some strains have this toxin?" asked Elizabeth.

"We have a unique organism that is programmed to ignore one of our toughest antibiotics and at the same time destroy tissue rapidly after infection. A variant of the organism, one seen in only eleven patients in U.S. hospitals between 2002 and 2010, has never spread to a second person. It's always been acquired in hospitals, and has never been seen in the population at large. Our strain has some characteristics of the community-acquired staph strains seen infecting healthy citizens in several countries as well as the unique antibiotic profile of the eleven resistant strains in the U.S. It also has one more special feature: ours has caused an epidemic.

"Because of all the improbabilities, I think that a microbial hacker is a serious possibility, even though I'm reluctant to advance such an idea publicly. I'm concerned that I may be wasting your valuable time, and in the end, perhaps some will say that I overreacted, but all things considered, I'm more comfortable bringing you in early."

On hearing the words *microbial hacker*, Elizabeth clenched both fists astride her laptop, fixed Chris's eyes with hers, and asked, "How certain are you that this organism has been manipulated? That it's not just an accident in nature?"

Chris responded soberly, "I'm afraid the features of this organism are so unusual and so varied, that it's beyond any reasonable likelihood that it's an accident. I'll be able to confirm this in the next series of laboratory investigations."

"Then, if your tests rule out a natural accident, we're dealing with a criminal act," said Elizabeth. In her judgment Chris Rose was no hysterical type. His was a sobering statement, clearly the result of thoughtful consideration. Terrorists could be involved here. There was no telling what the targets were, how many people would be infected or killed, who might be behind this – or why. *Are all hospitals in London the focus? Why? How quickly can these two physicians offer clues?* She would need to start planning a counter-terrorism operation immediately.

"So we may be dealing with a biological hacker who has created a deadly organism," Elizabeth mused out loud, "and if it gets loose it could be extremely dangerous."

"If my findings confirm my suspicions, a very skilled hacker," responded Chris. "It's as though someone is trying to see how many harmful genes he or she can successfully add to the bacteria."

Harmful genes had special meaning for Elizabeth Foster. One year ago her husband, a successful barrister, had been diagnosed with Huntington's Chorea, a dominantly inherited and progressive neurological disorder. A dominant gene from one parent always trumped a recessive gene from the other parent, and half of the couple's children could be expected to be affected. It began with some facial twitching and a sense of depression, and it was a psychiatrist who first considered the diagnosis. Their two children were checked and weren't affected, but her husband was expected to have progressive movement disorders, soon lose his ability to walk, and eventually suffer from dementia. "He will probably die in the next five years," the neurologist had said. It was their secret, and neither Elizabeth nor her husband confided in anyone outside the medical profession about his fatal illness. In the short run and the long run, she had to be super MI-5 agent, super mom, and super wife.

All heads nodded in agreement. This time Elizabeth smiled briefly, revealing evenly spread white teeth, and suddenly she appeared to be younger than her forty-one years. Jake mused that she would rate highly on the scale of the perfect sexual partner, as defined in London's pubs by his classmates ten years earlier.

"Jake," said Elizabeth, "anything you can provide through statistical analysis will be very helpful. Here's my card and secure cell phone number. Please call me when you've identified the final risk factors – including any individual identified – in your initial analysis. Chris, here's my card for you, too."

"Thanks, Elizabeth," said Chris. "I need to tell you that our administrator is extremely concerned about adverse publicity. He will surely want your advice regarding the management of a likely press meeting. I don't wish to bias you, but you need to know that he may not have an open mind about dealing with this outbreak in a transparent fashion. What's more, he may show some reluctance about having MI-5 at the hospital."

"Well, we all need to be prepared," said Elizabeth. "For now I will suggest that he announce that an epidemic of serious *Staphylococcal* infections has occurred and that experts are involved in its control. Only when we all are more confident that a biohacker, as you say, is involved do we go on with another announcement. I will take it from there regarding any criminal investigation. However, the administrative approach to controlling an epidemic in a hospital, I'll leave to you two experts."

As she walked out the door, Elizabeth turned to Jake with a critical question. "How long does it usually take for an epidemiologist to solve the riddle of an outbreak?"

Jake knew the answer – days to weeks, if all goes well – but tried to hide his emotions with the noncommittal term, *variable,* knowing that weeks are usually required to complete such work. He felt anxious about the situation, suddenly recalling his quarrel with Deb the night before he left California. Deb's words had been unequivocal: no excuses for missing their wedding anniversary, as she had something special planned, and this time no playing with the natives in London. As Elizabeth and Chris exited, he reached into his coat pocket for the ibuprofen. If he left London on time to celebrate his twentieth anniversary, Deb would be delighted. However, if the situation was what they suspected, then he wouldn't be able to leave. Here was the opportunity of a lifetime, the pinnacle of a thousand medical careers. This could be the ticket to a prize at Stanford and a professorship at Harvard, possibly a larger salary and even more time with the family. Surely Deb would understand if he delayed his return with so much at stake.

IV

Lunch was organized by Chris and set up in his office for the three members of the newly formed investigative team. There were fish and chips prepared by the hospital's kitchen, Earl Grey tea, and vanilla biscuits. Elizabeth sat between Chris and Jake at a small round table "originally designed for Lord Lister," Chris noted proudly.

Jake asked Elizabeth if she would mind describing MI-5's range of responsibilities, to help him understand what happened in these circumstances.

She explained that MI-5 – the MI stands for military intelligence – had its history and name from the early 1900s in the Home Section of the Secret Service Bureau, and had the responsibility of investigating espionage. A complementary organization known as MI-6 was created to conduct counter-espionage outside of Britain. MI-5 and MI-6 worked together, for obvious reasons. She worked for the G-9 branch in International Terrorism.

To Jake, the intrigue of tracking down the cause of an epidemic had some features akin to tracking down a serial bioterrorist. There must be some special behaviors that indicated the cause in either arena. He used epidemiology bolstered by science, and Elizabeth employed pattern recognition bolstered by forensics. This was a once-in-a-lifetime experience for an infectious diseases epidemiologist. What made the whole thing even more exciting was that he was intrigued with this attractive woman and the dangerous world in which she worked.

31

Jake then summarized his preliminary analysis. "Four variables show up as statistically significant on my first run, which I've just completed this morning: exposure to a single anesthesiologist; a delay of twenty minutes between the posted or expected starting time of the operation and the time of first incision; exposure to operating theatre number 2; and exposure to one operating theatre nurse."

"But Doctor, which is the most important of the four exposures?"

"My question, too. So the next step is to go from looking at one variable at a time – a so-called univariate analysis – to looking at all of the variables at the same time – a multi-variable analysis. The latter statistical test identifies *independent* exposures, or what you may think of as causes. I'm running that analysis on my computer as we're speaking."

Not pausing to question the analysis, Elizabeth called her chief and, with his concurrence, initiated an immediate stakeout at the homes of the two people who were identified in Jake's initial epidemiological analysis. Anything unusual would be reported immediately to Elizabeth. "I had an uneasy meeting with the hospital director," she said to the person on the other end of the call, "who may turn out to be a weak link in this case. He is unpredictable because of his concerns about adverse publicity and lawsuits, and I believe he has a short fuse in the face of stress."

Overhearing the conversation, Chris had difficulty suppressing a smile.

"Fortunately, he straightened right up when I acknowledged that I was not really asking for his permission but demanding his cooperation with the full force of law. Apparently, he does respect forceful authority."

"Teams of two agents will be in place shortly, parked across from the flats of each of the two healthcare professionals implicated so far. All four agents are relative newcomers to our organization, however, and I think it would be helpful and safer if we had an experienced team of two agents as soon as possible to replace them. I'll arrange for that later. I can have the two teams in place by morning," replied Ronald

Ellis, the district commander of MI-5. "I'll also assign four agents to the case who'll be prepared to meet you when you are ready for a briefing. Keep me informed and take care of yourself. If the physicians are right, this could turn out to be quite dangerous."

Ellis's message had a paternalistic tone, not unexpected for the aging senior member who had recruited Elizabeth to the team twenty-one years earlier. But she let it pass and allowed him to continue. "I'll also run an immediate check on each of the principals and ask Interpol to join in."

"Thanks, sir. I'm set to meet the entire operating theatre team this afternoon after the cultures are reviewed by Professor Christopher Rose. I'll pose as one of the new administrators helping the doctors. But I won't acknowledge that I'm at all focused on the two professionals identified in the initial epidemiological analysis. Instead, I'll meet separately with all fourteen – four surgeons, four anesthesiologists and six nurses or techs. No one will discuss the possibility of a crime. In the meantime, Professor Rose has requested nasal cultures of each one immediately to see if any are carriers."

"Be vigilant, Agent Foster. I'll be in touch." She returned to her seat at the table.

Chris, who had been paged out of the room when Elizabeth was speaking with her supervisor, returned with a disappointed look on his face. He announced that the two women implicated in Jake's analysis – the nurse, Ms. Jeanne Whitcomb, and the anesthesiologist, Dr. Diana Kontos – failed to show up at the Employee Health office for their cultures. Each was called at home after it was learned that they reported not feeling well, and each said that she would return to the emergency department, where one of the nurses was assigned to take their vital signs, do nasal and hand cultures, and carry the samples directly to the laboratory.

Elizabeth called MI-5, and the agents who had recently parked outside at Dr. Kontos' home in Wimbledon confirmed her arrival just after noon. "No sign of her having left the flat since then."

She then placed a call to the agents observing the home of Ms.

Whitcomb. She, too, had arrived and had not left her flat in Swiss Cottage. Both were advised that replacements would arrive by the end of the night shift.

Elizabeth turned to her new colleagues and began to inquire as to why a hacker would pick King's to introduce a designer strain of bacteria. "Is there a particular interest or a research focus on organisms that might be useful for bioterror? A policy analyst or a national or international figure at King's, who has been outspoken? Anyone who has strong opinions about Islamic extremists?"

Chris replied quickly, "I'm not aware of any high profile scientist or policy figure at King's. I can't speculate on who would do this, but would say that the molecular biology skills needed to modify the organism of interest would be substantive." Chris also uttered the phrase *bioterror.*

Jake asked Elizabeth and Chris if it were possible that King's might have been chosen as a testing ground for the manipulated organism. If the testing passed this phase, perhaps a larger, more horrific event would be planned.

Elizabeth said she would ask one of her partners at MI-5 to look into the possible social connections between the surgeon who died and the two health care workers who were identified in Jake's initial univariate analysis.

Jake excitedly gave the results of the multivariable analysis that identified the key predictors for infections in patients. "Exposure either to the nurse, Ms. Whitcomb, or to Anesthesiologist A, Dr. Diana Kontos, *remained significant*," said Jake. "So patients who had anesthesia performed by Dr. Kontos *or* who had surgery when nurse Whitcomb was present in the operating theatre were 4.5 times more likely to be infected with *Staph aureus* than patients exposed only to other anesthesiologists and other nurses. It turns out that Dr. Kontos and the OR nurse, Ms. Whitcomb, frequently work together, so it's difficult to know if one is more important than the other. And they usually work in operating theatre room 2."

Jake described the implications of the analysis. He explained that after correcting for exposure to the two health care workers, exposure to operating theatre room number 2 fell out of the model. The analysis suggested that there was nothing about the environment in the OR that was critical, and that their focus should be on the two health care workers.

Elizabeth took in this information attentively and paused a moment before responding. "Tell me what you think of the significance of a single surgeon's being infected, Jake? What's the connection?" asked Elizabeth.

Admitting that he was speculating at this early phase of the investigation, Jake replied, "Either he was involved directly or he had the ill fortune of being exposed accidentally – caught in the random cross-fire of the organism and the targeted individuals, the patients. However, the early analysis suggests that he's not a key risk factor. I did a quick review of the OR schedule earlier; it looks like he was a workaholic who spent hours performing surgery. I doubt that he would have had the time or background experience to be directly involved. It is possible, of course, that if one of the two people – the nurse or the anesthesiologist in the operating room – were a carrier, Professor Allen might have picked up the organism during surgery from direct contact. Alternatively, he could have contracted the infection from a patient who was a carrier. Since his nasal culture was negative, it would appear he wasn't a long-term carrier, but perhaps he had picked up the organism in the last few weeks, possibly in the last seven days.

"At this point, I see a greater likelihood that Professor Allen was a victim and not a perpetrator. However, he was such a high-profile surgeon and was apparently interested in the Middle East; you may have to consider the possibility that he was a deliberate target. Of course, it could just be bad luck, like being at the wrong place when lightning hits, but I deal with odds, and this seems oddly unusual."

Finishing lunch, the three sketched out their respective tasks for the afternoon. The interviews with the twelve available operating theatre team members would take most of the afternoon, and both Jake and Elizabeth agreed to be in the room to listen to ideas each team member would offer. Meanwhile, Chris would oversee the microbiological testing already underway.

Jake's primary role as he reviewed it for the team would be to ask if anything in the standard practice had changed: Any new drugs given? Any new equipment used? More importantly, any new personnel with access to the OR? Any skin or eye infections noted by one or more members of the operating team? Anyone with family members with boils, styes, or skin infections? "These are the kind of infections that staph could cause, Elizabeth."

Jake would of course conduct the inquiries, attempt to allay unnecessary fears, and emphasize handwashing and other assiduous infection control practices. If new patients were identified, he would outline appropriate isolation procedures: a single patient room; gown, gloves and mask worn by all healthcare workers exposed to the patient; and negative air pressure in the room relative to the hallway as an extreme precaution to avoid airborne spread within the hospital. Elizabeth said she would carefully observe the responses, seeking insights into the personalities of each individual, based on their statements and the cadence and timbre of their words. She would observe the degree of eye contact, what wasn't said, and each person's body language.

Jake and Elizabeth sat on the same side of a square table in a small office near the operating theatre. Each member of the operating room team sat across from them and, after a series of questions, was asked if she or he had any ideas about the infections, any concerns, or anything else to say.

In general, there were no surprises until the last two persons to be interviewed discussed their concerns. A male nurse said he had a few things to get off his chest. Todd Ayliffe was a fifty-year-old man who appeared to be quite earnest and concerned, speaking in a loud whisper. He recalled that Professor Allen and one of the OR nurses had a disagreement about ten days ago during a difficult nodal dissection in an obese woman with advanced breast cancer. Towards the end of the operation Professor Allen had been feeling for the tip of the curved needle that he was delicately pushing through the tissue when the nurse hit his arm, causing the needle to penetrate his hand. "It looked like she did it on purpose, Professor Evans. It may be that that is how he became infected. I've written down the name of the nurse, Ms. Jenny Pickens, in case you think it's important."

Jake thanked him for his openness and assured Mr. Ayliffe that every angle would be pursued.

Before the last person to be interviewed came in the room, Elizabeth asked Jake if that accident or purposeful error had any relevance. Jake replied that it put the surgeon at risk for blood-borne infections such as HIV and Hepatitis C but less likely for *Staphylococcus* infection unless the woman had the organism circulating in her blood. Checking his computer, he found that she had never developed a fever during her entire stay. Furthermore, Ms. Pickens was not identified in the analysis as a risk factor.

Then an anesthesiologist named Dr. Graham Rogers entered, and he had a concern. He was strident in his response. "Is it at all possible that Professor Allen was the victim of a deliberate bacterial infection?" He knew that at times Allen had raised money for Jewish causes but was very much a moderate, showing sympathy for all factions of the Middle East. "His even-handed views got him into some bitter disagreements," said Dr. Rogers. "I attended one of the fund raising events, and someone in the crowd said that it would be better for the famous surgeon to be dead than showing the least bit of sympathy to Israel's enemies. I stopped going to the fund raisers after that night."

The comment took Jake by surprise. He stiffened his back and bit his lower lip. After Dr. Rogers left the room, Jake stated, "If there's merit in that statement, Elizabeth, it would account for the motive behind the introduction of an organism to the OR. But how would an assassin do this?"

"Too early to tell, and I need to establish if Dr. Rogers himself is free of conflict. It's an alarming insinuation, but I'll take it seriously, and follow up with Dr. Rogers about the details behind his concerns."

The interviews pointedly suggested that most of the operating theatre crew had significant anxieties about the cases because of the rapidity of the deaths and because one of their own, Professor Jeffrey Allen himself, had fallen victim to the devastating illness. Each seemed somewhat assured by the responses of the American expert and his confidence that this problem could be managed.

Six o'clock had arrived quickly, and all three principals met over dinner at the hospital, in a private dining room arranged by Chris. An Indian meal was served with samosas, basmati rice with saffron, chicken tiki masala, mango chutney and Cardamon tea. The air was completely filled with a delightfully savory vapor, and the flavors ranged from the floral taste of the rice, the varied spices of the masala and contrasting fruit, and the slightly bitter taste of chutney. While the meal was a working dinner, all three were aware of how comfortable they were in each other's presence, exploring each other's thoughts, building a team.

Elizabeth summarized what little there was in Dr. Kontos' personnel chart: "An excellent anesthesiologist who has been on the staff for two years. Completed graduate training and a fellowship at Frankfurt University in Germany. Her referring letters were strong. The file contains no details about her undergraduate training or place of birth. She is thirty-six years old and listed as single. She is variously described as aloof yet highly professional and extremely competent."

Elizabeth passed around a photograph that showed Kontos to be remarkably attractive, with olive skin, large brown eyes, black hair, and a prominent dimple on her right cheek. Her annual reviews by the professor of anesthesiology were laudatory, even remarking on "her strong work ethic and quiet and respectful personality."

In the report, she was also described as technically quite skillful. A few annual reviews noted her "great dexterity in intubating patients" about to receive general anesthesia before surgery. Furthermore, with a delicate touch she could insert a needle into the thread-like vein of a premature baby or a deeply traversing and invisible vein of an obese adult. Her colleagues thought so highly of her skills with a needle that one of them recorded with obvious hyperbole that she could "place the needle or its contents between individual cellular layers of the epidermis."

Elizabeth continued, "Ms. Whitcomb is of African descent, and both parents had emigrated from Jamaica. She grew up in Surry with close family ties and married a neighbor and school boyfriend when both entered nursing school in London. They have three children, and there is no record of their having traveled outside of the U.K. Husband and wife are quite active in the community. Once or twice a year they have, in fact, joined Professor Allen in some fund-raising efforts."

The interviews with the operating theatre staff were unrevealing, and further laboratory tests would not be available until the next morning. Jake said that he needed to call his wife, and Chris thought that a full night at home with his family was proper. Elizabeth said she would return to her office to meet the four colleagues assigned to assist her directly with the investigation. She would caution the two agents newly assigned to each of the suspects about the seriousness of the task and unknown risks. Thereafter, she would be joining her husband, informing him that there could be some long days of work for her ahead.

Elizabeth's cell phone went off, and the agent at the other end said, "Dr. Kontos has returned to the flat, having gone to the hospital for her cultures."

"Why didn't you notify me immediately when she left?" inquired a vexed Elizabeth. She knew that the more senior agents scheduled to arrive would never let that happen.

"Sorry, ma'am, I was intent on following her myself. She's back, and I have her under surveillance."

Elizabeth hung up and related what had happened to the two physicians.

Chris immediately phoned the Casualty Department and asked to speak with the nurse who obtained the hand and nasal cultures. He had inquired if the local staff members were sure that Dr. Kontos had arrived to be cultured. They had responded affirmatively, assuring the compulsive microbiologist that swabs of her nares and her hands were obtained for culture. Apparently there was no sign of illness and she had no fever. Her reason for being away was that she had had a backache. The nurse also noted that Ms. Whitcomb just arrived for her cultures. Chris then said that he might know by the next afternoon if the cultures were positive for staph. If so, he would run the DNA fingerprinting to see if it was the special strain of staph in which they were interested.

Elizabeth's cell phone rang again, and this time it was her boss. "Agent Foster, as you requested, we're looking to see if there are any social connections among the surgeon and the two people you have high on your list.

"In the meantime, nothing unusual checks out for Ms. Whitcomb. She is a solid citizen, on several civic committees and church groups. Keeps mostly at home and manages the children with her husband. We are seeking any connection between Professor Allen and either of the two women other than the obvious: their work in the operating theatre. We don't yet know where Dr. Kontos was born. However, what we know so far about Diana Kontos is that she was raised as a teenager outside of Athens, subsequently went to the American University in Beirut, and then to medical school and anesthesia training in Germany after sitting for a PhD in Lebanon. Her doctoral field of study in Beirut: molecular genetics and microbiology."

V

The central hall of the Convention Centre – about one-third the size of a football field – was abuzz with the activities of delegates arriving mid-morning, registering for the meeting, and queuing up for their name badges and backpacks laden with the Powerpoint handouts and key references from the scientific literature supplementing the three-day conference. Amid the cacophony of noise and laughter, people who had not seen their colleagues for a year or more strutted from group to group, offering sound bites on their latest research findings. The repetitive blinking of camera flashes among smiling trios and quartets of delegates telegraphed the renewal of friendships in the crowd. A number of sprightly young women in forest green sport jackets and matching knee socks, white blouses, and grey woolen skirts guided the international guests to the proper queues, depending on whether the delegates had pre-registered or instead arrived needing to complete the proper forms for onsite registration. Some of the hostesses were ferrying around silver trays amid the sea of guests, serving tea and biscuits to the newly registered delegates, generously seeking eye contact while weaving erratic paths through the hall to avoid bumping into people.

The staff of the Convention Centre were highly trained and organized, and in recent years they had hosted international conferences ranging from a convention on space exploration to an Islamic and Christian religious meeting to a convention of international trucking associates. Jake scanned the framed posters of these earlier conferences on the

41

wall of the hall. On electronic calendars at four locations in the hall was the list of future conventions; in the next three weeks there would be meetings of the International Stock Exchange, the Chemical Society, the culinary societies of France and Italy, and the Israeli-American Medical-Legal Association.

Jake stopped a moment to admire the striking three-story structure, especially the architecture of the central hall, which reached to a completely glass roof that peaked at the center. The gleaming white light piercing through gave magnificent illumination below. On a wall just inside the door of the hall, he noticed a diagram displaying convention rooms of varying sizes, from the 1500-seat auditorium for plenary sessions to three 500-seat rooms, equipped with the latest audiovisual technology.

Several placards held the outline of the days' activities: the plenary session on infection control would begin at 4:45 p.m. with a procession and several welcoming addresses, first by the chair of the organizing committee and then by the mayor of London. In the large auditorium Jake Evans would be introduced to give the first of the four daily keynote talks, after which numerous brief presentations from the international delegates would begin. A senior colleague from Geneva would provide a glowing thirty-second summary of his career.

Jake's credentials were impressive. He was a full professor by age thirty-six. Supported by NIH during a career which was notable for a record of prolific epidemiological studies, he had pinpointed the cause of over ten major epidemics in several U.S. hospitals. He would be recognized for his leadership in advising the NIH as a member of the National Research Council and for his extraordinary funding from the National Institute of Allergy and Infectious Diseases in Bethesda, Maryland. Most of his basic science work dealt with mathematical modeling of the transmission of infectious diseases.

Jake's jet lag and fatigue were constant companions, and he thought about his call last night to Deb. He telephoned to say that he had arrived, the flight was comfortable, and he had already run into Chris, who had asked his assistance with an infection control problem.

He could imagine Deb sitting on a chair in the center hallway, next to a small maple table with inlaid mother of pearl, when the phone rang. Thanking Jake for his call, she exhaled the next sentence with sharp edges, etching instructions to her husband. "Jake, you know our twentieth anniversary is on the day after you return. So don't you dare miss your flights for any reason."

"No problem, Deb. I'll be back in plenty of time," he responded unemotionally, checking his watch – 9:30 p.m., he noted.

"Well, I hope so. There's more to your life than medicine, your international talks, your fellows and patients. You have a family – in case you've forgotten."

"Deb, I haven't forgotten. You can count on me." Jake said this while breathing deeply through his nostrils, as though he thought all of the admonitions were unnecessary. But even the argument the night before his flight about his expansive travels for lectures had ended unsuccessfully. Furthermore, despite all of his apologies and complete focus on his wife's concerns, his subsequent romantic overtures were rebuffed with Deb's reminding him repeatedly "not to play with the natives on this visit to the U.K."

Deb responded with a pent-up litany: "Do you know how many of our children's birthdays you have missed, how many Christmas mornings you were away seeing patients in the hospital, on how many of our anniversaries you were traveling? Yes, we live well, you are a fine doctor, and when you schedule time on your calendar for us, you are here some of the time. But even when you are with us, your goddamn BlackBerry seems more important than conversation with the family. You can't even set it aside for dinner!"

"Deb, you have no worries. I'll be home for our anniversary and look forward to returning home. I love you."

After saying good night, Jake set his travel alarm and prepared for a quiet evening. Having again swallowed a three-milligram pill of melatonin, both for jet lag and its hypnotic effect, he collapsed heavily into bed at ten o'clock in the evening, descending into a deep sleep.

Jake awakened to a blustery, gray but dry morning. After showering, he spent an hour doing emails and reviewing his presentation. He also made initial revisions on a manuscript he had brought along before taking a twenty-minute walk and returning to his room.

He had felt a little groggy earlier with a slight headache, but a one-hour nap, three ibuprofen capsules, and two cups of espresso at an Italian bakery had fired him up for an animated thirty-minute Powerpoint presentation.

Jake approached the stage from a seat in the front row near the edge of the right aisle. This was a critical time. His talk was good, but he knew that it would have to be great to get media attention. He needed to be crisp, scientifically critical, and provocative. He would especially look for an opportunity to provoke the audience, to create a newsworthy event for reporters listening to the talk. His recent discussions with the dean were blunt but encouraging: If *The New York Times* picked up his story, the award was likely to be his. What he didn't tell the dean was that if he won the International Award, a professorship at Harvard would be offered, and he would be leaving for the East Coast. Only Deb knew this.

Red carpet covered the four steps leading to the oak podium with the computer screen facing him, a mouse with a pointer, and keyboard to advance the slides. He bent the necks of two microphones upwards so that they would be closer to his mouth.

Jake's presentation began with a summary of the problem of antibiotic resistance in U.S. hospitals, increasingly riddled with microbes susceptible to fewer and fewer antibiotics. He made the point that few pharmaceutical companies had remained in the business of anti-infective discovery, just when countries all over the world were observing more microbial resistance.

He reminded his audience that in the 1930s and 1940s, there were four new classes of antibiotics discovered, each with novel antibacterial targets: sulfa drugs, penicillin, and the aminoglycoside drug called streptomycin – the first wonder drug for tuberculosis. Each of the three discoverers of the first three antibiotics won a Nobel Prize. Then there was chloramphenicol – the first effective treatment for typhoid fever. In the 1950s and 1960s, the most prolific period for antibiotic discovery, six more classes became available.

"The bad news is that in the 1970s, 1980s, and 1990s, no new classes of antibiotics were available and all 'new' drugs were merely derivatives of earlier classes." He noted that no novel targets on the bacteria were identified and successfully followed by new antibiotics to hit those molecular targets. Only in 2000 and 2003 were two new classes of antibiotics introduced – linezolid and daptomycin.

"Meanwhile, Aventis and Roche spun off their anti-infective business; Bristol Myers Squibb, Eli-Lilly, Wyeth, and Proctor and Gamble ended anti-infective discovery; and GlaxoSmithKline downsized their antibiotic research enterprise."

He added that with fewer drugs, clinicians were facing more menacing bacteria causing infections to occur in hospitals; half of staph infections all around the globe were resistant to methicillin.

"For the first time in history," he said, "we are seeing safety-net drugs like vancomycin fail – though rarely." He felt himself cringe at his last statement, knowing that he could not announce to the audience of almost a thousand that microbiological history was being made right then in London.

Jake briefly described the eleven fully vancomycin-resistant staph isolates in unrelated patients in Michigan, Pennsylvania, Delaware, and New York state. "Fortunately, in each case there were no serious outcomes for the patients and no secondary transmissions, but vigilance is critical. There is an office at CDC continually monitoring these rare infections and an entire laboratory dedicated to studying the biology of these bacteria," he said with equanimity.

"Early in the twenty-first century, we are facing a crisis in the interaction of man and microbe."

Jake went on to describe the microbial traffic of organisms from the hospital to the community and, more recently, in the opposite direction. "In most U.S. cities, a special form of methicillin-resistant staph has emerged in the community – quite distinct strains from the usual hospital-associated organisms. In young adults, cosmetic body shaving has emerged as a risk factor, as has spending time in a communal hot tub. Epidemics involving prisoners have occurred, and infections are now increasingly seen in professional and collegiate football players and wrestlers in the U.S. The sharing of towels and soap is thought to be important in some outbreaks. Some individuals have lost their lives."

Jake then began to ad lib in an attempt to provoke the audience. "Suppose we are faced with no effective antibiotics to treat life-threatening infections? Imagine that we clinicians are pushed back to the pre-antibiotic era, when the mortality of bloodstream infections due to *Staph aureus* was over eighty percent. Once such a resistant organism gains entrance to our hospitals, it will march through our ICUs like wildfire! Infection control would be effective at some hospitals but would be practiced without discipline in others. My friends, without vaccines and effective antibiotics, our field itself will become a vestige of internal medicine, a relic of historical interest only." He banged his fist on the podium, feeling the fervor of a religious leader.

Suddenly he caught the strident, almost evangelistic tone of his own message and viewed a startled audience – all eyes on him as though wondering what drug he was on. He dialed back his volume and softened the delivery.

"We need expert, worldwide surveillance to detect the movement of resistant strains; we need to be much wiser in limiting our excessive use of antibiotics and much bolder about enforcing handwashing, proper isolation, and effective infection control measures."

During the question and answer period, Jake found the audience to be less than friendly.

The first person with a question at the microphone identified himself as the professor from Birmingham and instead of addressing Jake as Professor Evans, noted that he took exception to the doomsday scenario of a nervous colleague from abroad. Did the gentleman expert from the States see the end of the world coming, an apocalypse of marching microbes engulfing mankind? Could he not entertain the idea of science rising to the rescue in a responsible and calm fashion?

To Jake's embarrassment, there was modest applause after the professor's questions. He felt the need to backpedal and say only that he was giving a worst-case scenario. But he realized that his free comments, the result of fatigue, had possibly undermined his message.

A physician from Basel then stepped up to the microphone, identified himself as a member of industry, and once again Jake was taken to task. He, too, never referred to Jake as Doctor or Professor Evans. "I fear the Americans have lost all sense of the free enterprise system. Do they not realize how much money – between one hundred million and a billion euros – it costs to bring a drug to market? Do they not realize how many lifesaving products the pharmaceutical industry has produced? Are we supposed to give away our technology and creativity? I regret the speaker's failure to appreciate the successful efforts of dedicated scientists in one of the greatest industries in the free world!"

This time there was sustained and loud applause. Reporters in the front row were typing notes frantically, and a few photographers rose to take Jake's picture, capturing an awkward frown. Not feeling up for a fight in a foreign country, Jake apologetically responded that industry had certainly produced useful products, and that was the reason he had hoped they would re-engage with the field of infectious diseases.

After receiving a small applause himself at the end of the Q and A period, Jake remained at the Convention Centre only briefly, avoiding several reporters hotly pursuing him to follow up on his remarks, hoping to make something of the controversy he had created. Instead, he ran outside for a cab ride to King's. In fact, he began to think that his talk was a disaster, a feeling he would confide in Chris.

Chris's reverence for the inherent beauty of microbiology was expressed in the hallway leading to his office, in a simply-framed graphic of the penicillin molecule discovered by Alexander Fleming almost a century before. To Jake, it looked like a child's drawing of a simple, two-story house with a peaked roof and an attached, rectangular, one-story garage. Framed on an opposite wall was the outline of the twisted-ladder model of DNA originally proposed by James Watson and Francis Crick. "Men of discipline who made their reputations in science," Chris would reiterate to his PhD students in microbiology, "continually optimistic in the pursuit of knowledge despite repeated experimental setbacks. But when discovery came their way, both had what Pasteur called the *prepared mind*."

Chris welcomed Jake, who immediately recognized from the ashen look on his face that Chris was distressed. "Mary just called, Jake, to say that she found a lump in her breast and wants to know immediately what the diagnosis is. She scheduled a biopsy herself with one of Professor Allen's colleagues at King's. I told her we would talk tonight when I arrive home, but hinted that we may want to wait a few days. I couldn't say over the phone that I would be terrified to have her undergo a breast biopsy here and now."

Chris changed the topic from his wife's discovery to focus on the outbreak, imploring Jake to stay on as long as possible until this epidemic was solved.

To Jake, the stakes were raised with an explosive epidemic of thirteen patients including the infection of a healthcare worker, the leading surgeon who died so quickly. Jake was hoping he could make a difference, and he could sense the adrenalin racing throughout his body. He would have to stay on. What and how would he tell Deb remained a question.

Jake began to ask questions about the late Professor Allen, who was so revered. Like an old army horse hearing the call of the bugle, he was now ready, and he rattled off a series of epidemiological interrogatories, "Was he in any way immunosuppressed? On steroids for any reason? Any history of chronic illnesses? A transplant patient, by chance? Any history of repeated skin infections or styes? Any possibility of his being an IV drug abuser?"

"Nothing we know about, Jake."

There were two immediate issues: how did the surgeon get infected, and how would fear be managed, the fear naturally expected from the hospital staff? The outbreak was already serious: patients were involved, and now a leading surgical professor was dead. There would be continual fear, the kind that had gripped hospitals from Hong Kong to Toronto during the SARS outbreak, an acute illness that claimed the lives of so many physicians and nurses taking care of infected patients. The same fear was seen in the spring of 2009 among Mexican health workers when the H1N1 virus – swine flu – hit the capital city. Jake knew that part of the task would be to communicate accurately and transparently to the hospital staff, patients, and visitors. Each group would need to be assured that everything possible was being done to protect their health.

"Chris, what *do* we know about Professor Allen?"

"Well, he was a national leader in breast cancer surgery and breast reconstruction. Came from a wealthy family. He was a major fund-raiser for various Jewish organizations, although he was a vocal champion of peaceful coexistence of *all* religious groups in Israel.

"To be blunt, he was an outspoken critic of American policy in the Middle East. The two goals in his mind were security for Israel and sovereignty for the Palestinians. However, he thought that both goals were elusive so long as the U.S. was both a partner with Israel and the major peace broker. In his mind, the sooner the U.S. got out of the peace process, the sooner the prospect of peace would occur. I don't mean to offend you with that statement, but you seem interested in knowing the real person."

"I take no offense," said Jake, who felt hard-pressed to define the U.S. and Middle Eastern policy.

"He has a son who is a talented graphic artist, but father and son became estranged about ten years ago. Not sure of the details. Phillip was the apple of his father's eye – an excellent student, a star on the rugby team, a handsome and engaging extrovert who was a political activist for the disenfranchised from his mid-teens on. He was particularly sensitive to the lack of access to healthcare among people in Africa, those in former colonies of England.

"The rumors are that when the son came out of the closet in his late teens, the paternal reception was not so friendly. Apparently, it must have been more than an ambitious surgeon pursuing a high-profile career could bear in a family member, and a source of personal embarrassment for the professor. The son and his partner still live in London, I think. Most people who knew Professor Allen well say that that was the time when he began to bury himself in work. I don't know anything else about his personal life. He tended to keep his activities away from the university quite close to the vest."

Checking his BlackBerry, Jake opened a note from Deb. *Hi Honey. Sorry for being so crabby on the phone. I just arranged a special venue for our anniversary celebration. It costs a fortune, but we'll only do this every 20 years. Think of me in diaphanous silk holding a bottle of champagne and two flutes. Don't leave me stranded at the B&B! Love, Deb.*

VI

At a small, second-floor flat in the Wimbledon section of London, two women were having an argument. The roommates were anxiously facing each other, clutching the forearms of one another, each trying to reassure the other that now was the time for calm, for resolve, that all would eventually be fine.

Each was dressed in cotton pajamas, one an apricot color and the other a pale yellow shade. They were sitting up against the headboard of the king-size bed, which was covered with a white, fluffy duvet, bordered with a wide blue meander pattern of repeating lines at ninety-degree angles every twenty centimeters. The women were sitting on top of the duvet, leaning back against two side-by-side stacks of three pillows encased in brilliant white linen covers.

"You are usually so careful, so meticulous. What in God's name hap-happened?" asked one.

Diana Kontos responded, "I have no idea. I just don't know. What I *do* know was that microbes hide in skin crevices and can occasionally evade handwashing, but I followed the protocol diligently. I took no chances that I knew about. I'm as puzzled as you. Possibly I became colonized in the nose and on the hands."

"I tol-told you before not to wear artificial na-nails when you socialize. You should have listened to me, since that may have been the weak link. You need to add the antibiotic cream immediately to your hands after re-removing the nails and then to-to your nose," said Sasha.

"I have already done so, dear," said Diana in a reassuring tone.

"How will you handle the American epi-epidemiologist who is working with the microbiology professor?"

"There are always outbreaks of staph after surgery," said Diana, "so that's not a problem. And with luck, it's over."

"What if Professor Rose starts examining the staph isolates in some de-detail?" asked the roommate.

"Hopefully, if he recognizes it's unusual, he'll chalk it up to bad luck or to randomness. If he does more, we'll have to rely on our contingency plans. I'll call Ata right away. Don't worry; he'll take care of everything. He's always given us good advice. I love you, and you are safe."

"I love you, too."

After making the phone call, Diana came back, fully relaxed, and hugged Sasha, who was still sitting up in bed. Diana told her that they should both get some rest. "Ata said that he would look into matters immediately and prepare for all contingences." To calm both, Diana said that she would recite Sasha's favorite story from childhood, a local village interpretation of an ancient myth.

Once upon a time on the edge of a beautiful river there was a tranquil village that began to be terrified by a menacing Minotaur who chased young maidens through the winding streets, threatening to devour them. The Minotaur would suddenly appear from a hidden alley, bare his threatening teeth and smile, and inquire if the little girls wanted to race on the way to their homes. A race seemed like a good idea since all the young girls were trained to run swiftly in that village.

The Minotaur was delighted to race the village girls, but told them that they had to join him for dinner if they lost the race. He knew all of the twists and turns of the labyrinthine streets of the village by heart.

Several of the little girls lost the race to the surprisingly fleet Minotaur and were never found again. The fear and dread in the village rose, as increasing numbers of schoolmates no longer showed up for class. So one of the young maidens came up with an idea to fool the Minotaur: they would dress up like boys and wear long pants, cut their hair and speak in an artificially deep voice.

Very soon the Minotaur could find no little girls to ask to race home, and two years went by without any maidens disappearing.

One sunny day a handsome young man from another town proudly rode into the village on a large, white horse. He had a long, silver sword by his side, and he announced that he was looking for a Minotaur that had ravaged his own village before being chased out over four years earlier. In fact, the Minotaur had devoured his beautiful girlfriend before fleeing.

The handsome young man was surprised to see only young boys in the village and no young maidens. As he rode near two young people, the disguised girls revealed the truth and that they were fearful of the Minotaur. The man on horseback listened attentively, and he was told that the Minotaur ran through the village square every day at three o'clock, and since it was 2:45 p.m., he would surely arrive soon. The handsome man thanked the young girls and rode off to the village square in a brisk canter.

Just as the bell rang three times and the Minotaur approached, the handsome young man drew his silver sword, charged the Minotaur, and thrust the sharp blade into the belly of the beast. As soon as he did this, out came twenty-one maidens, all joyous at their release and the death of the Minotaur. One of the maidens was the girlfriend of the strange and handsome man, and she was pulled up onto the horse next to him to return to her village.

To commemorate the event, all young maidens once a year wear long pants and pull their hair behind their heads to appear like boys when they congregate at the village square.

The two women smiled at each other, embraced, and kissed each other tenderly.

Feeling better, Sasha went to the dresser and opened the bottom drawer to view a framed photograph of a woman and young girl from an earlier time.

So many deceptions, so many promises and lies at that time, she thought. They had lost it all – family, land, home – and then were forced to live in another country, and oh, so crowded! And the family still had the keys – useless keys to the front door, kept for decades.

Staring at the photograph, she wondered how it was all possible. *And now they humiliate those left behind, crushing their homes with bulldozers, crushing their will with a wall, denying our people good medicine, a right to vote, a right to seek a good job, a right to live like a person. Where is humanity? And where is justice?*

Tears welled in Sasha's eyes as Diana moved closer to embrace her. "I know what you feel, but we need to be optimistic." She kissed her again, tasting the salinity of the falling teardrops.

Outside the building, two MI-5 agents in a 2004 Citroën were sipping tea from their respective thermal containers, listening to the odd conversation between two women at 11:30 p.m., having placed a bug in the apartment earlier, with the landlord's help. They had been dispatched to the area at 11:00 p.m., replacing their younger colleagues. They were parked beneath the canopy offered by a sycamore tree diagonally across from the main entrance to the brick, four-story building, which was one segment in a series of rowhouses that had been converted into upscale apartments some years back. Having finished their preliminary surveillance earlier, they knew there was a back entrance reserved for the tenants living on the ground floor; all others left by the front door.

"No need to watch a rear entrance," said one officer.

The other nodded and remarked, "By the way, congratulations on the birth of your son! You've got some strong set of goolies to be a parent again at the advanced age of forty-five!"

"Thank you, Eric. But since this is my second marriage and my wife is only thirty, she was quite eager to get pregnant and have a child of her own. I plan to spend more time with this one than I did with my older two."

"I know what you mean. My bird wants me to retire this year. Get a jolly safer job part-time so we can travel. I plan to tell the boss at next month's meeting."

At four-hour intervals they would phone in to a control officer. For fun they wagered on the point spread of the upcoming football match between England and Ireland. Both, of course, were confident that England would prevail. Each week they would place a wager on one of the football games, but because they were friends, they placed a two-pound limit on the bet.

Across town, Jake was calling Deb, thanking her for her email and special plans for an anniversary celebration, yet imploring her to be understanding. He told her that he was pulled away from the meetings unexpectedly because of the "problem" at King's. He briefly mentioned again his embarrassment after his talk and alluded to meeting a "senior woman in MI-5" because of a fear about the organism.

Deborah Evans told her husband curtly, "Three things you need to know. I will not accept your missing our anniversary; you need to be sure that you don't create any international ill will through overconfidence too early; and again, no affairs – and I mean it!" She then said, "Good night," and hung up the phone.

Jake placed the phone back on the receiver and felt a heavy sense of fatigue. He fell into a deep sleep shortly after swallowing a small melatonin tablet. It seemed like only minutes went by before the alarm went off at 6:00 a.m., and he prepared to join Chris at the hospital.

At 7:00 a.m., Chris was pacing back and forth when Jake arrived, arms flailing, appearing almost electrified with some new information.

Jake immediately asked how it was with Mary.

"She indeed has a small lump, about a centimeter in diameter and hard. But it's not fixed to the overlying skin. I told her it could be benign or malignant and explained the problem here and my fears about a biopsy at King's. After I reviewed the usual rate of growth and suggested that a week would not be a long delay, she was still worried.

So we'll plan on a biopsy at Oxford tomorrow, which I arranged through a colleague last night."

Chris had arrived at the lab to check his experiments and said his hypothesis was confirmed. He knew he had seen a microbiological feature never before witnessed.

"What are you talking about, Chris?"

"Jake, do you know anything about the term *quorum sensing*?"

"I've seen the phrase, but I don't know much about it. Something about the way bacteria communicate to each other."

"Yes, that's it. Until recently no one knew that bacteria actually have a system that recognizes each other's presence. New studies show that, in fact, they can. Imagine this scenario: A colony of bacteria grows on the inside of a plastic IV catheter or on a prosthetic hip device or mechanical heart valve, building its numbers over a period of time. At a crucial concentration of bacteria – a quorum – because of the production of certain chemical signals that we know to be like pheromones – all organisms signal each other to produce toxins simultaneously in order to kill the host.

"What I'm saying is that when the quorum is reached, suddenly the bacteria are essentially able to send out a kind of microbial broadcast email and immediately transform a large number of individual predators into a disciplined army. It's as though they had waited patiently until their numbers became so great that they could kill the host before the host knew they were there, offering little time to mount an immune response. It is hard for a single organism, one bacterium, to make it in life. But if many organisms can learn to function like a multi-cellular species, survival is enhanced. What is interesting is that each species has a specific language. An *E. coli* can tell how many other *E. coli* are in an area and also how many total bacteria of all species. Thus, bacteria are bilingual in their communication."

"What's that got to do with our organism?'

"When I ran some molecular studies, in one of the isolates I found the quorum-sensing mechanism was jacked up a hundredfold. Jake, we knew we had an organism that is resistant to a key antibiotic, and

I also detected the virulence factor, PVL, in four isolates. The latter is not so unusual for some staph species. However, when I ran tests on all isolates, I found two isolates with incredibly high concentrations of PVL. I then reasoned that, because the production of PVL seemed so magnified, maybe there was some stimulation of the quorum-sensing activity. And Jake, that's it! That's why a few victims died so quickly. It's not just that PVL is present in four isolates, but in the two patients who died rapidly – Professor Jeffrey Allen and Janet Woolsey – its production was revved up tremendously from baseline. I'll try to understand exactly the molecular biology behind this, but quorum sensing is the key to this organism's virulence."

Jake realized that Chris's findings explained why some patients had such a relentless downhill path to death. They also explained the especially virulent nature of the infection in the last victim, Professor Allen, whose rapid demise was associated with extraordinary lesions in his heart and brain.

"Here's another point, Jake. Of all the isolates I've now tested, only two have an abnormally high quorum-sensing activity, only four have the presence of any PVL production, and all have the gene for vancomycin resistance."

"What do you conclude from that?"

"To me," Chris said resolutely, "this is firm evidence that we are observing a series of experiments in which a talented molecular biologist is rapidly adding new features to an organism. First, a gene for vancomycin resistance was inserted, then a gene for PVL production, and finally a gene to increase dramatically the production of PVL. The organism made unusually large concentrations of PVL because its production rate was accelerated. Productivity was enhanced by an aberrant stimulation of quorum-sensing activity. This is essentially a *Staphylococcus aureus* on performance enhancing steroids!

"In short, we are witnesses to a longitudinal series of increasingly complex experiments. Most importantly, this finding indicates a molecular hacker with potentially Nobel-Prize-winning skills."

Jake suddenly felt disoriented, and a chill overcame him briefly.

He had read speculative reports about bioterror labs in dark corners of remote parts of the world, but he'd never seen any conclusive data about molecular enhancements of serious pathogens. Furthermore, he had never imagined himself involved in an epidemic involving a criminal.

"Chris, I appreciate your work and believe you may be right about this being a case of bioterrorism. I've never worked on anything like this before, but seeing what's been happening here at King's, I'm ready to do what I can to help you and Elizabeth. Count me in!"

"We'll need each other's skills, Jake. And I hope you'll be flexible about your return."

Jake just nodded nervously. He didn't want Chris to worry about Deb's insistence on a prescribed return date. Chris had enough to worry about, both in the lab and at home.

"Another thing occurs to me, Chris. When you finish examining all of the isolates, would you give me the names of the patients and the genetic profile of the organisms? Then I'll try to link the clinical presentations and the outcomes with the genetic repertoire of the bacteria in a statistical analysis."

"Brilliant. I'll get you the information as soon as I finish my studies."

A knock on the door indicated that Elizabeth had arrived. "Gentlemen, there have been new developments, and we may have to move quickly." There was an intense seriousness in her voice. "First, what do you have, Chris?"

Chris briefly reviewed what he had just covered with Jake and listened anxiously as a distressed Elizabeth described the failure of the two senior agents stationed outside of Diana Kontos' flat to call in at 6:00 a.m. as expected. She had immediately dispatched an investigating team to the site, and the surveillance car with the two agents was missing. "Only a few fragments of glass were found and evidence of blood on the glass – nothing else. The glass will undergo analysis this morning to see if it matches the windows in the Citroën. It would be a gross understatement to say that I'm worried." She was clenching both fists tightly as she finished speaking.

Now the color faded from Jake's face, and a mounting fear crept over him. People were dying in the hospital who should have lived, and now a surveillance team of officers had disappeared and might have met a bloody demise.

For his part, Chris was equally frightened about the new level of threat.

Both physicians retreated to the comfort zone of their expertise. Chris proceeded to the incubator and pulled out the culture plates of the two health-care workers who had been screened the day before. "No staph yet, which means that they will probably all be negative. We'll be able to confirm the data this afternoon."

Jake looked puzzled. Since the epidemiological data seemed to pinpoint Dr. Kontos, he would have thought there was a ninety five percent probability their cultures would be positive if she were involved.

"I'll double check with the nurse in the Casualty Department who did the cultures," said Chris.

Dialing Casualty, Chris asked for the nurse who obtained the swabs for cultures and then inquired, "Are you sure that you cultured Dr. Kontos and that you brought the correct specimens to the lab yesterday? Forgive me for being so persistent, but I just need to be a little compulsive by asking."

"Yes," responded the nurse. "I don't know Dr. Kontos personally, but I have seen her occasionally in the hospital cafeteria, and I definitely know what she looks like. She is the one I cultured. I personally delivered the swabs to the microbiology receiving area myself."

When Chris repeated the information to Jake and Elizabeth, Jake had to admit plaintively that "epidemiology is a great screening tool but occasionally is not perfect. Yet the data are so strong that we shouldn't dismiss this individual yet."

A call on Elizabeth's cell from Agent Ellis, her supervisor, interrupted the conversation. "We found the Citroën only ten blocks from the apartment, with both side windows shattered and bullets lodged in the seats, which are grossly bloody. No sign of the agents, and no sign of the tapes of the conversation. We won't even know what they heard, and obviously it doesn't look good. I fear the worst."

Elizabeth paused to repeat what she'd learned to Jake and Chris.

Jake realized that his dark anxieties were confirmed. People with no publicized connection to the outbreak had died a bloody death. Did the killer know about the workup going on at King's? How far would the killer go to end the investigation? Could he and Chris be *obstacles* in the eyes of the criminals? Obstacles that needed to be eliminated?

"Thanks, sir," Elizabeth said, returning to her call. "I have to assume that their cover was blown, and maybe the bugs hastily placed in the flat with the help of the landlord were somehow identified. I'd like to examine the flat after the doctor leaves, but we'll want plenty of backup support. Is there anyone living with Dr. Kontos?"

"We've checked and have no record of anyone sharing the flat with her. The landlord confirms this."

"Thanks again, Sir. I'll keep you informed. Goodbye."

Elizabeth immediately placed a call to one of the surveillance officers and reviewed the information with him.

"Do you want us to pick her up now, ma'am?" asked the officer.

"Not yet. Wait until we have more agents on location. However, if Dr. Kontos emerges, do pick her up for questioning, and I'll meet you at the office at that time. For now I'd like to see if there are any accomplices, but I plan to join you soon to look over the flat. At this time, it looks as though the nurse is not likely involved, but we'll wait to see what the cultures show and continue to observe her. If our investigation rules her out, we'll discontinue surveillance and focus everything on Dr. Kontos. I'm extremely disturbed about the missing agents."

Elizabeth faced her two new colleagues and said grimly, "Our experience with missing agents after a stakeout is that few return. Worse still, one-third undergo the horrors of torture."

Dr. Jonathan White entered the room and introduced himself as a senior registrar who specialized in internal medicine. He said he was covering the house for new admissions, and having finished a clinical consultation, he had some news himself. "Sorry to bother you, but I just examined one of the patients afflicted earlier with the staph infection and released after an apparent recovery, Ms. Phyllis Everly. Her daughter accompanied her to the emergency room when she began having lower extremity weakness."

"Does it look like a problem related to staph infection?" asked Elizabeth.

"I don't think so. She has no fever and is not toxic," answered Jonathan. "The neurologist suspects a polyneuropathy, probably Guillain-Barré syndrome, and I agree."

"What is that?" asked Elizabeth.

"Well," said Jonathan, "this is a disease involving peripheral nerves, and we don't know the cause. Patients sense a severe weakness in the muscles, usually beginning in the feet and legs and later rising to include the chest and arms. Sometimes it can lead to total paralysis, and they may need to be placed on a respirator to breathe. Many cases of Guillain-Barré polyneuropathy that we recognize follow a common intestinal bacterial infection caused by *Campylobacter*. But it can occasionally follow other infections, or even vaccines. Five hundred Americans developed Guillain-Barré syndrome in 1976 after a swine flu vaccine program began. It was a disaster!"

"Have you ever seen a case following a staph infection?" asked Chris. Jake responded that he had never read of a case, but to be sure someone should examine the available literature with a computer-assisted literature review. "I'll do that myself," he volunteered.

"So this is just bad luck – a coincidence?" said Elizabeth.

"It appears so," said Jonathan. "And unfortunately, not all patients regain full neurological functions afterwards."

Jake was focused on the word *coincidence*. It was a coincidence that he was in London to give a paper when a serious outbreak of infections occurred. A coincidence that the outbreak was so complicated and might take days or weeks to solve, yet his wedding anniversary was rapidly approaching. A coincidence that a victim of the extremely strange infection had a new and rare syndrome. *There have to be some threads tying most of these events together,* he thought. His being in London was an opportunity to do something special.

VII

In two separate cars on opposite sides of the street, a new team of four agents waited outside Diana Kontos' flat. Even by 11:00 a.m. she had failed to leave the building. Keeping notes, they recorded the following: *The tenant on the second floor left at 8:10 a.m., and the landlord went out at 9:03 a.m. Two women in the neighboring building left at 9:07 a.m. and 9:17 a.m., respectively, followed shortly thereafter by a large, elderly man.*

But since then no one had come or gone.

Feeling restless, the agents rang the central office, and asked for and received permission to approach the flat. They quickly climbed up the three stories to the second floor, first pressing the wall-mounted, round, white button the size of a hockey puck that turned on the stairwell lights for ninety seconds.

One agent knocked forcefully on the door to the flat listed as belonging to a D. Kontos. There was no response. Cautiously, the agents entered the flat with a key provided the day before by the landlord. All four men, hands on their weapons, announced their arrival as law-enforcement officials, inquiring, *"Is anyone home?"* They received no answer. They scattered quickly throughout the rooms. To their utter surprise, a complete search of the flat revealed no one, and nothing suspicious was seen. Dr. Kontos had literally evaporated into thin air. They checked for the six-centimeter, round listening device placed under the kitchen table, but it, too, was missing.

The living room was essentially a library with three of the four walls occupied by nine-foot tall, white bookcases filled with Greek and Middle Eastern history books, pieces of art and small sculptures. There were red Persian rugs scattered throughout the room, a modern dining room with a glass top table and four chairs with chrome bases and plastic seat covers. On the walls throughout the flat were several framed photographs of old, partially destroyed stone village homes, still standing amid the rubble all around them. The black-and-white images were somewhat faded. One showed a group of four thin boys with dark skin and hair playing football in an unpaved road, kicking a dirty ball towards a goal marked by two mounds of large rocks. One of the agents paused curiously for several seconds to examine the photograph. He couldn't help but notice the glee that the boys showed despite the spartan surroundings.

Behind the dining room was a small kitchen with stainless steel pots and pans of every size hanging like decorations from silver-colored hooks on the walls. There was a well-organized cabinet with over a hundred spices arranged alphabetically in five rows. Some were written in both English and Greek: mint, cloves, cinnamon, Persian cherry, nutmeg, and others. The hallway stretched to the bedroom at the far end of the flat. Across from the kitchen was a small bathroom that had a separate door leading to a bedroom.

In a separate reading room were two white, leather lounge chairs facing a thirty-inch flat-screen television. Two Greek Orthodox prayer books with black leather covers were resting on the small table nearby, one stacked on top of the other. A small, flat-screen computer monitor was sitting on a square table, but when one of the agents pulled on transparent latex gloves and checked its contents, he found that all programs had been deleted. There was nothing on the hard drive.

On either side of the bed were closet doors leading to a long storage space with a woman's shirts, suits, skirts, dresses, and shoes lining the entire distance behind the bed. On the back wall was a thin black curtain running the length of the huge closet.

Returning to the living room, two agents systematically moved the couch and chairs, patted down everything, and rolled up the rugs to look for any trap doors or movable panels. Meanwhile, the other two agents examined the walls, one at a time, tapping from one edge to another the way a physician might examine a patient's chest. They then began lifting up any pictures hanging on the walls. Systematically they removed the books in the bookcase, shelf by shelf, looking for a secret door.

Having examined the living room, they explored the dining room, kitchen, bathroom, and reading room in the same meticulous fashion. "Nothing unusual, no leads," said one, feeling especially puzzled and frustrated. "All the back windows look secure, locked on the inside. She didn't escape that way."

Two of the agents re-entered the bedroom, applying the same discipline. Examining the long closet behind the bed, one of the agents pulled the strings to the light bulbs that illuminated each end, and systematically tapped the curtain-shrouded back wall with his fingers. The closet space was two meters high and about one meter deep. It extended for about three meters in length. Near the middle of the wall, the resonance elicited by the tapping fingers sounded hollow, more like the tapping of the skin over a large kettle drum, suggesting an open space beyond the panel. Cautiously they turned to the edge of the black curtain and pulled the draw strings, which opened it from the middle to both sides. Behind the curtain was a door with no knob, instead just a flat metal lever recessed into the dark wood. The door opened toward the agents. In unison, the men instantaneously drew their weapons, fixing their eyes on the door, as one slowly pressed the lever down and quietly pulled the door towards himself.

Patiently inching the door open, the agent in charge noticed that there was a second door directly behind the first, that opened away from them. With the same caution, the agents pulled the lever down, slowly edging into a new room, both of them taking shallow, quiet breaths. When the second door was pushed fully open, the agents registered shock on their faces. One of them immediately phoned Elizabeth.

"Ma'am. No one came or went out of the flat, so we entered when no one responded to our knocking. There is absolutely no sign of the tenant. We made a careful examination of the flat. In the only bedroom, there's a closet with a hidden door, which opens to a neighboring flat in the next building. These old row houses share a wall, you know. As it turns out, though, it's not a proper flat at all. Instead of a living room, there's a modern laboratory with what looks like chemistry benches, glass and plastic equipment, several microscopes, sterilizers, centrifuges, incubators, and culture plates, and a small wash room with cleaning equipment."

"Don't touch anything!" shouted Elizabeth. "I'll ask the doctors from King's to come over to the flat with me. Just stay put. If Dr. Kontos returns, detain her there with you."

Jake was observing Elizabeth closely during her phone conversation, noting the subtle retraction upwards of her eye lids and slight dilatation of her pupils. Her respiration seemed mildly accelerated, and her lips parted slightly. This kind of response in a seasoned law enforcement expert told him something was terribly amiss.

Elizabeth returned her cell phone to the side pocket of her jacket, and quickly explained the call. She asked Chris and Jake to bring whatever investigative and protective equipment they needed and to accompany her to the Kontos flat.

Elizabeth summoned her driver, and shortly thereafter a black 2006 Audi sedan arrived at the hospital's entrance, siren blazing and mobile emergency light flashing on the roof. She entered the passenger side door, quickly locking her seatbelt in place. The two doctors crowded into the back seat with culturing material, masks, gowns, and gloves that they had hastily gathered from Chris's lab. Racing to the Wimbledon section of London, dodging the lines of traffic that were politely giving way to their emergency light and siren, both felt awkward in the uncertain situation.

"Elizabeth," said Jake anxiously, "Knowing what you know now, can you put this together?"

"At this stage I would still be guessing. Until I know more about who's behind this, I am in the dark as much as you." Recognizing his discomfort, Elizabeth turned with a brief smile, "Don't worry, we'll get to the bottom of this, Jake."

Jake had brought alcohol in plastic containers and a basin for the agents to disinfect their hands carefully. He announced that it would be important to watch them closely for several days in case of any illness, although the likelihood was low. He also brought red plastic bags for all contaminated materials and admonished everyone to wear gowns, gloves, and masks as a precaution, even though the main risk for acquiring staph is by getting the bacteria on one's hands.

Chris followed with a review of his tasks. He would examine the lab, take away proper culture materials, and do some surface cultures of the environment, looking for any traces of the organism causing havoc at King's.

Elizabeth called her office to ask for a listing of all tenants in the building and requested the front office to check on neighbors on either side of the Kontos residence.

Arriving at the flat, the driver parked the car directly in front. The four MI-5 agents greeted her at the front door of the flat and looked relieved to see the trio of experts arrive. Jake splashed alcohol liberally over the palms of the agents and instructed them to massage the liquid on both sides of their hands and wrists, rub a generous volume of alcohol from their elbows to their finger tips, and then repeat the process two more times. Everyone then donned the isolation materials.

Going from the bedroom closet to the flat in the adjoining building, Chris was greatly impressed with the elaborate nature of what he quickly concluded was an ultra-modern microbiology laboratory.

"There are people funded by the U.K.'s Medical Research Council who would give their right arms for this equipment!" Chris said, his voice somewhat muffled by the mask he was wearing. "The latest gene-sequencing apparatus, confocal scanning microscopes, and microarray setups to do the most sophisticated molecular genetic experiments in the world are here: hundreds of test tubes, numerous agar plates, two microbiological hoods to manage dangerous organisms, and a fan to vent the air through high efficiency particulate air filters to the outside. This is not cheap!"

Mentally recording Chris's reactions, Elizabeth led a careful search of the apartment. Behind the laboratory was a living room, a bedroom, a closet full of men's clothes only, a kitchen, and a bathroom.

"So it would appear that Dr. Kontos has a male accomplice, perhaps one who is also a microbiologist," said Elizabeth. "Judging from the waist, collar, and shoe sizes, he's a large man, well over twenty stones."

While explaining all this, Elizabeth was wondering, *Who is Dr. Kontos? Who lives in the flat with the laboratory? Kontos probably left the building through the adjacent apartment, but who lives here, and why did she leave through the flat with the laboratory?*

Reviewing the notes of the agents, she realized that the two women and large elderly man who left the adjoining flat were most likely Dr. Kontos and one or more accomplices. "If so, who is the woman with her?" she asked out loud. She alerted her office to look for a large man and a woman, or a man with two women. "Send the alerts to all airports, train stations, and bus terminals."

The central office had Diana Kontos' license plate number and a description of her personal automobile, but Elizabeth surmised that she and her accomplice were clever enough to escape in another vehicle. She concluded that she would again contact Interpol, recalling the view of the secretary general and his statement about there being no criminal threat with greater international impact than bioterrorism. *They need to be notified immediately,* she thought.

In the connecting flat, the steam sterilizer was running, and Chris immediately went over to turn it off, his hand encased in a padded glove to avoid heat damage. He was hoping to recover organisms before they were killed by the intense heat and high pressure. A few minutes later he opened the round door to the autoclave by turning the steering wheel-shaped lock counterclockwise. He then reached into the open, tubular space while holding a hot pad and pulled out stacks of agar plates with organisms on them and rows of cloudy solutions within a rack of test tubes. He had brought stainless steel containers to safely transport all the specimens for testing.

"I'll take these back to my lab to perform Gram stains and attempt to grow them on various media in order to ID them. If they turn out to be staph, we'll see if it's the same strain that killed our patients and Professor Allen. I'll also get some swabs from the benches and the flat leading into the lab." Turning anxiously to Elizabeth, he said, "When I finish, Jake and I will wait outside. We have a disposable box for all the used gowns, gloves, and masks."

Elizabeth returned to Diana Kontos's flat and examined the clothes to see if there were blouses, shoes, or dresses of different sizes. They were quite similar, she noticed. The woman lived by herself, she concluded. Noting the huge collection of Greek and Middle Eastern history books, Elizabeth again wondered out loud, "Could this be Al Qaeda or Hamas? Why here and now? Is a more serious, calamitous event in play? Why King's Hospital?"

One of the agents asked Elizabeth about a white sculpture on the living room table. It stood about fifteen centimeters long and ten centimeters high and resembled a weird animal with a huge head and almost human body.

Elizabeth recognized the figure immediately. It was the Minotaur. She continued directing the activities of the criminal investigation and issuing orders to the agents, who were now wearing light blue gowns and surgical caps, slightly darker blue masks, and pale blue latex gloves. "Dust both flats for fingerprints, look for any blood, get DNA samples from toothbrushes, and take numerous investigative photographs of everything. I want both buildings sealed off until we get to the bottom of this. Check again for any computers, discs, CDs, film, photos, letters, and any paper files. Bring all the evidence to our crime lab. Find out who manages the apartment building with the lab and interview both that person and the landlord of Dr. Kontos' apartment."

From the bottom of a drawer in Dr. Kontos' flat, Elizabeth pulled out a set of two very old keys and, next to them, a framed, black-and-white photograph of two women. Both appeared to be Mediterranean, possibly Middle Eastern, she thought. Perhaps a mother and child. She noticed that behind the two, who were sitting on a cement bench, was a barbed wire fence.

The older woman, perhaps forty-five, was looking plaintively at the younger one who was perhaps ten years old when the photo was taken. Both were dressed simply, with no jewelry, and wore light-colored blouses and dark scarves on their heads. The older woman's eyes seemed glazed and somewhat sunken into her orbits. There was no smile, and the lines of her face suggested a deep sorrow. She looked as though her spirit had evaporated years earlier.

Chris was on his way out when he noticed the picture. "Look at the photograph! The older one closely resembles Dr. Kontos, but clearly it couldn't be her. Perhaps Dr. Kontos' mother, grandmother, or aunt at an earlier time."

"I might be wrong, but that scene resembles a refugee camp," said Elizabeth. "I would date the photo from the early 1950s. I'm sure that this is important. It doesn't seem to match anything else in this flat. I'll work with our forensic people to see what we can make of this.

"If the date and location of the photograph can be determined, we may begin to figure out a motive. In any case, we can't ignore that photograph. Even if it's fifty years old – maybe *because* it's fifty years old – we might find it tells us something valuable, and that the other photos hanging here are also clues to understanding what Diana Kontos is up to." She turned to look at the photograph of the young boys playing football, wondering why it would be important to Diana Kontos. She needed to hear more about this microbiologist-anesthesiologist, Dr. Diana Kontos. *Who is she, and who is her accomplice? Furthermore, what happened to the two agents who disappeared?*

Again her cell phone went off and Elizabeth picked it up. It was her chief. "Agent Foster, we have new information. According to the landlord, the entire flat next door is let by a Mr. Ata Atuk. He's often seen in the company of another woman and sometimes two women. The landlord says he assumes one woman stays with him. We ran him through our computers. He's originally from Kurdistan, and the woman, whose name is Sasha Rhodos, is apparently from Greece. Get this, however. She was enrolled at the American University of Beirut at the same time as Dr. Kontos. Sasha was a degree student of pharmacy and toxicology, and her family name is Abbas. This may be an alias, however. We're checking to see if Ata Atuk was in Lebanon at any time."

"Thanks, sir. I'll appreciate any follow up. However, this just complicates our puzzle. Looking around the Kontos flat, I'd say it was occupied by someone who may be an expert chef, who has an abiding love for the Greek islands and mythology, and for the culture of the Middle East as well. The occupant may have strong religious ties to the Greek Orthodox church and be associated in some way with a person or people in the adjoining apartment who have big secrets. The photograph of two people probably in a detention area or refugee camp is particularly intriguing and may yield important insights into what's driving this person's actions. Furthermore, although it's possible Mr. Atuk may have a live-in girlfriend, only men's clothes were found in his flat. Yet Dr. Kontos has a king-sized bed in her own flat. Would you see if you can find any information on Dr. Kontos's sexual orientation? Thanks."

Elizabeth thought the answers to many of her questions about the perpetrators and their motives were right there in the flat. For the moment she could discern only a vague outline of what they might be like, and why they were intent on engaging in some act of bioterrorism. Hopefully, as she had time to think and to analyze, the picture would become more clear. The first step was to take all the photographs to the forensic team. Someone might be able to pinpoint the locations – perhaps Greece or the Middle East – then suggest who the people in the photos were, and what organizations might be represented in these camps (if these *were* camps) and from that she could consider possible motives.

This was already feeling like the biggest case of her career, a special opportunity for a woman at MI-5. She also sensed that she needed to take the next step up the career ladder in the next year, two years at the most, before she had to cope with a neurologically disabled husband. Time was the enemy; there was none to waste. There was too much at stake for screw-ups.

VIII

Ata, Sasha, and Diana were in a tan 2004 Fiat four-door sedan, traveling on Route 2 just past Canterbury, heading for Dover. Traffic was heavy, but Ata found himself weaving aggressively from lane to lane, paying no attention to the horns from lorries and passenger vehicles forced to apply their brakes abruptly. He insisted on driving, placing both women in the back seat. Intermittently, he would reach over to the passenger side of the front seat for his dark glasses as the sun sporadically broke through the cumulus clouds.

Each woman wore a different colored wig. Sasha's hair, a reddish-brown color, was flipped back on its sides and Diana's sandy blonde hair was pulled in a ponytail. Ata's bald head was topped with a frizzy grey wig. Earlier, while walking to his car with his makeup on, hunched over and keeping his elbows flexed like a senior citizen, he had appeared to be twenty years older than his forty-three years.

Ata thought about how he had purchased the car earlier in the year from a Pakistani grocer he had met only once. The man had a home-made *For Sale* sign in the car window in front of his store. Ata rarely drove the car and instead had saved it for just such a contingency. To be safe, he had used false identification papers in its purchase and paid cash.

"Just to take no chances," said Ata. Rolling his "Rs" with a heavy Middle Eastern accent, he added, "When we reach the dock, we'll separate and board the hydrofoil for Ostend separately. I thought it would be safer to avoid airports."

"Ostend is an inter-resting place, ladies, a thousand-year-old city on the North Sea coastline in Belgium, noted for its beaches and casino. So if anyone asks why you are on the ferry, simply reply that you are going to rest on the sand and try your luck at gambling in the nights." He explained that it was quite natural for people in London to get away for a few days' holiday in Ostend. He had looked into this carefully as a possible escape route and thought it would be easy for them to blend in with the crowd. The authorities might be looking for two of them, or all three. He would remove his makeup, so if they were searching for an older man, he would not attract attention, but he would leave the wig on and walk without stooping.

"When we get to our destination in Belgium, our friend Elaina will be waiting to drive us to a safe house in Brussels, where we need to stay for a few days before returning. I sense that we need to be away for a few days until the investigation at the hospital is over. That is why we needed to leave so quickly. But it is only tempor-rary."

Ata was a burly man about six feet tall and weighing 300 pounds. Even hunched over, his nineteen-inch neck and broad, round shoulders were positioned above a chest of fifty inches. He had dark, bushy eyebrows, and the lines in his round face were deeply furrowed. The menacing stare of his grayish eyes and pin-point pupils made him look like an alien. He walked stiffly with an almost undetectable limp, the result of pain from premature osteoarthritis in both hip joints. His arms seemed long even for his huge frame, and both hands were remarkably large and out of proportion to his body, like the sculpture of Michelangelo's *David* in Florence.

Ata was attempting to assure Diana that all was not lost, just postponed. He had listened with empathy as she talked of a lifetime of planning, years and years of studying and working, and experimenting. Ata said there would be time to retest the final isolates of staph once more before deploying them.

Peering into the rearview mirror, Ata could see that Sasha and Diana were not even talking with each other. They had argued all night about Diana's error and her affair with the chief of surgery. "You should have remained friends, not lovers!" Sasha had said the night before. "You should have consoled him but not slept with him! All of your talk about wild sex in the tiled shower, and now he is dead." Before the evening was over, she and Diana had been crying in each other's arms.

"The affair was necessary if we were going to be invited to the international meeting," Diana had argued. "And he was such a kind and lonely man. He also was one of a few who really understood the history of our mother's birthplace and the unfairness, the atrocities that plagued our family. He understood the ignominy suffered daily in Palestine today. It was just bad luck that he became infected, very bad luck – *Inshala*, as God wills it."

Diana had tried to explain to Sasha that she and the professor of surgery had enjoyed a close professional relationship for years in the operating theatre. After his wife had left him, they had talked frequently over tea between cases, and Diana had learned of his interest in philanthropy, especially dealing with Israeli agencies. He was a rare man who believed that people of different faiths could live together peacefully. She had expressed a warm sympathy for him after the divorce, and he was grateful. Jeffrey was always careful to protect his privacy, but as the two became better friends, she received more frequent invitations to his luxurious home on Hampstead Heath.

Ata recalled what he knew of the affair. Five months ago after a night of champagne and a Middle Eastern meal that Diana had prepared, the couple made love for the first time. The affair had blossomed, and in the interim she had traveled with Professor Allen to a few surgical meetings, each time anxiously awaiting his return to the hotel room after his scientific presentation. Earlier, Diana had told Ata, "I'm not sure that I love the professor – *Jeffrey* – but we share a certain feeling of loneliness, a sense of life's inequities, a deep-seated sadness, and a feeling that we each have more to accomplish in our lives."

When they learned that the American physician had begun to screen the operating theatre team for nasal cultures, it was Diana's idea to have Sasha go in her place to the Casualty Department to be cultured. Ata had agreed when Sasha called him to explain the sisters' rationale.

"Very likely," said Sasha, "Diana is a staph carrier of the designer strain, but I have not worked in the lab with staph. My own studies are completely different and done only at my workplace. The Casualty Department nurse at King's wouldn't be able to distinguish us."

On hearing the plan, Diana had immediately placed an antibacterial cream into both nares twice daily with Q-tips to eradicate the staph and reduce her own risk of infection. Removing artificial nails, which she wore only socially, she carefully scrubbed her fingertips with alcohol before applying the antibacterial cream lavishly over the skin of her hands, beneath the nail folds, and in the webs between her fingers. She was aware from reading the scientific manuscripts of American investigators that forty percent of nasal carriers of staph have the same organism on the hands.

Trying to keep the women focused, Ata knew just the chord to strike. "Remember your mother and grandmother, ladies."

Diana closed her eyes and began reminiscing as the car made its way towards Dover. Their mother was ten and their grandmother thirty-seven when the people of Jerusalem became targets for the belligerent occupants of Palestine in 1948. Mother told them of the daily ordeal of walking to school and having the Zionist soldiers fire bullets over her head, eventually driving her into a near-catatonic state for weeks. It didn't help when her mother's father – Diana and Sasha's grandfather – or her mother's uncle would accompany the ten-year-old, since their fears returned when the bullets began flying again, forcing them to cower behind stone walls for hours at a time.

The Zionist soldiers told their mother, Jawhara, who was only a child, and their grandmother, Rana – a young woman – that they needed to leave their village for a few days so the soldiers could protect their homes from the terrorists. In a fate common among many of their neighbors, all the members of their family huddled together under a single blanket on the cold ground in the nearby hills. They had little food and no extra clothing. When they returned after three days, all of their household belongings were missing. Everything gone! The keys were on the ground near the front steps. The house had been ransacked.

Even worse, the soldiers had taken away all the men, including their grandfather and his father, saying that they were being questioned about their terrorist links. They never returned.

Rana and Jawhara were left behind to find their way to Lebanon with similarly ill-fated neighbors. Only later, in the refugee camp, did the two hear about the shallow graves containing the bodies of the men, including those of Diana and Sasha's grandfather and his father. All had been shot in the back of the head.

Ten years of life in a refugee camp had made Jawhara and Rana broken and humiliated; but the women vowed to get revenge if ever an opportunity arose. A young Greek man and his uncle were kind and warm toward them, however. God had willed this change of fortune. They told many stories about good and evil, and Rana shared these nightly with her teenage daughter. Years later, in Greece, she would do the same for her granddaughters.

In the last few years in the camp, Jawhara and Rana helped a fledging group of angry men who called themselves the *Fedayeen*, cooking for them, sending messages, and bringing equipment for their raids into Israel.

Eventually one of the *Fedayeen*, who loved the young girl and had family in Greece, arranged for an escape from the Middle East.

Aided in their safe transport to the airport by an ambulance, they made their way to the Beirut airport. There a cargo plane belonging to Olympia Airlines received the passengers, who flew to freedom amid huge wooden crates. Jawhara later married the man, who came and went frequently to Beirut to help the new group of warriors.

Hoping each would have a better life, Rana would tell the stories almost nightly to Sasha and Diana, who shared a bed when they were young children growing up outside of Athens. Each of them did achieve scholastically, and both were excellent athletes. But both vowed to avenge their family.

Diana, who had heard so much about life in the refugee camps and the illnesses – especially from infections – was drawn to medicine and microbiology. She had determined that one day she would work in

Palestine, providing accessible medical care. Sasha, too, had an interest and skill in science, but she chose pharmacology and toxicology as her field, always taking courses in the same university as Diana. Eventually she received a doctorate degree from the American University of Beirut. To help support her education, she apprenticed with master chefs in Athens, Paris, and Frankfurt whenever there were summer session breaks. In London she worked as a University of London laboratory manager for a team of scientists working on the actions of various toxin-producing bacteria.

The two sisters had frequently shared their experiences with Ata, and he knew of their vows to avenge the cruelty done to their family members. For his part, he always treated them kindly and with apparent respect. Their anger had grown to hatred and then rage as daily television and print news stories chronicled the fate of the miserable Palestinians. Ata was pleased that he succeeded in having the women focus on their families and not the hasty trip to Belgium.

All three Londoners boarded the eighty-one-meter Seacat ferry without incident for the two-hour trip to Ostend, blending in with approximately 500 other passengers. There were billowing, dark-blue cumulus clouds in all directions and blustery winds. The North Sea waters to Belgium were choppy on this late summer day, and the captain requested that all passengers lock their seatbelts in place for much of the duration of the hydrofoil trip. The winds kicked up to over thirty knots, and the steel-grey waters were roiling, whitecaps slapping into each other from all directions.

On the ride to Ostend, Diana began to reminisce about the way the sisters' friendship with Ata had grown. Besides protecting them like a big brother, he always remembered their birthday; he brought two bouquets of white roses and arranged for a special celebration dinner at a favorite Lebanese restaurant in central London. During the times they shared in Lebanon and subsequently in Germany, Sasha – cautious Sasha – had her doubts about Ata. She had been suspicious of his solicitousness and his general reluctance to discuss his feelings as the two women wanted to do. Gradually and reluctantly, she accepted his confidence, suppressing the thought that there was a hidden motive behind his attentions.

One of the events that had won them to him was when he took some of the favorite old photographs of their mother's early days in Palestine and had them expertly enlarged and framed beautifully. He had presented them as Christmas gifts almost two years ago, recalled Diana.

Diana had thanked Ata for his understanding and protection. She had fears of failing, of not completing her life's goal, really the goal of several generations. What would her father do in this situation? Should she try to reach him? Would this all blow over as Ata had suggested, and everyone could return to London? Or would she and Sasha become nomadic fugitives, forced to run to safe havens in a different part of the world?

On arrival, the relieved group of passengers was slow to disengage from their seat belts, apparently a little disoriented after a rough voyage. None of the three fugitives acknowledged one another, even as they disembarked unsteadily in the port city of Ostend and entered a black 2007 Volvo sedan.

The woman driver smiled wryly, announced to her guests that food and drinks were on the floor of the back seat, and said that it would take less than three hours to get to Brussels. Introducing herself only as *Elaina,* the driver had an accent that sounded Iraqi or Turkish to Diana, with the harsh *R*s and clipped cadence of her speech. Apparently in her late thirties, she was short in stature and had a bulky midsection; yet she had a pretty face with a warm smile, pouting lips, and luxurious dark hair that flowed to her shoulders. She was dressed conservatively in dark blue slacks, black loafers, and a dark blue blouse over which she wore a black leather jacket. She lit a cigarette and passed a small bundle of materials to the sisters in the back seat.

"The new passports are clipped together with open economy class tickets to Frankfurt if we need them. From there, we can discuss further options," she said.

The two Interpol agents working in Belgium had been notified of the trio of fugitives but had arrived just as the suspects' car was leaving. Having earlier been dispatched to travel from Brussels to Ostend, they now opted to trail the four at a safe distance. Auspiciously, they had been alerted by an unusually observant agent at the Dover station after he was shown pictures of Diana Kontos. What raised his suspicions was a bit of curious behavior on the beach while he was smoking a cigarette on his break. As he told the story, he happened to notice one of the fugitives stepping out of a car with a large man and another woman, and then the two women hugged each other, but strangely, they walked four or five minutes behind each other in the same direction. Each entered the hydrofoil separated by at least twenty people. None of the three talked to each other, and he thought that was especially odd.

"It is fortunate that Agent Foster had also thought to alert all port authorities," said one of the Interpol agents to the other. "Unfortunately, it was too late to intercept the three fugitives in Dover, and she thought it too dangerous to approach them in Ostend. We have opted to set up a trap with sufficient reinforcements along the way."

In London, Elizabeth did not know what to expect in terms of the microbiological risks from the fugitives. She had implored the two physicians involved in the investigation to accompany her on a private jet to Ostend. At 8,000 meters altitude the flight of the cramped aircraft was smooth. Elizabeth was sitting behind the cockpit facing the rear of the plane, her knees touching Jake's as he faced her. To offer more space, Jake separated his legs slightly, straddling the outside of Elizabeth's thighs. Without a sense of self-consciousness, she thanked him. Jake nodded his head. "No problem," he said, enjoying the soft pressure of her knees against his own thighs.

Chris sat across the aisle from Jake. On the way, Jake asked if it was likely that a psychopath was behind this plot.

"Well, there are many possible motives," Elizabeth answered.

"Powerful ones: love, jealousy, revenge, and the insanity that may sometimes accompany a criminal mind. Psychopaths, as you suggest, see the world as being full of symbols that are invisible to the rest of us, but they act on their interpretations of the symbols – the whispers, the visions, the electrical signals that pulse through their brains, and the odd smells they sense. Psychopaths are loosely tethered in an alien world, spinning through fog, bizarre colors, discordant sounds, and unpredictable connections. Eventually we're able to define this thinking disorder, but we never fully comprehend it. Judging from the professional success she's enjoyed, I don't think Dr. Kontos is a psychopath."

"Could some form of hatred – of patients or other physicians – be driving her? As difficult as it is for me to understand any antipathy for the medical profession, I know it happens."

"Some disagree," noted Elizabeth, "but I think love is the most powerful motive for people, and obviously it's not original thinking on my part to say that hatred follows unrequited love in some people, especially those who fail to cope with its loss. Many who kill in the name of unrequited love see their entire life converging at lightning speed on a single relationship. It's a do-or-die situation literally, and all meaning ends with the breakup. There's no future, no present, only the past – which they see as a fraud. Anger, despair, and the drive to eliminate and erase the pain all seize control of a person's thinking."

"What about some jealous situation in the operating theatre? We all know that day in and day out, with six people crammed into a space the size of a single office, soap opera-type scenarios can develop," inquired Chris.

"Well," said Elizabeth, "did the doctor get involved in a love triangle that went awry? If so, what are the roles of her accomplices? Jealousy is an obsession that never leaves a person. Everywhere the jealous person looks, he or she is confronted with unwanted intrusions on their thinking, often accompanied by a sense that others nearby are watching, laughing, snickering, or pointing fingers at him or her. The jealous person can't escape the feeling of embarrassment or abject rejection. It's like a child lost in a house of strange mirrors, distorting the reality of the outlines of the body. They suffer a profound loss of face, and they feel a deep need to regain control and self-esteem. What I need to understand is which one drives our suspects in this case. In addition to the main cause for their actions, there may be subplots that play out, often defined by personal experience. Are our suspects talented but insane – bent on destruction for its own sake?"

His curiosity aroused, Chris asked, "Could some form of revenge be motivating them? If a person feels he or she has been repeatedly slighted, at some point there could be a psychological eruption."

"I agree, Chris. Revenge, too, is an obsession," said Elizabeth, "more powerful than jealousy and occasionally hidden or suppressed. But it can surface in a second, sparked by a single word, a gesture, or a curl of the lip that is interpreted as demeaning. Revenge is rooted deeply, somewhere in the labyrinthian recesses of the brain, inaccessible to the rational side of the criminal, yet continually pulsating in his or her mind. The person sees vengeance as a release. The mind that seeks to avenge sees itself on the side of good; people justify their actions based on the natural order in life as they imagine it. They wait for the opportunity with the vigilance of a sentinel. But satisfaction can be short-lived, and they need to produce even greater consequences to demonstrate their anger.

"So the questions I need answered are the following: Are one or both women victims of jealousy? What is the role of the man often seen with them? Are we dealing with a hatred that has transformed slowly over the years into a mania for revenge? If so, how are the three tied together? Is the photograph of the woman and child critical to understanding a motive? Is there a meaning to the ancient keys found in the drawers?"

"I'm curious, Elizabeth," said Jake, "about the strange sculpture in Dr. Kontos' flat. Is that sculpture simply a piece of artwork, or does she attach some special meaning to that monster?"

"Of course we can't be certain," Elizabeth replied. "But the figure of the Minotaur prompts some interesting speculation. The story goes back to ancient Greek mythology, and true to myths, there are numerous versions of the story. Briefly, the monster you describe is called the *Minotaur*, the offspring of a beautiful bull sent by the god of the sea, Poseidon, to be sacrificed by King Minos. However, when Minos thought the bull too handsome for sacrifice, he killed another in its stead. Angry at Minos's failure to obey his wish, Poseidon then created in Minos's wife, Pasiphae, a relentless passion for the bull so powerful that she contrived a way to make love with it. She enticed her friend, Daedalus, to place her inside of a wooden makeshift cow with an entrance for the bull. When she later became pregnant and eventually delivered, the offspring had a head of a bull and body of a boy, and was named the Minotaur.

"Of course, this unspeakable event was so intensely embarrassing to Minos that he hired Daedalus, his greatest architect, to construct a labyrinth to enclose the creature forever. Sadly, because Minos's son had been killed earlier by an Athenian, each year the citizens of Athens were required to send as tribute to the Cretan king seven young men and seven maidens. Instead of keeping them as his bondservants, Minos would place them in the labyrinth. Unable to find their way out, they would be devoured by the Minotaur.

"The Minotaur was eventually killed by Theseus, who would later become king of Athens. As fate would have it, Theseus was aided in his escape by Minos's daughter, Ariadne, who learned about the secret exit from the labyrinth from Daedalus. So Daedalus was the key to an escape."

"And you think that story may have important meanings for Dr. Kontos?" asked Jake.

"It's impossible to know for sure, but I suspect it does have great meaning for our fugitives. Of course, it's always possible that it simply represents an attractive piece of art for Dr. Kontos. However, because of its prominent location in the flat and her apparent attraction to Greek art and architecture, it's more likely that it represents something extremely significant. It's important to recognize that fairy tales and myths prepare young people for the world they will face, in some large or small way influencing and organizing their thinking. Myths allow people of different cultures to cope, to give some meaning to life, to imagine a sense of order and fairness in the world.

"Fairy tales and myths are recognized worldwide. For example, if I go to the airport and ask one hundred people to name Ian McEwan's latest book, only one or two may know of it. However, if I ask if they ever heard of *the wicked stepmother*, all would say ,'Yes, of course.' So it's more likely than not that the tale of the Minotaur has relevance. However, in exactly what way, we may only know when we catch up to the fugitives."

Elizabeth refocused her thoughts on the matter of apprehending the trio. "Since we now have photographs of Dr. Kontos and Mr. Atuk, these have been distributed by Interpol to every airline in Europe. Our colleagues in Ostend have said that three people – including Mr. Atuk – and their driver are on the highway headed towards Brussels. Regrettably, we have no photograph of the third person.

"They are obviously dangerous people, and probably armed. You two need to stay out of the way until I call for you. Please remain with one of our agents inside the jet on the Ostend tarmac. We'll call for your expertise if needed, since I need professionals available whom I can trust in case of a biological attack. You'll fly back to London if the three are captured or if you can comfortably rule out the probability of a new outbreak. In any case, I'll have you both back to London by this evening. I'm grateful for your expertise and help. Eventually I'll understand these people's thinking, and when I do, I'll know where to find them."

Reflecting on the story of the devouring monster, the victims trapped in the labyrinth, unable to find their way out of the maze, and the panoply of potential motives of a biohacker, Jake decided at that moment that he would stay in London until the case was solved. He was simply not able to leave early, despite his family obligation. As a witness to the unfolding of an unprecedented outbreak, Jake viewed these events with a sense of historical proportion. This epidemic required his expertise and therefore demanded his involvement.

But something else was happening that influenced his decision as well: he was sensing a strong sexual attraction for Elizabeth. He was imagining her thighs straddling his.

IX

On the passenger side of the moving car, Ata Atuk was uncomfortable, his large body cramped tightly inside. His completely bald head was the result of an unidentified illness characterized by persistent fever, which began twenty-six years earlier at age fourteen in the Kurdish plateau of Iraq in the town of Kirkuk. He had recounted the story frequently to the two women in the back seat. Because he was extremely sensitive about his baldness and about the pale green, wavy tattoos high on both temples, remnants of a teenage gang ritual, he had always worn some type of wig as an adult. Both huge hands were placed on the dashboard as though pushing his body away from the front of the car.

"How long might you stay in Frankfurt if we leave Brussels?" asked Diana kindly. "I know you wish to return to your homeland in Iraq as soon as possible."

"I am not sure," Ata responded with his guttural Kurdish accent. "I cannot possibly go home. The American occupation and the escalating civil war are obstacles." He recounted that he had not seen his family since 1991, when the Iraqi forces crushed the Kurdish uprising after the Persian Gulf War. He would return as soon as possible, but only to battle the Iraqi dogs who had killed his mother. "My long hope is to see my country and my home once again. I wish to gaze at the open land of my childhood. Just imagining its beautiful sunsets gives me hope."

Ata recalled how he lost his father soon after he was born, how he was raised by a domineering and strong-willed mother, who did whatever was necessary to save the family of four children from starvation. She could look a man straight in the face and tell him that the quality of her weaving was the best in the land, when in fact it was machine made with nylon and wool mixed fabrics. Her cunning was artistic, and she was very much admired by men in his town.

She taught me to consider what might happen on the next day and to anticipate the problems that might arise, he thought. *And to consider how I might respond to each one. I think she taught me about security, the long-term need to be independent and safe. And I learned the value of money from her.*

One event stood out in his mind. When the teasing about his bald head was so severe in school, his mother asked his uncle, who was a butcher, to teach him how to fight. Later, when he won his first fight in the school yard when he was fourteen, his mother praised him highly, kissing him on the lips and hugging him to her breasts. She then told him to take the money out of the pocket of the boys he beat up. It was a just reward. Before he was sixteen, the teasing ended, but very few boys in the village were close friends, only those who formed a small group that never fit in.

But he still missed his ancient birthplace. He reminisced about the Hasa River glistening nearby, those few Kurdish friends he did have, and the times when his grandparents were coming home from the oil fields to cook for the family on weekends. He could still smell the oil on their clothes. This is what he yearned to see and experience again.

"We know why you are bitter, Ata," Sasha said warmly. "We, too, understand repression and humiliation. We know about restraint, timing, and planning for justice."

"Thank you, ladies. It was a good day when we met in Beirut."

Ata's cell phone rang. "Hello?"

"Hello, Ata. Did you cross to Belgium safety?" the man with a Russian accent asked on the other end.

"Yes. We are leaving Ostend for our next destination," Ata responded cautiously.

"Are you free to talk openly?"

"Not yet," said Ata unemotionally.

"Then let's agree that you smile and answer in 'yes' and 'no' responses. Do your friends have samples of the material?"

"Yes, that is correct," said Ata.

"Do the sisters have any inkling of your design?"

"No, I cannot imagine that, thank you," replied Ata, remaining cautious.

"Do they know you found a listening device in the flat, and that you had to deal with the men in the car outside?"

"No, that never presented a problem. Thank you," said Ata.

"Excellent. The buses will be in place very shortly from now, as we planned. Go safely, Ata." He then hung up.

Ata said to the two women that his friends were ready to help if needed.

Glancing repeatedly into the rearview mirror, Elaina spotted a black sedan that seemed to have been following them from the time of they left the dockside at Ostend. "Ata, we may have company."

"Not to worry, Elaina. We have a turn in four kilometers, and several buses will assist us."

Ata was giving directions. Driving east on route A-10, Elaina slowed to take a left turn exit onto A-14 towards Antwerp, then quickly accelerated around two tour buses. When the pursuing agents attempted to pass, the bus driver last in line pulled beside the other tour bus and in front of the pursuing sedan, causing it to slow down almost to a crawl. Intensely frustrated, the agent slapped the horn a few times, only to have the two buses slow down, side by side, to thirty kilometers per hour just as they entered a tunnel. The agents found themselves trapped behind two buses travelling at an exasperatingly slow speed.

The Interpol agents were incensed, the driver now honking the horn furiously with his fist and frantically flashing his bright headlights repeatedly. Both men lowered their windows, and each raised an arm erratically, hoping the bus drivers would see them and make way. They were screaming at the bus drivers in French, "Get out of the way! *Merde!*"

The agent driving the sedan hit the horn again with a renewed fervor but to no avail, and Elaina sped off and made two ninety-degree turns to a small side road towards Brugge and the coastal town of Knokke. Still in the tunnel and now two kilometers behind, the Interpol agents were unable to notice the fugitive car's circling retreat.

Having accelerated to 120 kilometers an hour for over fifteen minutes and seeing no one behind, Elaina began to breathe more comfortably. Still no one was in sight after another twenty minutes, and she slowed down to eighty kilometers an hour.

In an effort to deflect any worries his passengers might have, Ata began a new conversation. He seemed to know where their deep passions lay. "What do you think about returning to Greece? Or do you really want to go back to your family's homeland in Palestine? Do you miss your father?"

Ata knew well that the sisters completed secondary school in Athens, where their father had taken them. Sasha and Diana had needed a few extra years to finish because of the poor education they had received in the Lebanese camp, but they were excellent students. Their father was a Christian Palestinian who came to see them every few months from his business abroad. They saw their father only for a few days at a time, and he was very loving, saying that the girls needed to look to the future. He always said that there would be a time when the winners became the losers. So each woman could never forget and would never forgive the people who committed such atrocities against their family.

The women had recounted to Ata that in a single bed, lying side-by-side growing up, they had listened to their grandmother and mother tell the story of their flight from Palestine to the refugee camp called Sabra. The sisters had given up almost all social life to become dedicated and accomplished professionals. Always they kept their goals in mind, always they knew they were destined to carry out a special mission – initially unclear, but more sharply focused once they found the molecular keys to bacterial genetic engineering. Sasha's expertise in pharmacology and toxicology allowed them to combine their talents.

When neither of the women answered him immediately, Ata

spoke again. "You could have a good life in Greece, a family, financial stability, peace – if you gave this up and moved on. You are intelligent and beautiful women."

Sasha responded quickly, "I never thought of myself as beautiful. Just the opposite." She had told this story many times. When she was growing up, many people thought that her mother was beautiful also, but she told the twins she thought she must be ugly. "Otherwise, she told us, 'Why would the Israelis shower bullets over my head in Jerusalem? Why would they murder our relatives when I was a child?' Mother would say to Diana and me, 'I must be a horrible person; why else would they have tried to kill me? I did nothing to them.' Grandmother used to tell us that Mother and we were all beautiful victims, but we never were convinced. Grandmother also said that we can never forget, never forgive, never fail to avenge these horrible wrongs no matter how long it takes."

Diana continued, "Then when Sasha was sexually attacked in Beirut, she thought that she could never be attractive to any man. The sugar of their words just coats their lust. Only you, Ata, have been a friend and a protector."

In the moving car Diana turned to face Sasha. The two sisters clasped fingers tightly and looked at each other with a deep affection. Each had a stare as though fixed on a distant horizon, with a sad recognition of something still missing in life, possibly to be won in the future if their life's mission was successful.

––––––––––––––

Ten kilometers behind, the enraged and embarrassed Interpol agents trailing the fugitives called Elizabeth's secure cell phone. Elizabeth was walking on the tarmac of the Ostend airport in the direction of the main building where one of her pilots was arranging for a car. There was an unseasonal chill in the air on this grey day. The contour of her breasts could be observed beneath the grip of her black sweater, and her dark sweater and trousers provided a sharp contrast to the colorless sky, tarmac, and grey building.

"Agent Foster, we followed closely but lost the car with the three suspects. I think they're making a rush to the Brussels airport, but we're flashing our lights to try and get two tour buses out of the way."

Frustrated, Elizabeth asked, "Do you think the bus drivers are part of this? If you can't see where the fugitives went, pull over the drivers and bring them in for interrogation. I'll arrange for additional help while you do that."

"We'll do that, ma'am. I'm very sorry we messed this up, but we'll have agents all over the Brussels airport, just in case they're heading in that direction."

After twelve more kilometers, Elaina made a right turn to a small two-lane highway, now slowing to sixty kilometers an hour. The two sisters in the back seat looked puzzled.

"Where are we going?" Diana asked Ata.

"Don't worry. We needed to avoid a pursuing car, possibly Interpol agents who arrived at Ostend to detain us for questioning. It could be embarrassing. I always have another plan, so just rest awhile, and I'll have us all safe within an hour, then on to Brussels in the dark. I can make some calls to associates who are on the highways and know when it's safe to move on. We just need to be patient."

Just then, Elaina slowed down and made a sharp right-hand turn into a single-lane driveway lined with tall poplars astride canals on both sides of the asphalt road. Two minutes later she came to a full stop at a farm house. To Diana, the structure seemed to have been built in the late eighteenth century, as evidenced by its high entrance door and U-shaped design around an open court yard. Stone and cob walls lined the boundaries of the farm about thirty meters on each side. A barn and stable from the same period were off to the right of the farm house, where the car came to a stop. Lowering her window, Sasha inhaled the sweet smell of hay.

Ata stepped out of the car and opened the right back door. "Don't worry about anything, ladies. We'll rest here for an hour until the way is safe. You need to trust me."

The color drained from Diana's face, and her neck became tense; Sasha saw the change in her sister's demeanor. Sasha, too, was uneasy, her pulse quickening as her breath became more rapid and shallow. She could sense the appearance of tiny beads of sweat, moistening the hairline of both temples. She leaned over to whisper in Diana's ear, "Wh–why are we he–here?"

Diana whispered back, "I don't know. Let's listen and see." The sisters began to feel and look nervous and a bit confused.

Ata tried to reassure the women that all was fine. He had prepared for years for this scenario by building their trust in his promise to fulfill their desire to inflict pain – the best way they knew how – to make appropriate retribution.

"The meeting at the London Conference Centre of 350 Israeli medical-legal experts and delegates joined by 400 or more Israeli supporters from the U.S. would be the perfect opportunity," Ata had said repeatedly. In fact, Ata took pride in his creativity in planting the seed for Diana to have the affair with Jeffrey Allen, who would be invited to the meeting because of his generous donations to their society and its cause. He rehearsed his commitment to their aspirations whenever he saw them, and each time they were reassured of his friendship and commitment to their common cause. The outbreak at King's had created an unexpected problem, but he focused on alternative plans, knowing there were other ways for him to achieve the aims *he* had in mind.

"But Ata, do you think our cause is lost now?" asked Diana.

"Not at all, my loves. Ata always has a new plan. In fact, we'll arrange to return by private plane to London in a just few days. While the outbreak at King's is being investigated, it's good for us to rest. Very likely, there will be no connection between you and the outbreak, and you can say that you needed to be away to manage the illness of a relative. And if in some fashion you are connected to the infections at King's, that, too, will not be an issue. The law enforcement author-rities will assume we have escaped to a foreign country, never to return," he said, trilling his *R*s. "That is what usually happens when sleeper cells are discovered. The car following us may be nothing important, but we need to remain cautious until I have a chance to read the newspaper. On the way, we can talk about how we'll use the organisms you have."

Diana smiled uncomfortably, while Sasha kept both hands in her coat pockets, worried and withdrawn. Her face wore an agitated expression, unable to mask a growing sense that something was amiss.

Diana and Sasha exited the car and followed Ata hesitatingly to the side entrance of the barn. The heavy wood door closed with a loud click, indicating an automatic lock. At the far end were two old tractors, and on the walls hung various farm tools – hoes, saws, sledge hammers, metal rakes, and scythes. An acrid smell and a pervasive dampness heightened Sasha's sense of apprehension as she stood on the hay-strewn mud floor of the barn. There were a few dirty windows at the second-floor level allowing grey shafts of light to flood parts of the floor and north wall of the two-story structure.

Diana had hoped for a sign that her anxieties were misplaced, but instead, one look to her right magnified all her trepidations.

Inside the barn was another man whom the women had never seen before. The only light shone in from both sides of the loft above, and his face was obscured. Sasha surveyed the strange man carefully, noting that he was stocky and short, about five foot seven, she thought. With dark hair and olive brown skin he might be from Eastern Europe, she surmised.

Without a word, Ata and Elaina walked hastily to a side door and exited. Neither had looked back. No word was uttered. Now there were three in the barn, the two sisters and the foreigner. Diana took in a deep breath, more of a gasp, feeling a choking terror rising high in her neck. Her legs felt weak. She didn't think she could run. She fought off alternating waves of light-headedness and vertigo. Sasha never moved her eyes, which were fixed on the strange man. She slowly removed her hands from her coat pockets, placing them by her sides. As the strange man pulled back his jacket to his sides, placing both hands on his hips, both women could see the bulge filling his right-sided shoulder holster.

92

Behind the barn, having fetched the Styrofoam container with the lab isolates from the car, Ata and Elaina ran briskly in the direction of a twin-engine plane whose propellers were just beginning to turn. They stepped up into the plane by way of the metal, drop-down entrance steps and moved to their respective seats. Just as the pilot was closing the door and the steps retracted to the inside of the plane, the muffled sounds of two shots were heard coming from inside the barn.

X

Prompted by a call from a Belgian police officer responding to instructions to detain all drivers of recently made, black Volvo sedans, Elizabeth, one of her pilots, and the two physicians raced towards the A-13 near Maastricht. They, themselves were in a tan 2007 Volvo sedan, hired at the airport, heading for one of six roadblocks set up after Interpol agents sighted the fugitives. The two women being detained by the police officer claimed to be Italian tourists.

The pilot was speeding along the motorway with Elizabeth next to him, Jake in the back seat behind Elizabeth, and Chris behind the driver. Jake's outstretched hands rested on Elizabeth's head rest, her hair falling onto his knuckles and fingers. She turned to ask Jake a question, her left cheek pressing gently against his hand. For a few seconds she did not say anything. Then her cell phone rang.

While Elizabeth spoke on the phone, Chris and Jake began discussing the possibilities of a continued outbreak at King's as well as the new danger of cases possibly related to a spread of staph by the three fugitives to passengers on the hydrofoil.

Jake concluded that person-to-person exposure on the hydrofoil was unlikely to transmit the infection. To him, it seemed more probable that the trip across the North Sea to Belgium was a hastily planned escape, not part of a bioterror plot. Still, caution was needed, and certainly it would be prudent to alert the Belgian authorities to consider imposing a home quarantine – or at least some surveillance – on all passengers until local physicians observed them for three days and cultured them and their immediate household contacts. If no one became ill and cultures were negative, the period of observation could be lifted. Of course the worst scenario would be a transmission that set off an epidemic in a new country.

Chris agreed to contact his colleagues in the Health Department to request their full support, asking them to keep any staph bacteria cultured from the passengers for his lab. He would need to study each strain of staph to see if it was the unusual clone capable of producing an epidemic. If there were infection control issues, however, he would ask Jake to be available by phone for the Belgian team, at least initially.

Of course it is exciting and important, thought Chris, *and a pleasure to help, despite the possible risks to our reputations, and, in this case, even personal risks.* There are always risks in medicine, but an epidemic always gave them both a great adrenalin rush. With a brief smile, he said, "And you, Jake, are among a handful of people with whom I would hunt tigers."

Elizabeth interrupted abruptly. "Not much good news to report. In fact, no good news at our end. Our agents arrived just a little too late in Ostend to arrest the fleeing trio and driver, but they were able to follow them closely while calling in reinforcements. However, the group eluded them within five kilometers of our first roadblock and are missing. Our team members arrested four tour bus drivers who were paid handsomely to block our agents' way, but they were naïve young men who said they accepted money to help two married couples evade pursuing relatives. Our fugitives probably doubled back on a smaller road. We have five cars looking for them and a helicopter coming in from Brussels very soon.

"If that news isn't bad enough, we found the remains of our two surveillance officers in a roadside ditch twenty kilometers north of London. They were killed at close range, and both had multiple bullet wounds. A few of our team now have to visit each of the agent's families with the news."

Jake felt his throat constrict on hearing about the bloody death of two agents who had been staking out the flat he and Chris had visited so recently. This was a new experience for him, and he felt a slight headache and a discomforting heaviness enveloping his body. In Elizabeth's company he felt secure, but how much risk was there when he was alone? Reaching into his pocket, he unobtrusively pulled out two ibuprofen tablets, tossed them into his mouth, and washed them down with bottled water he had picked up at the airport.

"The positive news," said Elizabeth, "is that I've been working with a former colleague of mine who transferred to Interpol, and I now have some insight into the man, Ata Atuk. He was born in Kurdistan to an impoverished father and mother. He was a below-average student in school and nearly flunked the master's degree course in marketing in Beirut. He received a degree, but unofficially the professors noted that his two bright women friends helped him, possibly by writing his thesis. Unfortunately, school officials had no proof. Apparently, he befriended these women early in the course when he began to receive poor grades, and things improved. We just learned that they are identical twins, Diana and Sasha Kontos. The name is Greek. Their Palestinian mother married in Athens."

Both physicians were surprised by the information, but Chris found it especially astonishing, since no one at the hospital had ever mentioned Diana having a sibling, much less a twin.

"The two women are very attractive," said Elizabeth, "and thus were not popular with many local Lebanese women, who were envious of the attention they received from Lebanese men. One man, however, began to harass them both and sexually assaulted Sasha. Both sisters went to Mr. Atuk, who gave the man a brutal beating. He so terrified Sasha's attacker that no charges were filed against Atuk. The man said he couldn't characterize his assailant and was himself arrested for rape. Authorities found his 'inability' to identify the man remarkable, since Atuk is a huge man with a totally bald head with both temples full of wavy tattoos. So it should have been easy to identify him as the assailant of the rapist. Even at the trial for the rape, the man's facial anatomy was so distorted from being pummeled that his family did not immediately recognize him. After this incident, the friendship of the trio blossomed. But we're not yet sure about the timeline of Atuk's movement from Beirut to the U.K."

Elizabeth told the two physicians that Atuk had never used his marketing degree in a large business enterprise but instead managed a small store in Swiss Cottage that sold foreign newspapers, cigarettes and cigars, and sundry food items. The store was owned by a man who originally came from Bangladesh and who appeared to have been a model citizen, raising a family successfully. The Bengali man also had a second, apparently legitimate business; he owned a large furniture warehouse in central London, not far from the Convention Centre. Apparently, Atuk helped him with this enterprise as well, but it was unclear what use Atuk had for the old building. Elizabeth added that she was looking into the possibility that Atuk subsequently used the small store as a front for some illegal activities. There were some initial hints of ties to an Eastern European mafia – hints of money laundering and illicit drug trading. Some of her agents thought that Atuk was linked to a radical Kurdish group planning to take over key cities in northern Iraq to form a separate state, Kurdistan, after the Americans left the country.

"The only other thing so far is that Ata Atuk is known to hate Iraqis," said Elizabeth, "and our team thinks his hatred is longstanding, possibly related to deaths of relatives in various clashes between Kurds and Iraqis."

Elizabeth continued, "Let's hope the Belgian authorities have the two women we're looking for."

Chris asked, "How is this new information from Interpol helpful?"

"We can safely say that in Atuk we are dealing with a violent individual who will do whatever is necessary to fulfill his goals. There's no question that he's dangerous. The poverty he experienced as a child may be driving him to pursue financial security, but it's too early to be sure.

"It does explain the fact that I recognized only a single size of clothes in the Kontos flat. Clearly the twins live together, one of them routinely entering their flat by way of the Atuk flat and lab. Exactly what the motive is for this arrangement and the relationships among these three are unclear – still a bit unusual and mysterious."

An idea suddenly came to Jake. "Elizabeth, if Dr. Diana Kontos was a carrier of staph, do you think it's possible the other twin – a non-carrier – went for the screening in Casualty? The nurse there might not have been able to distinguish the two. No one knew Diana had a twin! So what I initially thought was a failure of epidemiology in pinpointing the key risk factor may have been instead a clever, calculated scheme."

"Spot on! It makes perfect sense!" said Elizabeth. She reached around to clasp his left hand, which was still resting on her head rest, in an affectionate way. She recognized his desire to be helpful in the investigation, enjoying a sense of her being needed by a man for her professional expertise – this man especially.

Momentarily distracted by her thoughts about Jake, Elizabeth broke from her reverie and turned her attention back to the case. She called her home base, asking to be patched into the agents who would deliver the news to the families of their murdered colleagues. "Take whatever time is needed to listen to their grief and deal with the shock, and answer any questions the family members will have," she requested somberly. "This is the worst news anyone can receive. Let the family know we have grief counselors available who will come to their homes. Please tell them we will formally honor both agents at a special memorial ceremony in the next few weeks –whenever they feel comfortable. Most importantly, let them know we will not rest until the person or people who did this are captured and brought to justice."

Elizabeth continued briefing the agents, stating that, later that night, she would make a formal report on television, taking full responsibility for letting the public know that MI-5 would hunt down and catch the perpetrators. At this time, she would not provide information about what possible motives these people had for killing the agents, or how it might be tied to some larger plot. Of course, she would not link their deaths to the infections at King's.

Jake admired both the equanimity with which Elizabeth managed all the news and her remarkable empathy for the family of the slain team members. He also respected her abilities to outline the character of a villain analytically from the limited clues available. It was clear she was adept at synthesizing information, and her objectivity suggested she would have made a fine scientist – maybe better than he was. *In fact, she is more like Chris,* he thought. Jake recognized his own limitations when it came to understanding human behavior. In contrast, he viewed Elizabeth as both intelligent and unemotional. *She is also beautiful,* he thought, briefly focusing his eyes on the tiny lines on either side of her lips as she turned to speak.

"There is some good news," said Elizabeth. "A report from forensic specialists who analyzed the photograph of the two women that we found in the Kontos flat confirmed my hunch. It's from a refugee camp in Lebanon called Sabra. When we magnified the photograph, we were able to read information on a signpost, giving us the identity of the camp. We've now learned that the mother and grandmother were forced out of their hometown in Palestine by the Zionists in the spring of 1949. Several male family members were murdered, and the two women were forced to flee for safety. Many of the Palestinians kept the keys to their original homes. We've also matched the style of keys found in the Kontos flat to those from homes in Palestine in the late 1940s."

Elizabeth felt that now she had identified a likely motive for the women's actions – a smoldering hate and a drive for revenge that had persisted but lain dormant for years. Current events in the Middle East and the continued isolation of the Palestinians could have easily sparked them to act now.

Elizabeth told Chris and Jake that she always considered the Middle East as full of contradictions and intrigue, and she had some sympathy for the Palestinians. In their barren, sand-covered desert, they had seen the mirage of hope vanish on several occasions. Subjected for hundreds of years to the harsh rulers of the Ottoman Empire, they had sensed the advent of freedom at the end of the First World War as the empire began to fail. The powerful British Empire told the Palestinians they would help them push the Turks out; but the British deceived them and stayed on to rule them. Hope again faded.

Eventually, the international lexicon granting rightful control of Israel to the people called Zionists was supported by the Americans, and the Kibbutzim were systematically developed, creating Jewish settlements across the land. Elizabeth thought it incredibly ironic that a people who had suffered the most unspeakable horrors ever recorded, the systematic killing of generations of Jews followed by the stealing and looting of their homes in Europe, would sponsor so much fear. Who would imagine that the same suffering people would in the late 1940s relentlessly drive out the Palestinians, killing them and looting their property and possessions? But, in fact, that was what happened.

"To understand the Zionists, however," she noted, "one has to recognize that over 100,000 Jews in Europe who survived the Holocaust had no desire at all to remain in Europe. Then when they were courted by David Ben-Gurion to emigrate to what is now Israel, they did so eagerly. Their fear of Nazism was still palpable, and the smell of the ovens in concentration camps still reeking in their noses."

She recounted that some factions of the Zionists – only a few – thought that violence was needed for survival. They led the way quickly during the Exodus from Europe. One could imagine that the European Jews' thinking was a complex mixture of fear, desperation, hope, and quest for survival. After Israel won the war with the Arabs, they then attracted many honorable Jewish people to their new land.

"Elizabeth," asked Jake, "how was it possible for Jewish people to be encouraged to move to a place where they knew they would suffer the hardships that must have existed in Israel, since many were already comfortable in their own countries?"

"I think appearances were deceiving," she answered. "You can get a glimpse of what conditions were like from the writings of Elias Chacour, the Palestinian Catholic priest and scholar. He and his family were forced into exile from their home in Palestine after 1948. Chacour said that prior to 1930, over 130,000 Jews were living comfortably in Iraq, a fact that seems incredible to Americans and Brits following the activities of the current American-led war. But in 1950, several bombs exploded in Jewish communities in Iraq, and rumors were rampant that a systematic killing of Jews was underway. Well, the Jews took this seriously – not surprisingly, considering the recent, terrifying images still vivid of Nazi Germany and the Holocaust. As a result of rumors, almost every Jew in Iraq fled to Israel; only a few thousand remained in the following year, 1951.

"Later it was rumored that the especially militant wing of the Zionists, the *Haganah,* had, in fact, set off the bombs, killing their own people and subsequently designing a propaganda program to drive the Jews to the new state of Israel. This was later discovered to be a Palestinian hoax, but many Palestinians thought it was true. So the Palestinians, whose land had comprised over ninety percent of the Israeli-occupied territory prior to the 1948 declaration of statehood, have had hundreds of years of insecurity, deception, illusions, and sadness – sometimes of their own making."

"I must say, I'm embarrassed," Jake said. "I know so little of this history."

"Well, it's not gotten much attention except by a few Jewish and Palestinian scholars who are still hopeful and optimistic about a fair settlement in the Middle East, and who oppose the minority of radical militants on both sides. Those of us in the U.K. and America tend to be even handed in our thinking of the Middle East. We can understand the desperation of the Jews immigrating to Israel in 1948, literally rising from the ashes of Nazi terrorism. We can also have sympathy for the Palestinians who lost their lives and future afterwards. But we have no sympathy for terrorists, whether Israeli or Palestinian sympathizers. What few in the U.K. realize and, I suspect, few in the U.S. acknowledge, is that the jihadists are a small fraction of all Arab populations, and even among the jihadists, the most violent are a small subset. So gross labels distort reality and thwart solutions."

"So bias coming from the Middle East may be the source of a motive?" asked Jake.

"Absolutely," Elizabeth replied. "But remember this if you think bias is limited to the Middle East: When Shakespeare was alive in London, it was dangerous to admit that one was a Catholic. Such a person might be hanged on the banks of the Thames. We now have increasing evidence that Shakespeare was indeed a Catholic with a close allegiance to the church. Imagine the outcome if his religious beliefs had been revealed and he had been hanged! It takes a long time for such prejudices to die out. Some may argue that four centuries later we still have remnants of anti-Catholic bias. You can see why it's so difficult to read current events as an outsider and why militant feelings are so deep."

Elizabeth said that she had also had her team review all Dr. Kontos' foreign travel. "She generally took a ten-day holiday outside of the county each year. Three years ago to Greece, two years ago to Canada and a year ago to the southeastern U.S. We're trying to get more details."

The car raced through the Belgian countryside as the driver swerved to avoid inpatient travelers on the A-13, cutting into and out of traffic lanes. He began to pull out to the passing lane, narrowly missing a collision with a speeding silver Mercedes sedan whose occupants, two women, appeared angry that anyone would be in their lane. The oncoming driver pressed her horn furiously, causing Chris to cover his head, fearing an immediate crash. All four seemed relieved that an accident was averted, and Elizabeth said they would be pulling over in approximately one kilometer to examine the passengers of the Volvo that had been detained by the Interpol agents.

Parking a hundred meters behind the police barricade, the driver and Elizabeth exited the car, having instructed the physicians to remain inside. As they approached the two women who were standing next to the black Volvo, Elizabeth quickly realized they were not the fugitives. They were obviously a mother and daughter who bore no resemblance to the twins. Elizabeth thanked them profusely and wished them a good holiday. She also thanked the Belgian officer for his quick thinking, then returned to the car and for the trip back to the Ostend airport.

Chris and Jake agreed to organize a brief meeting of local physicians at the hospital in Ostend later that day, and to ask local medical personnel to arrange a follow-up of the hydrofoil passengers. Elizabeth would meet briefly with her Belgian counterparts to attempt to develop a strategy to capture the microbial hackers as quickly as possible, before they could do any more harm.

"Once things are set up, you should probably return to London to complete your studies. I can arrange transportation anytime, and we'll be in touch," said Elizabeth. "I don't know what those ladies have in mind."

At the airport, Elizabeth patted the back of Jake's shoulder with her fingers as he prepared to enter the plane. She could sense the American physician's interest in her and was flattered by his attention. Her ability to make him feel more comfortable in her world of law enforcement was strangely erotic for her. She decided not to discourage him.

In a telephone call back to his laboratory before takeoff, Chris learned from his chief laboratory tech that Cecil Barnes had held a brief press release. Reporters from the *Times* and *Guardian* were present, and cameramen from the BBC were at the hospital to record the statement. Ms. Keyes read the press release to Chris. It refered to the outbreak as "a small cluster of post-surgical infections caused by an antibiotic-resistant *Staphylococcus aureus*." It went on to say, "There have been no cases in the last three days, but we are taking all precautions. We have an expert epidemiologist from America assisting our own expert laboratory microbiologist at King's. The organism is considered common and dangerous, and we have had several deaths. We are working on this around the clock." Cecil Barnes apparently declined to answer any questions and could not be reached by the press for further comment.

Ms. Keyes also said that several members of Parliament were expected to comment on the problem at King's and that some were quite concerned that the cause might be related to the several-hundred-year-old building, possibly due to poor disinfection of the walls and floors. After all, the building was filled with tiny crevices that developed over many centuries – perfect places for germs and viruses to 'hide.'

A BBC commentator announced that he planned to interview family members of those who were infected to ask if they would call for an investigation by experts at Colindale. He would also inquire if they planned to bring suit against King's.

Chris hung up and reviewed Barnes's comments with Jake. "At least he didn't lie about everything, Jake, but his limited information and distortions may come back to bite him." Both concluded that Cecil Barnes would need to be prepared for a further onslaught of uncomfortable press notices whenever Elizabeth thought that the time was appropriate.

Jake was feeling somewhat more confident now about his workup of the investigation. Doubts about the negative culture of Dr. Kontos's nasal passage could now be explained by the existence of a twin who was not carrying the organism. He could imagine the praise he would receive for a quick focus on the culprit. He, Elizabeth, and Chris would be photographed linking raised hands for their work. Maybe the conclusion was near. He was beginning to feel lucky and positive for a change. The epidemic of a lifetime quickly averted, with high fives all around. He fantasized that he might have time to seduce Elizabeth and still enjoy a timely return to the U.S.

Such optimism was short lived, however, and Jake's reverie was interrupted when Chris's phone rang. The casualty physician at King's called to say that two more patients were admitted with serious complications of soft tissue infections, and the Gram stains pointed to *Staphylococcus aureus* – cases fourteen and fifteen. They were friends and neighbors of Ms. Phyllis Everly, who had visited her in the hospital. Both husband and wife were on intravenous blood pressure drugs in attempts to reverse septic shock. They were being transported to the critical care unit.

XI

S asha Kontos looked down coldly at the man she had just disabled with her spring-loaded dart. When he dropped the thirty-eight millimeter revolver, she quickly gave it to Diana, who calmly fired two shots into the wall of the barn, assuming that Ata and Elaina would be listening. Soon thereafter, the sisters heard the dissipating roar of a propeller plane leaving the area. A furtive peek through the windows of the barn revealed no trace of either Ata or Elaina.

The would-be assassin had begged for help, acutely fearing his own death. To his horror, he could barely move his muscles and could sense only intermittent flickers of activity in his arms, wrists, and fingers. He could speak, but his voice slowly became garbled over the next ten minutes. His eyes revealed his fear, and he was muttering questions that neither woman could understand, but he seemed to express bewilderment, confusion, and terror.

Having no remorse for the stranger on the ground, Sasha knew that within minutes he would develop blurred vision after his pupils dilated widely and that his swallowing would become difficult and then impossible. This would be followed by the welling of his own saliva in the back of his throat, gagging him relentlessly. Later he would be seeing double, the result of new defects within his cranial nerves carrying erratic messages from the brain to the eye muscles and leading to a total loss of coordinated eye movement.

In the end, she imagined, his core body temperature could sink to a hypothermic range, his heartbeat would accelerate and become feeble, and his blood pressure would go through erratic cycles before plummeting in an inexorable downhill descent. Thereafter, his breathing would lose all rhythm, become shallow and weak, and chaotically come to a full stop as the nerves in the muscles of his chest wall and diaphragm ceased to communicate their messages to inhale.

Pushing the man's right hip while reaching into his back pocket, Diana removed the stranger's wallet in order to delete all traces of his identification and took what she estimated to be 10,000 euros. "Probably his prepaid reward for eliminating us," she said bitterly. She then reached into the pockets of his shirt, found a passport and passed it to Sasha.

"Although the passport is Hungarian, the name of the man is listed as Kasamorov – probably Russian," said Sasha. In his jacket, they also found keys to a silver Mercedes sedan parked behind the barn. The sisters decided to use the man's car, since they were sure the police would have a description of the Volvo that brought them from the port at Ostend into the countryside.

Leaving their victim intermittently gurgling on the dirt floor of the dimly lit barn, the sisters failed to notice the cell phone that had fallen out of its carrier, now resting by his left hand.

The two women exited the side door of the barn, walked briskly along the building's edge through ankle-high grass, and entered the Mercedes, Sasha slipping into the driver's seat. "Diana, do you still have duplicates of the isolates in your bag?"

"Yes, of course, dear. I, too, try to plan for the unexpected, although I never, ever considered that Ata would betray us." She realized this was her second error – and a huge one – but no one, not even Ata, could be allowed to go unpunished for the mortal sin of betrayal. She opened the passenger door again and vomited onto the side of the barn.

Diana lifted up her head slowly. Looking off into the distance, she continued, "We thought he was our prince, sent to save us. Another misguided myth; instead he was the Minotaur in disguise. Now that we know he's an impostor, there must be revenge – *an eye for an eye.* I know where he will go, and we can pay him a surprise visit – Greeks bearing gifts."

"So we shall drive to Germany?" Sasha asked.

"Yes. Ata always said that he had a backup plan, the clandestine laboratory and hideaway where he'll need the help of a skilled microbiologist. Perhaps that's the role of Elaina, I don't know. But I know where the laboratory is, and I'm positive he'll go there, at least for several days, and I know what I need to do."

"Why would he do this to us? I'm so confused by all of this," Sasha said, holding back tears.

"I don't know, love, but you always suspected he had his own demons, deeper and darker than I ever imagined, and apparently somewhere along the line he made a decision to deceive us. Ata must have thought he had discovered a special opportunity to advance his own cause. We were his ticket to a degree in Beirut earlier, and apparently now he's come up with some plan requiring the organism we created. I don't know what he intends to do with our creation, however. He knows virtually nothing about molecular biology – only its power – and clearly he'll need expert help if he has his own targets in view."

"This afternoon, we should drive just past the border in Germany," Sasha said. "We can stay at a *gasthaus*, rest briefly, and plan our early morning surprise for Ata and Elaina."

The two women found their way to the A-13, which they decided to take towards Maastricht, circling clockwise above Brussels to avoid any roadblocks that might have been set up. Initially feeling impatient, Sasha was driving at a very high speed, narrowly missing a tan sedan with three men and a woman inside. Instinctively, she pressed long and hard on the horn as she passed. Later she slowed down until she was driving just below the speed limit.

From Maastricht they took a small road going southeast to the border town of Aachen in Germany. On the way, they listened to news broadcasts to see if they were identified as fugitives and see if there were any reports from the U.K. They were still unclear about why Ata insisted on such a rapid departure from London.

As the countryside passed by, Diana could see a small school and brilliant-green football pitch where two teams of uniformed teens were competing. A young, blonde boy was springing into the air, heading the black-and-white ball towards the goal. Curiously, this pleasant image of youthful athleticism caused her to recall a story told frequently by the twins' mother and grandmother while the family was living in Greece.

In the Palestine of the late 1940s, when the men in the family had disappeared, a group of boys who were friends of their mother gathered to play football on a dirt road. Seeing their excitement, their grandmother had fetched an old Kodak box camera to catch the moment on film. She took several photographs to be sure to capture the joy of those young boys. Fifteen minutes later, the boys decided to move the makeshift goal and began gathering rocks to pile up on end to mark its boundaries. One of the boys thought that he had the perfect round stone for top of the pile. However, to his horror, as he grasped the object he suddenly realized it was instead the head of a man buried in the sand and dirt. Dusting off the man's face with her hands, Diana's grandmother recognized her brother, the victim of a gunshot wound to the head inflicted by the Zionist extremists.

Diana was overcome by an acute sense of fatigue, a heaviness that gripped her body and caused her to close her eyes and fall asleep. Fifteen minutes later, she awakened.

"I know of a small *gasthaus* off the Theaterstrasse near Wallstrasse," said Diana. "It's only a few minutes' walk from the cathedral where Charlemagne was buried."

The sisters knew Charlemagne as the greatest medieval king, whose leadership led to the conquest of Bavaria and Saxony in the name of Christianity. "*It was either baptism or death to those conquered,*" their teacher in Athens had told them repeatedly. Diana reminded her sister of the story.

"Unfortunately for them, Charlemagne's victory over Saxony came at a great cost to the 4,500 Saxons who could have chosen baptism but stubbornly declined; they were beheaded in one day," responded Sasha, now smiling wryly. "Charlemagne knew the value of loyalty, the need to

maintain it, and the proper way to respond if loyalty was threatened."
Both knew they were really talking not about Charlemagne, but Ata.

"Al-Hakim, *the Doctor,* espoused a similar code of right and wrong,"
said Diana. "It was a great day when he met our grandmother in
Lebanon in the refugee camp and introduced her to his Greek friends
and Greek Orthodox beliefs. He would never tolerate the selfishness of
an individual like Ata."

Sasha recalled their father, who had described mortal sin clearly
whenever he would see them on his surprise visits. For him, there was
no grey zone. The commandments said it was wrong to kill a man, but
the Bible said an eye for an eye. Some sins affected generations, so it
was up to the succeeding generations to avenge the successors of those
who harmed their ancestors. For strong families that had suffered
injustice, the present and the past were one. That was why they knew
their cause was just. History – past and current – reinforced the sense
of vulnerability and entrapment of the Palestinians.

*Ata needs to begin his long stay in the darkness of hell right here
on Earth,* reflected Diana.

Sasha continued, "Al-Hakim, too, could easily have enjoyed a
comfortable life with a large private practice in pediatrics, but he
chose instead a commitment to his people, the Palestinians. He is our
Charlemagne."

As the Mercedes crossed the border into Germany at the city of
Aachen, a twin-engine plane dropped its landing gear on approach to
the airport in Cologne.

"Was it really essential to eliminate the sisters, Ata? Do you have
any regrets?"

"Elaina, one cannot afford to have loose ends. I will have done more
good than evil by this deed. When I found the listening device under the
kitchen table in their flat, I was forced to make some quick decisions
involving the agents who were listening outside in a car. But I realized
that the ladies were now a liability. I knew we had to leave abruptly, but

I didn't let them know about the surveillance going on in their flat or that I had removed the agents. We needed to escape quickly; there was no time for sentimentality. However, I needed their prize organism. Vlad has been well paid, and he attends to details. As a result, we are free for the next phase of the plan. Just to be sure, though, I've asked Vlad to call me tomorrow at noon to let me know that all went well and that he has returned safely to Budapest. Even the pilots, who don't know our true identities, will return to France, and we have a rental car under a name that cannot be traced," said Ata.

The drive northwest from the airport to the small cottage just south of the huge cathedral at Cologne on the Rhine River took about twenty-five minutes. Ata told Elaina that he would make a brief stop in the central part of the city in the Heumarket section for bread, coffee, wurst, cheeses, and apple juice. He could get more groceries in the morning after he completed his morning routine: brief exercises followed by a walk.

Ata left Elaina sitting in the car and entered a small market store where various types of sausages were hanging by strings attached to the wall behind a glass display of various cuts of meats and cheeses from all over Europe. Quickly placing his order, Ata gathered his food, chose a wide loaf of pumpernickel to accompany the selection of cheeses and meats, and reached into his pocket for euros to complete the purchase. The shop owner recommended Kösch, the local beer, but Ata declined, causing the merchant to shrug his shoulders in confused disbelief.

Returning to the car, Ata mentioned to Elaina that the cottage would need some airing out. He had not been there for over a year, and even in the years since he purchased the building, he came there only intermittently after the lab was set up. When Diana was completing her medical training in Frankfurt, he found this house. The twins and he set up the laboratory over several months, eventually equipping it fully before moving to London. His ties with friends in the former Soviet Union allowed him a steady income. They had paid him handsomely for forging passports and other official documents and for providing reliable contacts in the drug trade business.

Twenty minutes south, they reached their destination. The five-acre lot was thickly wooded, effectively isolating the two-story building. The early evening sun was filtered by the tall pines behind the house, giving a tangerine splash of light to the front edge of the roof. No one had been in the building for months, and grass was growing erratically though the pebbled driveway, which extended almost a kilometer from the road. *The air is unusually cool for this time of year,* thought Ata as he exited the car with the bag of groceries.

The house itself was a cinderblock building with grey paint chipping off its surface, having been unattended for over ten years. Originally constructed just after the Second World War, it was functional but without any special style. On the ground floor was a small living room opening directly to a dining area, pantry, and small kitchen with a stone fireplace. The furniture was simple, the floors on the ground level covered with linoleum throughout, except for wall-to-wall carpeting in the living room. A couch and two arm chairs were placed near a low wooden table. The room smelled musty, the result of neglect and age. A single lamp beside the couch had a torn lampshade, offering enough light to see in the room but surely not to read.

Behind a bookcase upstairs was the entrance to a secret laboratory. "In the next few days, I will need your help, Elaina, as we prepare our work. When everything is ready for transport, I'll call the parties who are interested in what we have to offer."

"Of course," she replied. "We can discuss more over dinner and breakfast. A good night's sleep will also be welcome after the day we've experienced!"

Elaina sliced the brown bread, made a few cuts of the brie, Gouda, and Swiss cheeses, and placed the pre-sliced pieces of schinken, salami and bratwurst on to a plate for both of them to eat. They washed down the meal with apple juice. Ata boiled water for coffee, swallowed four small pills for his hip pain, and sat down with Elaina.

Ata admired this woman immensely because of her single-minded focus on business and her ability to detach herself from threat or hardship. In his mind, they shared a common heritage, a common language and culture, a common tragedy, and a common cause. Despite her thick body and wide jaw, he found her attractive. "You are especially beautiful, Elaina, and you remind me of my mother," he said, surprising himself about how open he was at that moment. As they both rose from the table, he placed his arms around Elaina's wide hips, pulling her close to him and kissing her lips forcefully. He thrust his tongue into her mouth, tasting the cheese, salami, and coffee in her saliva.

He buried his face into the base of Elaina's neck abruptly as his hands moved up beneath her blouse until he unlocked the clips of her bra. Pulling her bra down below her blouse, he brusquely tossed it onto the floor and cupped both of her breasts with his huge hands. Elaina threw her arms around his thick neck, yielding to him as Ata lifted her hips, cradling her in his huge arms as a father would a child, and they ascended the stairs together.

XII

An emergency call came to rescue workers in Ghent in northern Belgium. A man who claimed he was dying from some kind of poison gave directions to a remote barn thirty kilometers away. In broken French, he whispered in a staccato voice, "I . . . I . . . sick, weak . . . no breath . . . help please." He said that it was taking all of his energy to dial the emergency numbers on his cell phone. In his thick accent, he pleaded to be rescued. The listener initially concluded that the man was intoxicated or that the call was a prank. However, the caller denied drinking any alcohol. "No drug . . . no . . . alcohol . . . please send . . . help." Begging for assistance with a shuddering cough, he said that his body felt weak all over. He admitted he was terrified, and in a raspy voice said that he was now becoming extremely short of breath.

Twenty minutes later, Belgian medics arrived to find a forty-five-year-old male, almost speechless, with flaccid muscles throughout his body. Yet he was alert and appeared to know where he was. On the floor of the barn, they knelt down beside the man and recorded that his respirations were shallow and labored. A formal count of his inhalations indicated respiratory distress. His face was turned to the side, and he was drooling out of the corner of his mouth. When they asked his name, he could not answer. One medic picked up his right arm and let it go, catching it in mid-air, since the victim had insufficient strength to control his muscles. The same was true for the other arm and both legs.

One medic knelt down above the man's head and placed the fingers of each hand beneath his neck, his forefinger and thumbs gripping the lower jaw on both sides in order to pull the flaccid tongue away from the airway. He rotated the victim's jaw in an upward, circular thrust towards his head, extending his neck in an effort to open the airway maximally. The other medic placed a blood pressure cuff around his right arm above the elbow and repeatedly pumped up the bulb full of air while observing the pulsating dial on the round face of the instrument, indicating increasing pressure. The patient's blood pressure was significantly elevated at 180/94. Furthermore, the victim had no fever, yet his pulse was rapid at 118 per minute. The medic by his side called excitedly to his colleague, "Look! His eyes are moving asynchronously. His right eye is drifting to the right horizon and left eye is looking down and out. He cannot fix his gaze on us."

The medic by the man's head suggested, "He must have had a stroke, since he's having trouble swallowing his own saliva. He can't even take a deep breath."

His colleague by the victim's side now placed a stethoscope on the man's chest. His heart rhythm was chaotic. "It sounds like two horses trotting simultaneously. He must be sensing terrifying palpitations," said the medic. "God help him." Within minutes of the arrival the medics, the patient was too weak to speak.

When the patient looked as though he would soon stop breathing on his own, the medic at the head said, "I'm going to intubate him now." He placed the curved, plastic blade of the laryngoscope deep into the man's mouth, lifting up the soft palate with the attached handle at a right angle to the mouth and examining the two thin bands of muscle comprising the vocal cords with the light source embedded in the laryngoscope. Holding on to the handle of the laryngoscope with his left hand, he adroitly placed an endotracheal tube through the opening between the vocal cords and into the trachea, the main wind pipe leading to the lungs. He anchored it to the man's face with tape surrounding the tube at its exit from the victim's mouth. Attaching an empty syringe to a thin catheter, he pumped gently, pushing in a few cubic centimeters of air. This process inflated a small bulb attached to the tracheal part of the endotracheal tube, further fixing it in place. He then connected the airway tube to a black, air-filled ambou bag the size of a cantaloupe, which he compressed rapidly three times, forcing air into the victim's large airways and into the lungs. The medic was trying to keep him alive by repeatedly squeezing the round ambu bag with air and adding a high concentration of oxygen mixture coming from a small green tank connected via a plastic tube.

According to a local report, the *"unfortunate patient died of cardiac arrest on the way to the hospital."*

The police were subsequently alerted by the medical team and dispatched immediately to the location where the patient was found. Two members of the police force examined the perimeter of the barn, walking its exterior edges. They dusted the door knob of the side door and entered, cameras in hand, taking forensic photographs. Curiously, they noted two spent shells of a thirty-eight millimeter weapon on the floor of the barn and located the bullets lodged in the wooden wall. They phoned their office with the preliminary findings, speaking with their chief.

At a police office in Knokke, not far from the Ostend airport, Elizabeth had been receiving all reports of any suspected criminal activity. Having just spoken to the Belgian police, she immediately called Jake's BlackBerry number. Jake and Chris were still on the tarmac inside the plane at Ostend, nearing the time for takeoff. Elizabeth told him what she learned of the man's death, then asked Jake if he had any idea as to what might have caused it. "Jake, a dying man said that he was poisoned by two women in a barn not too far from the location where Interpol was pursuing our suspects." She described the scene as witnessed by the arriving medics, who recorded the story of the man who appeared to have a stroke.

"Jake, could a poison do this, and if so what kind? Can staph do this?"

115

"Since the victim had no fever and the primary symptoms suggest neurological problems, this is certainly not due to staph. Clearly, this is a poison that affects the neuromuscular axis – either just the muscles, just the nerves controlling the muscles, or possibly the junction of nerves and muscles. There are many possibilities. I'll call the poison control experts in London in the morning if you don't learn anything form the local forensic pathologists beforehand."

"Thanks, Jake. I'll ask the crime team in Brussels to review the toxicology studies at the morgue. We'll also send surveillance teams to focus on this area and to try and intercept the fugitives. I know you're anxious to return to London this evening so you can interview the new victims of staph infection."

When the Interpol forensics team arrived at the barn, they, too, were puzzled about the two thirty-eight millimeter shells and were surprised by the location of both bullets in the wooden wall of the barn opposite the side entrance. The more senior agent, rubbing his hand through his thick white hair, said to the other, "This is curious. No powder burns are obvious on the body of the man who died, and there are no entrance or exit wounds to indicate bullet penetration. In fact, the bullets were very close to each other in the wall, as though purposefully aimed in that direction, especially since they were only three feet above the ground. It seems to me that the person who pulled the trigger was not aiming at the chest or head of the victim."

Outside the barn was the black Volvo sedan that Interpol agents from Ostend had been pursuing earlier. However, the detectives noted fresh tire marks that did not match those of the Volvo. "Whoever did this," remarked one of the men, "probably escaped in another car. Perhaps if we take photographs we can determine the tire manufacturer and possibly identify the automobile."

The other responded, "That's possible, but there's also a short aircraft runway in the back. The grass has recently been matted down, and I suspect that a small plane was in the back of the barn. Our fugitives may have all escaped by air. We need to notify all European airports."

At the morgue in Antwerp, two forensic pathologists arrived to take blood and tissue samples for toxin analyses from a recently deceased man thought to have been poisoned. Snippets of hair and skin, four punch biopsies of muscle, and four biopsies of nerves were obtained. What each noticed was that now, sixteen hours after death, when *rigor mortis* should begin and the muscles fully stiffen up, in fact they were somewhat flaccid. Because of the mysterious death and the victim's statement about being poisoned, the police authorized detailed toxicology analyses in an attempt to find a cause.

Elizabeth was told by local authorities that it would take almost two hours for samples to reach the laboratory in Brussels, and three more hours before the mass spectroscopy tests would be completed. In response to her questions about the specificity and time requirements for the analyses, the lab tech told Elizabeth, "We'll know something useful in several hours."

Elizabeth had asked for a priority analysis, citing possible bioterror concerns.

At about 8:00 p.m. that evening, Elizabeth went before a BBC camera person who was dispatched to get a twenty second clip of her vowing to hunt down the killers of two MI-5 agents in a relentless fashion. She promised the families and friends that this would be a 24-7 effort.

Elizabeth received a call at 11:45 p.m. in her hotel room in Brussels, while she was still awake, reworking details of the case at a small desk. Speaking in clipped English with a soft French accent, the physician at the other end of the phone, a toxicologist, identified himself as Dr. David de Mol. He wanted to notify her of the results of his analyses, and he was quite confident about his findings. "Madam, the man found in the barn died of botulism. There can be no doubt! We found evidence of the presence of the botulinum toxin in extremely high concentrations in his blood and tissues. In fact, I've never observed or read of levels of toxin this high in any formal scientific report of botulism. Furthermore, the finding of the toxin matches the history reported by the victim in the clinical case, and I'm sure this is the cause of death. We'll have the results of our toxin testing in mice in the next two days and know precisely which toxin, A through E, was involved."

"Thank you, Dr. de Mol, this is very helpful," said Elizabeth, who immediately hung up and phoned London.

Jake was in his hotel room unable to fall asleep. His headache was gone, but he was restless, still awake despite having taken two melatonin pills an hour earlier. Lying on top of the covers, wearing only his boxer shorts and no shirt, he reached for the phone.

"Jake, I apologize for calling you so late, but I have an important question. I just heard from the toxicologist in Brussels. The man found in the barn apparently died of botulism. Just before he died, he said that a woman had poisoned him with a dart. Can you, as a clinician, make sense of this?"

"The dart must have had a lethal dose of the toxin manufactured by the bacterium *Clostridium botulinum*. The toxin doen't penetrate intact skin, so an assassin would need to inject it into the victim. A skilled microbiologist like Dr. Kontos might have prepared some kind of injection laced with botulinum toxin as a potent weapon. However, didn't you say earlier that Dr. Kontos' sister had a degree in toxicology? If so, this may be her footprint in the whole affair."

"How difficult would it be to inject someone with a deadly dose?"

"For a person with Dr. Kontos's apparent skill, not difficult at all. The lethal dose by injection is only a tenth of a microgram – ten percent of one-millionth of a gram. A dart with as little as a half a microgram could kill someone within minutes. It's also possible that the toxin itself was altered in order to bind rapidly to the receptors located in the juncture of nerves and muscles. To get a detailed evaluation, though, we'll need Chris's help, or guidance from a medical toxicologist."

"Jake, I'm glad I asked; you make it all so clear." She meant to flatter him. "It is horrible for the victim but useful for understanding what we're up against. You're right about Sasha, the sister. She does have a PhD in toxicology. I'm still trying to find out more about her, but MI-5 has just identified her employer as the University of London's Molecular Pharmacology program. In the morning I hope to know what she was doing there. I suspect I know the answer.

"By the way, our team has confirmed that the twins' mother and grandmother were Palestinians by the name of Khoury, which apparently means 'priest' in Arabic. Their mother was called Jawhara, meaning 'jewel', and their father's name is Hani, also an Arabic name. We don't know much more about him, or if the Greek name Kontos is an alias or not. We're also trying to find out if either parent is involved in current terrorist activities or if they have ties to radical Arab groups. In the meantime, we have Interpol helping us in our search for the Kontos twins."

On hearing Elizabeth's description of the Kontos' family history and her plans for continuing the investigation, Jake realized once more how much his life had changed in the few days since he had arrived in London. Besides the adventure of the epidemic workup, he had met an extraordinary woman, one who was comfortable calling him in his hotel room in the dark hours of night. In truth, he wished she had called from the lobby and was on her way up. He was fantasizing about her long legs wrapped around his hips.

"Jake, how did the two new patients look?" she inquired.

"Chris and I saw the husband and wife patients, and both are now in the ICU," he replied. "It looks like septic shock. Both are still on pressor drugs to try to reverse their low blood pressure. If both die, it will be seven deaths – approximately a fifty percent mortality with this outbreak. We have them on the only antibiotic known to be effective. We've limited the number of healthcare providers who will have contact with the patients, and all are experienced with infection control guidelines and isolation gear."

"What's the likely outcome?"

"There's a fifty-fifty chance of one or the other surviving. We also have them in strict isolation in hopes of preventing a new hospital outbreak."

"Thanks," Elizabeth replied. "Good luck, and keep me posted. I need to try and figure out what happened in Belgium. My guess is that the man who died was in some way threatening the women and was surprised when one of them caught him with a poisonous injection that eventually killed him. Surely the man who died is different from the heavyset man who lived in the Wimbledon flat with the laboratory. None of this is making sense yet, and every time we get close to some understanding, something else even more strange happens to disorient us!"

Elizabeth told Jake about the unusual finding of two spent shells and two matching bullets found in the barn. She wondered out loud that she would like to know whose gun fired these. If it was the man who died, why did he miss his victims? If it was one of the twins, why did they miss hitting the man, and why did they need to use the poisonous dart?

"Jake, anything else on your end?"

Jake said that for his part he was wondering if the twins began with isolates naturally resistant to vancomycin or instead added a new resistance gene. He would make calls to the labs in the U.S. that initially isolated the fully vancomycin-resistant staph and speak with his colleagues at CDC, who stored all of the isolates. He would also try to find out if anyone from outside the U.S. might have paid a visit and could have obtained samples of these isolates.

"Thanks," Elizabeth said. "Let me know what you learn. Good night. By the way, Jake, I made some calls and our investigators confirmed that Professor Allen and Dr. Kontos were seeing each other socially in the last year. Several neighbors noticed that she stayed through the night on a few occasions. We're not sure how he could be connected to the mystery, however, and we're not even sure if he knew anything. Nevertheless, it occurred to me that the superficial marks identified on Professor Allen's shoulders could have been the result of some amorous scratching during an affair with Dr. Kontos."

Jake paused a moment before replying. "It would certainly be possible for him to be infected directly from Dr. Kontos at the site of the scratches. That would mean he contracted the infection socially, – outside of the hospital, and not in the operating room. However, my analysis suggests that the patients who were infected very likely contracted their infections in the OR, from the anesthesiologist at the time of surgery. The case control study strongly suggests the importance

120

of Dr. Kontos in the transmissions.

"Elizabeth, something else just occurred to me. I have been worried about Ms. Everly, the patient who had the misfortune to have both staph infection and later Guillain-Barré Syndrome with a form of paralysis. I'm reluctant to suggest this without talking to Chris about how it might happen, but there's a possibility that Ms. Everly has botulism."

XIII

It was 5:00 a.m. when the silver Mercedes edged furtively towards the entrance of the wooded Cologne property on which the two-story cottage lay. Sasha brought the car to a stop aside a thick hedge three meters high and fifty meters to the north of the driveway, turning off all the lights. Whispering to Diana, she said cautiously, "Okay, it's now your time to meet again with Ata."

Diana gave Sasha final instructions. "Stay here until I return. I should be back in about one hour. We know Ata's habits well, and he will want to walk through the woods at exactly 5:30 a.m. by himself before breakfast. He's like clockwork with his routine, and I'll be waiting to surprise him.

"If anything delays me more than an hour, take no chances, gather your new passport and the money, go to the airport and book a flight for Athens. We have several friends of the Doctor there who will take care of you, and they can contact Father quickly. You must promise to pursue our mission."

"Okay, I promise, sister. But be care-careful. We've now become aware of Ata's duplicity. He's obviously cu-cunning and ruthless. He used us, and we severely misjudged him. He's probably run down and kill-killed many others like us who have gotten in his way. Please don't get too clo-close to him – and believe nothing that he says."

"I understand. Of course I'll be cautious," said Diana. "I hate that man; he took advantage of our loyalty. He must pay for this, and believe me, our revenge will be slow and sweet."

She patted both pockets of her sweatshirt as a final check and stepped away from the car. Over her right shoulder hung a wide, black strap holding a black canvas handbag, big enough to encase a large camera. Diana zipped the bag closed before moving toward the house. She would be barely visible, she thought, in her black sweat pants, sweatshirt, and running shoes.

Diana walked up to an opening in the hedge, then stepped ten meters to the right of the pebbled stone driveway in order not to be seen or heard. The unkempt woods were thick with pine cones, and she was careful to avoid a few trees that had fallen in earlier storms. The dim light gave faint evidence of rot and acid rain deterioration on the bark. With the unseasonably low morning temperature, Diana could see a small puff of her breath when she opened her mouth, and decided to breathe as slowly as possible and only through her nose. When she was within twenty-five meters of the front of the house, the sun was just beginning to rise from behind the driveway entrance, giving a rouge glow to the roofline above the pine wood front door.

A few minutes later there was just a sliver of morning light faintly outlining trees silhouetted in front of the house. Diana shivered briefly in the crisp air despite wearing her zipped-up sweatshirt with bulging pockets on both sides. She then moved the strap of the small canvas pocketbook to her left shoulder.

Fifteen minutes later, Ata emerged from the front door of the house with a walking stick. He paused on the stone entranceway to do some simple stretching exercises for three or four minutes, lifting his knees successively into the air while thrusting both arms alternately upward to the sky. First the right arm and right leg were raised, then the left leg and left arm. *There is nothing smooth about his movements*, Diana thought, remembering Ata's five-year battle with arthritis. But she could appreciate the power of his body, observing his thick knees push through the air like the huge pistons of an engine. He proceeded down three steps to the driveway, grinding pebbles beneath his large frame. Wearing dark pants, a sleeveless black shirt and sandals, he was more of a black holograph than a human at that hour. His huge deltoids and upper arms gave him the appearance of a professional wrestler. As was his custom on rising, he was not wearing a wig, and the early morning sun gave a slightly golden glow to his bald head.

Diana stood motionless in the woods and let him pass by her position. She fought back a few shivers created by the cold air, briefly folding her arms across her chest. Deftly avoiding the low branches of two trees, she moved closer to the driveway. Despite her best intentions, however, a high-pitched cracking noise from a broken twig registered at her feet. She froze instantly behind a cluster of trees, her heart pounding. She even wondered if Ata could hear her heart, which was exploding in her chest and sending pulsating sounds that she could sense like muffled jackhammers in both ears.

Ata turned abruptly and viewed the woods nervously but carefully, scanning the area with a radar intensity. Facing the direction of the driveway entrance, he was squinting slightly in the early morning sun. Then, seeing a squirrel prance across his line of vision, he concluded that the animal must have made the sound in its morning forage for food. More relaxed now, he took a few deep breaths, turned around, and continued walking down the drive with a slight hobble.

Diana had now edged within two meters of the driveway's border, only five meters behind Ata's position. She rehearsed the plan, telling herself that the discipline with which she trained needed to guide her and keep her focused on her prey. To her immediate and utter relief, she avoided stepping on a twig again, this time missing one only by inches. Gasping briefly because of the noise from her misstep, her warm breath against the cool morning air created a brief cloud of grey mist that was visible to Ata and betrayed her location. He squinted in the direction of the exhaled moisture, knowing without a doubt that someone was present in the woods.

Immediately, Ata saw the outline of a small figure and fixed his eyes on the intruder, his walking stick now held at shoulder level like a weapon.

Diana recognized that a critical moment had arrived, and she fought off her fright with a wave of newly channeled anger. "Good morning,

Ata," she said coldly. At that moment, she had transformed her fear into a single-minded determination. "You left Belgium in such a rush, we hardly had time for goodbyes," she said wryly. "Since we share so many visions, we owe it to each other to have a more formal farewell."

Although he could not see Diana clearly as he faced into the sun, Ata immediately recognized the owner's voice. Confused and utterly astonished, wondering briefly if he was hearing voices from the other world, he was now attempting to regain his equanimity, to make sense of the abrupt interruption of his morning walk. He began his conversation in a relaxed way, urgently trying to control the situation. "My dear, I hope you will forgive me. I've felt so guilty, and I should not have run off without you. It was a terrible mistake, a deceitful plan of Elaina's that in a rash moment I agreed to. Please forgive me. We can begin again without Elaina and plan properly for the Israelis' deaths. Elaina should be punished for brainwashing me against you. Oh, what a sad day when I met her! I promise you on the memory of my mother that I will do that, and we will continue with the plans you have."

Ata quickly dropped his walking stick in an attempt to defuse the situation, to convey to Diana an impression that she was in no danger. He was now walking slowly towards her, only three meters away, careful not to make an abrupt move. Stopping briefly, he forced a smile and placed both huge hands on his hips, still attempting to convince Diana she was safe in his presence.

"I've been in agony, thinking that some harm had come to you," he continued. "I could not sleep a minute last night. I am so relieved that you are well. Come inside and we can celebrate our good fortune. Please, let's have a cup of tea and start over."

He did not move for ten seconds, a period that felt like an eternity. Suddenly, sensing what felt like an insect bite to his chest, he decided to make a move to overpower her. With two broad, if somewhat feeble, strides Ata lunged forward to put his hands on both sides of Diana's shoulders and prepared to thrust his knee into her soft midsection, intending to disable her with one lethal blow. Yet for reasons he could not comprehend, he was unable to lift up his thigh.

Diana suddenly felt the huge hands reach up and surround her neck, and immediately she was gasping for breath. She felt weak and saw black spots in her field of vision, thinking that she had misfired and now was about to die. An excruciating stabbing pain now seized her throat. With every inhalation she made an uncontrollable rasping sound. *I now have stridor*, she thought, recognizing the braying sound of air desperately trying to enter a narrow airway, the result of swelling of the tissues lining the main windpipe and voice box. *The Minotaur's killed me!*

Just after he had made the split-second decision to lunge at the neck of his visitor, however, Ata was seized with an overwhelming sense of weakness. Now he also felt a recurrence of the small pain in the right side of his chest, the site of the contaminated dart. His grip seemed to evaporate into the air, his arms now lifeless. All of his power immediately drained from him. He could not even stand up; against his will, he fell limp and helpless to the ground, his head striking a rock with a dull thud, making a sound like a hammer hitting a watermelon.

Wincing in pain, Ata attempted to reach out for Diana's ankles, but she deftly evaded his clutches, and his feeble shoulder movements seemed to be without purpose. Diana was still feeling the effects of the deep constriction of his fingers on her neck, and her throat was burning with an intensely raw pain as though hit by the flames of a torch. She started coughing uncontrollably in fits of raspy explosions.

Now, in a voice barely audible and decidedly contrite, Ata said, "You've poisoned me ... but there must be an antidote!" He choked out his words between deep, racking gasps. "Please save me ... and I'll do ... whatever you want. We can work together ... on both of our projects, and you'll have ... all the money you'll ever ... need to succeed in your quest."

Ata tried again desperately to get to his feet, but none of his muscles were working, his body refusing to take orders from his brain.

Not wishing to utter a sound, Diana just stared at the wounded man for whom she now felt only repugnance and loathing. She wanted him to suffer, to remain in agony for the rest of his life – however long that was. *He does not deserve to die quickly. He has lied to us and betrayed us,* she thought. *An eye for an eye.*

Ata looked up to Diana, whispering and imploring her to help, pleading for mercy. His speech was uncontrollably garbled. He recognized that he was coughing weakly and felt his vision failing. His heart was pounding erratically, and he had an excruciating headache. He tried to scream for Elaina but couldn't, his breath and voice eluding him.

Diana bent down to whisper in Ata's ear, "Don't worry, I'll be back in a minute, and we'll have another chance to converse." Leaving him helpless on the ground in the woods, Diana entered the door of the house furtively, deciding to leave it open rather than risk making any noise. She ascended the stairs with soft, cat-like steps, and pushed on a partly opened door to a second floor bedroom, still not making a sound while clutching the inside of her bulging pocket.

Elaina had been asleep, but on hearing the door open widely and feeling a brief rush of cool air, she awoke. She had only just opened her eyes when a shot rang out of the thirty-eight millimeter revolver.

Turning immediately, Diana went to the bathroom, picked up a dry washcloth, and then entered the secret laboratory, which she knew well. She found all the specimens of the *Staphylococcal* isolates in the incubator along with a small motorized device at the bottom of the styrofoam container. Having gathered up the materials, she descended the stairs with great purpose and again moved outside toward the huge form lying on the driveway.

She quickly stepped along the driveway's edge, once again examining the pathway she would take toward Sasha and the Mercedes. After a few steps, she paused in front of the mass of the man she had just disabled.

Ata tried desperately to focus his vision on her and speak with his eyes. Now he couldn't believe what he was seeing – Diana was placing sterile latex gloves on both her hands. He could see Diana kneeling above his head, reaching into a canvas pocketbook and pulling out a thin syringe with a milky fluid in its cartridge. She placed the forefinger of her left hand on Ata's right eyelid, pulling upward, and with the left thumb she pulled the skin below the eye gently and purposefully downwards to expose the globe. Ata saw the syringe in her right hand and watched her slowly advance the needle to the edge of his cornea. He sensed an excruciating pain in his head as she plunged the needle deftly through the thin outer surface of the globe of the eye, as if piercing the surface of a grape. She emptied half of the cloudy material into the gelatinous vitreous cavity just behind the lens, applying pressure on the plunger with the precision of an expert. It seemed as if a bolt of lightning were hitting the back of his eye and hammering through half of his head, which was throbbing mercilessly. He could see a few crescent-shaped flashes of light in his right eye as Diana pulled the syringe back.

With the calculated dexterity of a seasoned anesthesiologist with operating theatre skills, Diana moved slightly to her left and punctured the globe of Ata's left eye, this time emptying the remaining half of the chalky fluid through the thin tuberculin syringe and needle.

Despite experiencing the most agonizing pain he could imagine, Ata could not move. Lying motionless, he suddenly realized that his life was taking a decidedly unexpected turn – not one he had bargained for. Only yesterday, he was on his way to achieving wealth and status, and was close to returning to his homeland. Now he was immobile on German soil, with searing head and eye pain, unable to speak or move – or to escape an unthinkable fate. His vision was gone; he was in complete darkness. He felt that soon he would also be unable to breathe.

"You wanted the *Staphylococcal* organisms. Now you are one with them, Ata. My gift to you for pretending to be my friend, a keepsake by which to remember me. Perhaps now you will have more insight into the virtue of loyalty." With that, Diana pushed the syringe and needle into a narrow rectangular metal container, closed and locked the lid, and placed it back into a red plastic bag. She removed her gloves, bathed her hands with a small container of alcohol, and carefully secured the materials in the bag.

Wiping the gun clean with a wash cloth from the house, Diana placed the handle in Ata's hand, wrapping his finger around the trigger.

"Should you recover some function, the police will want to know why you killed Elaina. They may initially conclude that an overwhelming guilt led you to stab yourself in both eyes like the tragic but heroic Oedipus, and your explanation of being poisoned will surely seem weak. Understand my sincerity in wishing you a long life.

"Now that we've said our formal goodbyes, I hope you'll forgive me for rushing off, but I must take my leave." Her voice was still strained, and the pain in her throat still haunted her.

With the cloth in her hand she went immediately toward the car, never looking back at the man who had befriended her and her sister in an earlier time and a distant place.

XIV

Entering Chris's laboratory, Jake was greeted by his friend. "Any word from the States on the vancomycin-resistant isolates?" asked Chris.

"I spoke with CDC, and they were inundated with requests to share the eleven uniquely resistant isolates. Almost uniformly, they turned down everyone, despite genuine requests from scientists interested in studying the biology and genetics of *Staphylococci*. After careful scrutiny, however, they offered samples to three distinguished laboratories in the U.S., which had appropriate biosafety hoods, and to two laboratories at the World Health Organization – nothing more.

"I specifically asked if anyone from the U.K. or anyone with the name Kontos had requested the isolates. The answer was no. They'll call me at my hotel if they forgot to tell me about anything that might be important."

"In that case," said Chris, "can we surmise that Dr. Kontos created the new resistant strain, somehow engineered the transfer of a gene for vancomycin resistance to the staph? It's actually been done in a lab one time before, right here in the U.K. But that was years ago, and only in a laboratory experiment. Genetically the organism is completely different as well. Nevertheless, with MI-5's assistance, I'd like to post our isolates overnight to CDC in a secure container to check the molecular fingerprinting against their eleven isolates. If nothing matches, at the very least they'll have a sample for their bacterial library.

"I also have some news related to specimens in the flat connected to

Diana Kontos's apartment. We found several *Staphylococcal* specimens, and in each case they were resistant to vancomycin. However, only five of fifteen separate isolates that we examined had any revved up quorum-sensing activity, and only two had a gene coding for toxic shock syndrome. All this confirms that Kontos was conducting a series of experiments in which new genes were continually being inserted into a vancomycin-resistant staph. This is all a work in progress, of course, which may explain why some patients died quickly and others did not. At this point, I don't know how Kontos was able to insert so many genes so easily. She obviously found a new technique that has not been reported in the scientific literature.

"I rang my laboratory colleagues in Belgium. None of the passengers on the hydrofoil is ill. All nasal cultures are negative so far for any antibiotic-resistant staph, and the Belgian authorities decided to lift all house quarantines. They plan to do a three-day repeat culture on everyone just to be sure."

Looking hopeful, Jake asked Chris if he knew how the two new patients in the ICU were faring.

"Not much change yet," Chris said. "They're still on pressors and considered in critical condition. The cultures are positive for staph, and I assume it's the same strain that infected Ms. Everly. So it should still be susceptible to timethoprim-sulfamethoxazole, which they're both receiving."

The chief lab tech interrupted to say that Ms. Foster had called. She was on her way from the front entrance and would be in the lab shortly. The two men rose and walked to the front end of the lab to greet their partner from MI-5. A few minutes later she arrived.

"Gentlemen," said Elizabeth, "We found Ata Atuk and are on the trail of the twins."

"Where did you find him, and what did he say?" asked Jake.

"Well, he didn't say anything, because he's on respiratory support in an ICU in Germany. There was also a woman named Elaina Raskin found bleeding from a chest wound inside the house where they were staying in Cologne. She was shot with a thirty-eight-caliber pistol, possibly matching the one that fired the bullets in the barn outside of Brussels. The gun was found in Ata's hand, and the German authorities concluded that Ata had attempted to kill Elaina and subsequently suffered a heart attack.

"What made this confusing was that when they examined Ata at the hospital, they discovered he had recent pinpoint puncture wounds in the globes of both eyes. An ophthalmologist is being called to see him, but the doctors are focused more on life-saving measures – hence, the respirator. So initially they assumed that the woman stabbed him in the eyes while he was asleep, and he got his gun to shoot her. The police psychologist had briefly considered the possibility that despondency had caused him to stab both globes with the needle on the end of a syringe, perhaps after shooting the woman in bed.

"Atuk was found by two neighbors when their dachshunds kept barking. He was in the driveway of a house just on the edge of Cologne. A rather sophisticated laboratory with a secret entrance was also found there, but appeared not to have been in use for some time.

"The woman was found in one of the bedrooms of the house. She was barely alive due to severe blood loss but apparently will survive. Ms. Raskin could speak and said that she awoke just a split second before being assaulted. She is sure it was one of the twins. That fact makes the theory of Ata's self-mutilation less likely."

Elizabeth wondered if one of the twins had been jealous of Elaina and had attempted to kill her. Perhaps Ata was involved romantically with both Kontos women. But what was affecting Ata's health, and why did he have puncture wounds in his eyes? How could a small woman disable such a huge man?

"I plan to fly to Cologne and interview her later today if possible. If Ata Atuk awakens, I'll try to speak with him also. In the meantime, we have Interpol alerted and hope to close in on the Kontos twins."

Jake shuddered on hearing the latest news. Where was this outbreak in London leading? When would it end? Now people were exposed in Belgium and Germany, and two new cases had surfaced at King's. He knew he would stay on as long as necessary, but recognized that he would be wise to look over his shoulder continually to see if anyone looking like the twins was nearby. He had reached that conclusion last night while trying to understand the cause of Ms. Everly's neurological condition.

Chris did his best to keep from thinking about matters he couldn't control and decided to focus on his lab work. "I've done some more work on the staph isolates," Chris said to Elizabeth, "and have a more detailed understanding of the mechanism of its revved-up quorum sensing. I just told Jake that it appears unequivocally that the twins were continually adding new genes to the staph to build a super bug. Although all had genes coding for antibiotic resistance, only some had genes for excessive quorum sensing and still fewer had genes for producing septic shock, the infectious syndrome creating very low blood pressure."

"Chris, I'd like to call Dr. Jonathan White to get an update on Ms. Everly's condition," Jake said.

Turning to Jake, Chris responded, "I'll page him to the lab." With that, Chris turned to ring the operator.

Moments later, Dr. White called back and said that Guillian-Barré was ruled out because of atypical signs. Now poisons were being considered. Suddenly looking excited, Jake said, "This is just what I was wondering! Could the clinical picture be compatible with botulism?"

"In fact," said Jonathan, "this diagnosis came up as a possibility, and we sent specimens off last night, but we never got a food history that was compatible."

"Please let us know what the results are, Dr. White. You've been a great help."

Hanging up the phone, Jake looked at Chris and Elizabeth, and asked Chris, "Do you think that it's remotely possible that Dr. Kontos inserted a gene for botulinum toxin into the DNA of staph? We know the twins have both the botulism toxin and the unusual staph, but for bioterror, staph is not an efficient organism. However, botulism is. Botulism doesn't spread from person to person, yet staph does. So if the twin geniuses of both Doctors Kontos were working on a bioterror weapon, this would fit the bill."

Chris saw the elegance of a single unifying theme immediately. "Bloody hell! I think that's possible, and I should have thought of it as well. I'll examine the organisms immediately for the botulinum gene, and we may tie this together."

"Does this help explain why King's was the initial target for this organism?" asked Elizabeth.

Chris said he still had no idea. Jake added that he, too, had no insights, but another thought came to him. "Chris, if you find the gene for botulism toxin on the staph organism, then we should advise the ICU physicians to begin prescribing botulism antitoxin as soon as possible to avoid their becoming dependent on a respirator for breathing after being inflicted with the paralyzing toxin. On second thought, they should take a risk of its side effects and go ahead now."

"I'll pass that on immediately," Chris replied.

"Well, gentlemen," Elizabeth said, "I have a car waiting to take me to the airport for a brief flight to Cologne. I'll return late this afternoon. If I can make it back before 8:00 p.m., could we meet for dinner?"

Chris said that he needed to be home with his wife, Mary, but Jake accepted.

"Brilliant!" said Elizabeth. "I'll make tentative arrangements for two at the Dickens Tavern on the Southside of the Thames. We can have an outstanding meal there and catch up on our collective thinking."

Three hours later, at a hospital in Cologne, Elizabeth was given directions to the critical care unit where two local police officers were sitting outside of the entrance. She was carrying her small laptop computer to take notes. She introduced herself, showed her MI-5 identification, and was escorted into a private room of the ICU to interview a groggy but alert Elaina Raskin.

Raskin was lying in her bed under a clean white sheet. A tube coming from her chest wound where the bullet had entered was connected to a suction device at the side of her bed. The nurse explained that it was needed to pull the air away from the chest so her lungs could fully inflate. Elaina took shallow breaths to avoid pain, but was comfortable speaking in a soft tone.

Elizabeth pulled up a chair next to the head of the bed, picked up Elaina's hand in a tender way, and thanked her for speaking so soon after her injury. She said she had a number of questions for her.

Elaina nodded as if to say she understood.

"Ms. Raskin, may I ask what your relationship is to Mr. Ata Atuk?"

"We share a common heritage and are close friends."

"Are you lovers?"

"We have become so."

"Did you and Mr. Atuk plan to kill the Kontos twins?"

"I knew about the plan. I told him I thought it was crazy, but he felt it was essential. I couldn't stop him."

"Ms. Raskin, many people like you get accidentally caught up in a crime that they didn't plan," Elizabeth said, employing a calculated strategy to gain Elaina's confidence. "You, too, are a victim."

Elaina began to cry. "Yes," she said.

"I feel sorry for you and want to help. If you help me, I can surely make the authorities know of your strong cooperation. Your sentence will be substantially briefer. Do you understand?"

"Yes. Thank you."

"You're welcome. Now, I need your help in understanding what Mr. Atuk intended to do with the special strain of *Staphylococcus*, where the twins may have gone, and what their intentions were originally for the special bacteria. Are you willing to fill me in on the details?"

"Yes, I am."

Two hours later Elizabeth left the hospital for her return flight. A press release would later erroneously state that Elaina Raskin was found dead in the Cologne house.

———————————

That evening in the business section of London, two of the three team members met at the Dickens Tavern. Elizabeth had driven her own car, and Chris had arrived in a London cab. They looked like good friends who had prepared for a month for a special night out on the town. Jake had returned to his hotel for a shower and shave. To Elizabeth's eyes, he was easily identified as an American: tan slacks, navy blue sport coat with white shirt, pale blue tie, and loafers. Elizabeth was wearing an aqua green pants suit with a starched white blouse, a silver pin on her lapel. To Jake, she appeared to be a model off the front page of a style magazine, not a brilliant MI-5 agent. They embraced warmly.

The inn was noisy in the first room, which was reserved for people wanting beer on tap and shellfish. The air was pungent from the smell of beer and dimmed by the thin fog of cigarette smoke. Passing through the hallway at the end of the room, the two were met by a maître d' who escorted them to a private non-smoking area off the main restaurant, framed on three sides by dark wood panels and stained-glass windows. Passing by the crowd, Jake noted an attractive woman with auburn hair who smiled broadly while making eye contact, squeezing her hand in the air as though to say '*Hello.*' The man beside her also smiled and in a Cockney accent said, "Good evenin', Yank." Jake paused to wave cheerfully to both, and he and Elizabeth quickly moved on. In a private room, a square, wood table with a brilliant-white table cloth and linens was already set for two, and a black folder containing the wine list lay on one of the places.

Elizabeth ordered a claret, explaining this red wine from Bordeaux, France, was a special favorite of the legendary English man of letters Samuel Johnson, who once said that "He who aspires to be a serious wine drinker, must drink Claret." The waiter suggested that both try the specialty of the house, Beef Wellington, served with roasted potatoes, haricots verts – tiny green beans – watercress salad, and Yorkshire pudding.

As the two were awaiting the arrival of the wine, Jake could hear the music from *Phantom of the Opera* coming through the loudspeaker. Elizabeth said, "Jake, this is one of my favorites of Andrew Lloyd Weber's musicals, describing the disfigured musical savant hiding in the deep recesses of the Paris opera house. Listen to this part by the heroine, Christine, sharing a boat with the Phantom, moving through the misty waters of the underground lake."

Jake closed his eyes and listened as the woman's voice swelled to fill the empty room.

In sleep he sang to me
In dreams he came
That voice which calls to me
And speaks my name
And do I dream again
For now I find
The Phantom of the Opera
Is there
Inside my mind

Then, a male singer joined the woman for a duet.

And in this labyrinth
Where night is blind
The Phantom of the Opera
Is here
Inside my mind

Hearing the word '*labyrinth*', Jake recalled Elizabeth's earlier explanation of the myth of the Minotaur. He said as much to her and asked, "How did it all conclude? Is there a happy ending?"

"Well, it does end happily – at least for a while. Theseus was born to King Aegeus and the daughter of King Pittheus, whose name was Aethra. When it came time for the third sacrifice of seven youths and seven maidens to the Minotaur, Theseus was so disturbed at the prospect that he vowed to go and rescue them before they were killed. As luck would have it, Minos's daughter Ariadne fell in love with Theseus immediately and convinced Daedalus to help him. The clever craftsman Daedalus suggested that Theseus use a ball of string to trace the way in and out of the confusing paths of the labyrinth housing the Minotaur. When Theseus found the center of the labyrinth, he killed the Minotaur with a sword given him by Ariadne."

The waiter brought wine to the table, and Jake offered a special toast to Elizabeth for her knowledge of Greek mythology.

"One wonders," said Elizabeth, "how much such stories influenced the behavior of our twin scientists – which I think is likely."

Jake told her that the medical microbiologists in Brussels reported no illnesses among the eighty percent of the Hydrofoil travelers whom they could identify and follow. It was improbable that anyone picked up the organism.

Elizabeth described her interview with the wounded Elaina Raskin. "We're fortunate that the Kontos' laboratory skills aren't matched by their ability to use a firearm. Apparently Ms. Raskin awoke just briefly to see a woman aiming a gun at her chest. She recalls nothing more. She confessed that she and Ata had contacted a man representing a financial group backing terrorists; these people were willing to pay one million euros for the staph bacteria. Ata made plans to have the twins eliminated, but Elaina said she didn't know how they avoided assassination. Ata and Elaina apparently planned to return to the Middle East at some time to live well in Kirkuk and assist the terrorists' plot against the Iraqis. She appeared quite sincere when she said she had nothing to do with puncturing Ata's eyes, adding that it was his dream to witness a free state of Kurdistan after the American army pulled out of Iraq."

"Why would the twins puncture Ata's eyes?" asked Jake.

"If he tried to have them assassinated, I suppose this was a chance to blind him in some way so he couldn't recognize anyone in a court of law should he survive," suggested Elizabeth.

"It's also possible," said Jake, "that the twins injected something into his eyes. Since *Staphylococcus* is their preferred organism, the hospital might consider this possibility. It can't hurt to give him an antibiotic to fight the bacteria in this situation." At this point they were being served the main course by the smiling waiter.

"Right," said Elizabeth. "We have to keep in mind that Diana Kontos is considered skillful with her hands, clearly capable of inserting needles into small veins. This is obviously something she could do." Elizabeth opened her pocketbook and pulled out an e-mail contact for the physicians in Germany. Jake used his BlackBerry to send an e-mail with his advice regarding antibiotics. They then turned their attention to the meal.

"According to Ms. Raskin," Elizabeth continued, "the twins confided completely in Ata, who learned about the years their grandmother and mother endured the ignominies of life in the refugee camp in Lebanon called Sabra."

Elizabeth gave Jake a thumbnail sketch of how those humiliating experiences at Sabra were instilled in the minds of the twins as they grew up in Greece. What the mother and grandmother experienced was not just the loss of family and home, but the abject loss of dignity. The twins told Ata about their mother's coming of age in a crowded house with no privacy, her growing breasts observed nightly by older teenage boys, who were also witnesses to her first menstrual period.

Elizabeth reviewed the history that she thought might be relevant. She said that in 1982, Israel invaded Lebanon on a peacekeeping mission, but hundreds of refugees in Sabra and another Palestinian refugee camp called Shatila were slaughtered. The refugees were not killed directly by the Israelis, but by Lebanon's Christian Militia, who were given access to the camps by the Israeli forces. No news media were given access. The Christian Militia intended to drive out the forces of the PLO in Sabra, but they wound up machine-gunning children and babies. Some distant cousins of the Kontos family who had not escaped to Greece in the 1950s were among the victims, according to Ms. Raskin. "One can only imagine what this information did to the psyches of the young women already predisposed to hate their oppressors.

"So we're getting a clearer image of the twins: their family history, their sense of humiliation, their need for retribution, their years of planning, their willingness to be patient, and their greatly submerged anger repeatedly fed by current events in Palestine," said Elizabeth. "In contrast, what strikes me most is the banality of the other two people now in Cologne, Ata and Elaina, despite their potential to wreak havoc. They were simply after the money they needed to return to Iraq."

"I just thought of something," Jake said. "If one of the twins fired at Elaina Raskin, why was the gun found in Ata's hand? In fact, did he really have a heart attack? Shouldn't we ask for a full toxicology analysis?"

"A good idea. I'll arrange for both a proper toxicology study," said Elizabeth. "Right now he's being maintained in a coma while on the respirator. I'm sure you and Chris know much more about this than I. If he responds to treatment, I'll interview him."

As dinner plates were cleared and dessert was served, Elizabeth continued, "What is more serious is the determination of the twins. Ms. Raskin told me the plan was to distribute the organism, possibly as an aerosol, at a crowded symposium coming up soon in London. On further questioning, she thought the meeting was international, involving Israeli physicians and lawyers. I then checked the list of conventions in London and found a notice for just such a meeting at the Convention Centre, where you gave your talk. She didn't know the date and time, so just before arriving at dinner I asked if one of the agents would get permission to enter the Convention Centre and obtain the schedule of events. I should hear back soon."

The business of the evening was concluded, and Elizabeth switched subjects in a way that raised Jake's hopes. "Jake, I have to pass by your hotel on my way home. Can I drop you off?" she asked.

"That would be great." He pulled out his wallet and lifted up his credit card.

"Dinner is my treat tonight, Jake. I appreciate all you've done," said Elizabeth, passing her credit card and the check to the waiter. "I know you wanted to host this tonight because you're grateful for my help. However, I think the real issue is terror, and secondarily an outbreak at King's, and so it's I who am grateful for *your* help. Please allow me to do this."

After the bill was paid, Jake reached over to Elizabeth's right hand in a gesture to help her rise from her chair, causing her to smile in recognition of his gallantry.

Jake began to think about his longing for affection, Deb's rebuff of his sexual overtures the night before his flight, Elizabeth's contrasting attentiveness, and his sense of freedom and adventure in London. Was he just fatigued from lack of sleep and the pressure of working so hard trying to determine the cause of the growing epidemic? Would he commit to an affair if the opportunity presented itself?

Jake excused himself and told Elizabeth he would meet her at the front entrance after a brief visit to the loo. She agreed and said she would fetch her car and offer him valet pickup service. Jake walked toward the front entrance with her and made a left turn down a long hallway to the rest room, where he passed the young woman and her escort whom he'd noted on the way in. This time the woman said, "Did you enjoy the meal?"

With a bright smile, Jake turned around to reply. Immediately he felt the steel edge of a gun pointed at his ribs. The man with the gun said, "We'll be exiting promptly through the back door here, Yank."

Feeling vulnerable and wishing he had never left Elizabeth, Jake followed orders, walking past the restroom to a rear entrance where he was ushered into the back seat of a dark van. The man slid in next to him. He was told to lie down on the floor, face down. The woman went to the driver's seat and motored away quickly. The end of the barrel of the gun was now resting on Jake's neck.

XV

Outside the restaurant, Elizabeth inhaled the crisp evening air and walked to her car, which she drove back to the front entrance of the restaurant. Surprised that Jake was not already outside, she turned off the engine and went inside to look for him, but he had vanished. Worried that something sinister might have happened, she dashed outside, only to notice a dark blue van spin its wheels and speed away from behind the building. The woman at the wheel and the man hunched over in the back seat immediately raised her suspicions. Instinctively, she wrote down the license number, recorded a description of the van, and phoned in an alert to the local police. She relayed the information about the van to them and asked that the vehicle be stopped and the passengers detained, emphasizing that they may be armed and dangerous.

A few minutes later, Jake found himself in the strange van, racing along the bank of the Thames, the gun still pressing against his neck. He felt a numbing sense of disorientation as the van slowed to pass a cluster of men alongside the dark section of road by the river.

Should he try to escape? To fight his abductors? Should he offer them money in hopes of being left alone? Were the man and woman tied to the agents of bioterror? If so, what did they want with him? Did they want to kill him for assisting MI-5? Did they mistake him for an MI-5 agent?

The woman driver skidded onto a dirt road heading towards the river about twenty yards from a bridge. Jake had no idea where he was.

The car came to a slow stop, and the man next to him said simply, "Get out!" As he stood up, he thought he saw a sign that read '*Embankment*'. In the distance he thought he saw a group of homeless people milling about by the river. Would he be killed instantly? Would death be painful?

Obeying the command, Jake stepped out of the van, the gun exerting a constant pressure against his body. He followed the woman, who was walking six or seven paces ahead. The man then shouted, "Get down on your knees! Close your eyes!"

Still uncertain of the motives of his captors, Jake did as he was told, feeling the gritty dirt and stones pressing against his shins. He was instructed to remove his wallet, passport, watch, and the entire contents of his pants pockets. The man then told him to remove his gold wedding ring, passing him some soapy material to apply to his finger. The man felt along Jake's belt line and took his BlackBerry, placing it in his own pocket. Now Jake was sure the kidnappers wanted to strip him of all identification in an effort to slow down any subsequent investigation. He wondered if his killers would chop up his body after they fired bullets into his head. How much pain lay ahead? So many unfinished projects. He would never see the new position at Harvard. Would Chris tell Deb about their efforts to stop terrorists in London? Would colleagues comfort her and the children? The irony of his dying without his BlackBerry would hit Deb squarely. He would miss seeing his son and daughter fall in love, marry, and raise their own families. Who would give the eulogy at the funeral and tell Deb how much she always meant to him? At that moment he was drowning in waves of dread, hopelessness, and isolation. He was short of breath, weak all over, his limbs feeling the dead weight of gravity.

The man gathered up all of Jake's identification documents, wallet and the contents of his pockets. The thought of his ignominious and premature death was terrifying. It just didn't make sense.

Now Jake could feel the barrel of a gun touching his forehead. The cold metal brought on a new wave of terrifying dizziness. He thought he was fainting. His body began shivering, then shaking uncontrollably.

Fearing death, alone and isolated in an anonymous corner of London, he thought he might cry or beg for his life, but no words came out of his mouth. Then, still pressing the gun above his right orbit, the man said forcefully, "Open your eyes!"

Jake did as he was told, anticipating a painful shot to his brain followed by instant darkness. Instead, he felt a brief stinging sensation in his eyes, the result of a somewhat sticky spray, the contents of a plastic bottle held by the woman. Both eyes began to tear profusely. Suddenly, a dense film covered his vision. He could not see! They had blinded him. But he was still alive, suddenly crying loudly as though some primal neural network had been activated, a howl released from deep below.

Jake was now on all fours, his muddy hands attempting to give him the orientation that he had lost when he was sprayed with the blinding liquid. He heard the couple run away, and immediately the van's engine revved up and signaled its departure.

His newfound relief was modulated by the continued blindness – and now something else as well. He could hear the mumblings of a crowd of men, probably the homeless people he had observed earlier.

He knew from talks at Stanford that many of the world's homeless were benign, but many, too, were schizophrenic or bipolar, and some were criminally insane. What would they do with him, obviously an American, unable to see, with no money to offer in exchange for safety? Would they take sticks and beat him to death in anger for his not having any money? Would they kick him to death and throw his half-dazed body into the Thames? How would Deb and the children receive the news?

With some newly discovered and desperate courage – or a sense that it was time to take a chance – Jake screamed, "I'm an American, and I've just been kidnapped and robbed of everything I own! Two people sprayed my eyes with something that caused me to lose my sight. Can you help me get to King's College Hospital?" His voice could be heard a hundred meters away.

Two or three of the men said nothing, but instead simply patted

Jake's head and face as though he were some exotic zoo animal. Jake felt a pair of hands touching his face, and he reached up to touch the gnarled knuckles of a person who had begun dabbing his eyes with a cloth handkerchief, making unintelligible sounds repeatedly. He heard a person calling on a cell phone, giving police directions to this blind man who said he had been robbed.

Ten minutes later, to his relief, Jake noted that his vision was beginning to improve, though it remained fuzzy. It was good enough for him to recognize the outlines of people. He could roughly discern a crowd of fifteen homeless Londoners greeting two policemen who had arrived, expecting to find the American physician. They had been alerted by MI-5 of the likely kidnapping and were unsure of the motives of the perpetrators. They had been told that an international group of terrorists might be behind the abduction. Then he saw Elizabeth exiting her car and quickly racing towards him.

Jake was standing now, the shame of his fright obviously visible, even in the dim light of the river bank. Elizabeth gave Jake a hug and told him she would take him back to the hotel. But first she insisted on a brief stop at King's Hospital Casualty Department where he could be checked out physically. Jake, still quivering, agreed with some reluctance.

Thirty minutes later, a young physician at King's used a series of saline washes to remove any remnants of the material sprayed into Jake's eyes. He then tested Jake's visual acuity, which had returned to normal. An ophthalmologist did a slit-lamp examination to look for superficial injuries to the eye and told Jake that the cornea had not been damaged. Both physicians assured Jake that he would suffer no long-term effects from the toxic spray. He could go back to his hotel if he wished. They gave him a single Halcion pill to help him sleep, telling him he should take it before going to bed.

Jake was still obviously distressed but comforted by his exam. Elizabeth knew it would take some time for Jake to recover from the effects of his traumatic evening. Although she wanted to debrief him as soon as possible, she knew the best thing she could do at the moment was offer him some comfort. Despite the pressure of time, she said they should spend a few moments together, perhaps briefly sharing a drink at a small wine bar on the way to the hotel.

Ten minutes later, Jake and Elizabeth were sitting across from each other, sipping vintage port, Elizabeth's hands gripping both of Jake's. She knew that circumstances had thrust him into the middle of a situation that, as an academic physician, he never anticipated experiencing. She wanted very much to comfort him.

For his part, Jake was overwhelmed by her kindness and grateful for his rescue. He knew she was physically attractive and found himself looking at her eyes, her warm smile, the skin of her forearms and youthful hands. He was seized with a desire to pull her to him, but in a conservative move picked up both of her hands, pressing them to his lips and kissing them. He became acutely aware of the absence of his wedding ring.

"Elizabeth," he began, "I've been enchanted by you since we met. You've probably seen me staring at you. There's so much I want to tell you about my feelings for you."

No words were needed and none were said. Elizabeth knew she was attracted to the American physician and wished that circumstances allowed for more time to try to make sense of her emotions. She wanted to share her secret about her husband's fatal illness, but that would break a promise she had made to him at home. She placed the palms of both hands on Jake's cheeks, kissing his forehead. He breathed in the refreshing lavender scent of her perfume; it reminded him of open fields of wildflowers. For a moment, time stood still.

Elizabeth retreated back to her seat, held up the glass of port and in a toasting gesture said, "Thanks, Jake. You are a fine man." A few sips later, she said she had more work to do, and sadly they needed to leave.

On the way back to the hotel, Elizabeth received a call and relayed the message to Jake that the police knew of the couple who had used the same M.O. in five previous abductions around London. The abductions and robberies had occurred in various locations, making it hard for the police to capture them. The couple was thought to be from central Europe, but beyond that, little was known about them. "The good news," said Elizabeth, "is that none of this has anything to do with the Kontos twins."

She did her best to calm an obviously shaken Jake, but saw that he was still traumatized by the recent memory of his experience in the underworld. How fast Jake would recover was uncertain, but she hoped quickly, since his assistance would be urgently needed in the morning.

As they were heading south on Baker Street toward the John Snow Hotel, Elizabeth's phone rang. It was her chief, who had reviewed the list of all symposia and meetings at the Convention Centre.

"Foster, I have the information you want. There's a meeting of Israeli healthcare workers and legal experts and their international supporters at the Convention Centre. Our window of time for response is brief; it begins tomorrow at 1:00 p.m.; registration opens at 10:00 a.m. If this is important, we don't have much time to prepare."

"You're right, sir. We'll need agents at every entrance and, if possible, in every major hallway. They'll have to be contacted tonight, and we'll send photos of the twins over the Internet, to their BlackBerries or other devices, and their cell phones. I'll let them know that each of our fugitives is capable of clever disguises, and that they may try to enter the conference centre separately.

"All equipment, all handbags and briefcases will have to be carefully examined – but without raising any alarm. We need to be there by 5:00 a.m. to set up surveillance cameras, a central control room, and a plan to work with the centre's administrators. That gives us only a few hours to sleep.

"I'll ask my physician colleagues to have ambulances ready and a team available in Casualty at King's to handle triage and manage exposure to biologicals," Elizabeth assured him. "I'll be sure to have my entire team meet me at 5:00 a.m. tomorrow at the front entrance."

"That seems like a sound plan," her supervisor replied. "Best of luck."

Although Jake had guessed the essence of the conversation,

Elizabeth reviewed the details with him. She was certain the twins, clearly obsessed with the idea of avenging the wrongs done to their relatives and their people, would attempt to carry out their nefarious mission, even if they thought their plans had been detected. She was also confident now that she had identified their true target.

"Jake, I'm very sorry to ask for your assistance after such a harrowing event, but if you're willing to help, I need you. Would you please contact Chris and work on a medical disaster plan this evening? Hopefully, we'll never need it, but we must be prepared. Perhaps we could meet at the Convention Centre at 7:00 a.m. to regroup. That would give me two hours to set up surveillance and instruct all of our agents, who will need to be in the guise of the convention support team. It's always possible that the two women are fleeing to a friendly country, but the determination they've shown is haunting, and the effort they've exerted suggests that we need to assume they'll return to London."

Elizabeth steered the car to the front entrance of the John Snow Hotel and brought it to a stop.

"You can count on both Chris and me," Jake responded. "If something needs to be done before morning, just call the hotel. I'm in Room 320."

Elizabeth moved over to kiss Jake on the cheek. "I know I can count on you. Thanks," she said. As Jake opened the car door and walked towards the hotel, the fragrance of her perfume accompanied him to the lobby.

Jake paused briefly as Elizabeth's car faded into London's indigo-colored fog and mist, trying to understand everything that had happened since his arrival only four days earlier. For a few moments, he stared in the direction of the disappearing car, hoping to prolong the special feelings he had developed for his MI-5 colleague. As he raised his hand to his mouth, the scent of perfume reappeared, still lingering on his palm.

The braying sound of a honking horn nearby disrupted his reverie. He turned to enter the hotel, first to call Chris and then Deb, who was in Palo Alto, a world away.

XVI

As she drove toward her home, Elizabeth began to reflect on the events that cast her and the two physicians together, about their shared frustrations so far in tracking down the elusive twins, the tragic deaths of two fine colleagues, and the terrifying after-dinner event that had left her American colleague so distressed.

She recognized her strong attraction to Jake, a handsome physician and vulnerable stranger in her world. What she felt tonight, she thought, was incredible lightness, adventure, intensity, and affection, all inspired by the focused attentions of a hardwired American knight.

Elizabeth quickly refocused on the professional issues at hand. The rain that had begun to fall when she dropped Jake off at his hotel was becoming more intense, and she moved the lever to speed up the windshield wipers. In the twenty minutes before reaching home, she organized her tasks: Spend a few minutes with her children and explain to her husband where the investigation was going. Then call her central office to plan for the next day's surveillance activities. Try to get a few hours' sleep and begin the next day at 4:15 a.m. However, just before taking the main turn onto the highway leading home, she decided instead to make a brief stop at her office to review the details of tomorrow's operation with her chief. He had generously agreed to make the late night calls to agents who would report at 5:00 a.m., ready to change into specific guises to blend into the surrounding neighborhood streets. They would have their cars positioned for any potential chase and arrest.

On the way, she phoned her chief to give him information and ask for further updates on anything that could be discovered about the twins. "Sir, have either our forensic team or Interpol linked the twins to any organized terrorist group?"

"No. Just the opposite. They've not been recognized before, because it appears they are working alone. No prior event to link them to terrorism. They seemed to be waiting to build something very big and then release it only when it could be overwhelming. Waiting until they could achieve surprise and inflict the right degree of harm."

Elizabeth mused out loud, "Like quorum sensing in bacteria."

"What did you say, Elizabeth?"

"Oh, sorry, sir. It's a term Professor Chris Rose used to describe some of the behavior of aggressive and cunning strains of bacteria."

"As you requested, we made several inquiries with our agents in Athens. We still haven't located the parents in Greece, but they may have distant ties to the Palestinian insurgency. We do have some interesting information, however. The mother of the twins apparently married a militant Christian Palestinian, who was the nephew of a leading Palestinian politician and militant himself, George Habash.

"Habash was born in 1926 to Greek Orthodox parents in the Palestinian city of Lydda, now called Lod, Israel. In 1948, he and his family were forced from their home and fled to Lebanon as refugees. He later graduated as a physician from the American University of Beirut and subsequently worked as a pediatrician in Pakistani refugee camps. Over a period of years, Habash became increasingly bitter and radical, founding the Arab Nationalist Movement and then the Popular Front for the Liberation of Palestine. He and his Marxist group of colleagues opposed any concessions to Israel and became particularly embittered after the Six-Day War in 1967.

"They then began a series of terrorist plots involving airline highjackings. You may recall the story of the 1968 highjacking of an El Al plane from Rome going to Tel Aviv and forced to land in Algeria. Not long afterwards, an Israeli aircraft was attacked in Athens. Then there occurred the highjackings of a Swiss Air DC-8, a TWA Boeing 707, a

BOAC DC-10 – all forced to land in Jordan. An intelligent El Al pilot foiled one attempt by sending the plane into a deep dive."

He said the man known as Al-Hakim, or the Doctor, had been close to the twins' grandmother since their eviction from Palestine in 1948. Ellis concluded that the seeds of bitterness were spread from generation to generation, reinforced by the continual humiliation of the Palestinians. Although the family had never been linked directly to terrorist activities, its ties to terrorism were strong.

"Sir, what do we know about the twins' father?"

"We suspect he continues to work for the Palestinians, and though he may be an active terrorist, he distances his work from his family, whom he loves. But his two children inherited an anti-Israeli philosophy. In the meantime, take no chances. Consider the danger of these beautiful women as real and imminent."

"Do we know where Habash is, or where the nephew lives?"

"Apparently the nephew, the twins' father, lives in the Middle East but travels secretly to Europe at irregular intervals. As for Habash, he died in January 2008 at the age of eighty-one. Apparently he had a heart attack at his residence in Amman, Jordan."

"Do we know where the twins' mother lives?"

"We've asked the Greek authorities to identify the home of the twins' mother near Athens, but we do not think she's active in any terrorist group, just supportive of her itinerant husband and his mania for revenge. Again, you need to be very careful, Elizabeth."

"I will, sir. Thanks very much." Although Elizabeth had already developed a clear idea of the sisters' motivation, the new information suggested to her that they were probably working alone and not in concert with a terrorist organization. But that remained to be proven. Influenced all of their lives by such people, they might be considered a small sleeper cell of two.

––––––––––

Earlier that same night, a silver Mercedes Benz with its two passengers was proceeding through the Chunnel from France towards the U.K. "I've made arrangements for us to stay overnight at a small bed and breakfast just after the tunnel emerges in the U.K. We can proceed to the Convention Centre later tomorrow morning," said Sasha.

It had been Sasha who suggested taking the Eurotonnel Shuttle so they could bring the car from France to England. At Sangatte in Northern France, they followed the signs for *Le tunnel sous la Manche* and entered the queue of vans, coaches and cars traveling to Cheriton in Kent. They would remain inside the Mercedes as the rail train sped up to 160 kilometers an hour at a depth of fifty meters beneath the sea bed at the Strait of Dover. Thirty minutes later, they arrived.

The two sisters had rehearsed their plan several times the day before while driving to London. The optional dispersing apparatus, the disguises, and the details of parking and approaching the Convention Centre were clear. They then reviewed their main plan for escape and several contingencies in case of surprises.

"Do you have the plan down: the disguises, the organisms, the decoy event, and the equipment we need?" inquired Diana.

"Yes," said Sasha.

"Your idea for the outfits is quite clever," said Diana. "We should have broad access to the Convention Centre, and although it's quite possible that some security officials might be looking out for the two of us, I think we'll elude anyone who might be conducting surveillance."

The night before, Sasha had watched the English television channel in Paris and saw that the police had found two people who had mysteriously contracted botulism, one in Belgium and one in Germany. They mentioned that one man in Belgium had died and another in Germany was on life support. But they gave no mention of a criminal act and, in fact, mentioned that contaminated food may have been responsible. "I only wish we could be in the ICU to see Ata," she said, "to witness his confusion and feelings of helplessness."

The news reports also mentioned that a woman named Elaina Raskin had been killed by gunshot in Cologne near the place where the second case of botulism had been discovered. There was nothing about an outbreak of infections in a London hospital, however.

"Although unlikely, it's always safe to assume that the police know about our involvement with the organism by now," Diana said. "They probably have no idea, however, of our ultimate goal. It is even more likely that they will assume we have left the continent. I also checked the newspapers from London, and so far there's little about the cases at King's. They had a brief column saying two more cases are being treated in the ICU. They are extremely worried that people in contact with infected patients are still at risk."

The path to our destiny, thought Sasha, *has been long and torturous, but it ends tomorrow, here in London.* She said aloud, "Our father, mother, and grandmother will be proud of us on learning of our exploits."

"Sister, you are right. And God is with us and has always been there."

Sasha leaned over to give a warm embrace and kiss to Diana.

In London Jake phoned Chris, planning to tell him about his eventful evening and Elizabeth's request for help the next morning. When Chris recognized his voice, he immediately blurted out, "Jake, I'm so relieved to hear from you! I just heard a BBC report of an incident at the Dickens Tavern. An American was kidnapped and robbed, but survived. It could have been you."

Jake paused for a few seconds to get his bearings. "Chris, it *was* me." Jake explained what had happened, and Chris offered his deepest sympathies repeatedly, feeling guilty for having convinced his friend to help with the outbreak. Jake then told Chris what Elizabeth wanted them to do to prepare for the following morning.

Chris listened attentively before responding. "Jake, we're assuming that the twins plan to expose the Israeli group to an unusual form of *Staphylococcus*. This is most likely the organism they will deploy. However, they've also demonstrated general but treacherous skills with botulism. It seems to me they could consider a plan to release some form of chimera, containing properties of both bacteria."

"I agree," said Jake. "We need to be extremely open-minded with this team of terrorists. We need to think about the modes of transmission they may have in mind – contaminated surfaces, food, water. Worst of all would be airborne, since that form of dispersal would be the most devastating, reaching so many people so quickly."

"I'll set up emergency services here at King's with all the biohazard equipment needed for such exposures," said Chris. "We'll plan to keep rotating teams in place for at least a week."

"Elizabeth has asked that we all meet at the Convention Centre at 7:00 a.m. I'll plan to spend the day in the key surveillance room with all of the monitors. If you need me before then, just call."

"Thank you, my friend, and try to get some sleep. Goodnight," said Chris.

Jake then dialed his home to call Deb, intending to describe the frightening events of the night, give her additional details about the outbreak, and offer his lost passport as a yet another reason for his needing to remain in London. Surely Deb would understand, and he needed some consoling words. While he was dialing the numbers, he wished Elizabeth was with him at the moment.

"Hi honey," he said when Deb answered. "It's been a terrible nightmare here. I need to tell you about the international implications of the investigation at King's – and about an incident in which I was briefly kidnapped and robbed. But the two events are not related."

"You were what?" Deb asked somewhat skeptically.

"On the way to the men's room at a restaurant, I was led at gunpoint to a van outside and taken to a riverbank where I thought I would be killed." He paused for a moment to let that news sink in before he told her something he was sure she would not want to hear.

"Deb, they stole my wedding ring." There was a slight tremulousness in his voice as he told this detail of his abduction.

Deb listened attentively as Jake described the horrifying details of the night and then reviewed the importance of the *Staphylococcal* infections. He apologized for not mentioning earlier to Deb all of the bioterror implications of the outbreak. But now, he said, he had two reasons for remaining in London longer than planned – he would need more time to help solve the outbreak and time to get a new passport. He paused nervously for Deb's response.

In a soft voice Deb began to speak. "I am sorry for what was surely a terrible experience. It sounds terrifying. But what upsets me is your commitment to stay in London when I told you how important it is to me that return." Her voice now became strident. "Now you say you were almost killed, that I was almost a widow and our children almost without a father. Yet you still want to stay, not return to us. It's nonsense, Jake! You're willing to break a promise to me, and now you add that your *wedding* ring is missing?

"First, I hope that what you're telling me is true. It sounds so improbable that I wonder if you're having another affair over there. But even if everything you say turns out to be true, none of it is important to me unless you return on time. The Embassy will help you get a passport within hours, we can shop for a new ring on our anniversary, and the world will still turn on its axis if the details of the outbreak are finally assembled after your departure.

"I need to tell you, too, that the Palo Alto newspapers covered your conference, and on page two they gave a summary of the exchange you had in your question and answer session. Unfortunately, you were ridiculed in the story. It may have a negative effect on your candidacy for the Dean's prize. Apparently you were foolish again. But that's not the end of the world.

"The choice is simple, Jake, your career or your family. You can sleep on that." Deb hung up.

Jake returned the phone to its receiver and closed his eyes, but couldn't sleep. *There's too much going on*, he thought. It was beginning to look as though he could please no one. His talk was a disaster, the outbreak was not solved, he had just experienced the fright of his life, and Deb was embittered. Now he found himself staring at the ceiling, feeling a heavy downward push in bed, the powerful gravity of fatigue. Exhaustion was a constant companion.

He thought he might be drifting off when he sensed the door to his room slowly opening. He was startled initially, but he relaxed when he recognized the familiar woman who entered, holding her index finger at right angles to her lips. She moved slowly and gracefully toward the bed and, with a bright smile, shook off both of her shoes. Jake said nothing and observed her with a curious sense of desire and guilt. Jake knew that the perfume he was sensing belonged to Elizabeth. He briefly smelled lavender, followed by the more complex aroma of laurel. Her hair seemed almost aglow with a greenish sheen, the reflection of the triangular nightlight. When she turned her head, the motion of her hair flowed in graceful patterns like undulating waves of fluorescence.

Elizabeth unbuttoned and removed her blouse. She then reached down and opened the buttons fastened around her hips, freeing her skirt to fall gracefully to the floor, like a parachute billowing slowly toward earth. The dim light emanating from the bathroom cast her long, athletic legs in silhouette. Jake could trace the muscular curves of her calves from her narrow ankles to her knees, then her long thighs that led to her panty line. Elizabeth reached behind her back to unfasten her bra and initially seemed to be having difficulty. Jake sat up and moved toward her, but, still smiling, Elizabeth quickly motioned with her hand for him to stay. Finally, the snaps were open, and the bra fell to the ground, revealing the outline of her supple pear-shaped breasts.

She reached for the covers. All of her movements seemed to be in slow motion. Removing her panties, Elizabeth entered into the bed, reaching her arms around Jake, pulling his head to her breasts.

Jake lifted his head and rested his lips softly against Elizabeth's neck, still inhaling the floral scent of her perfume while closing his eyes. With his arm around her waist, he placed his left hand on her abdomen, feeling the velvety texture of her skin, touching the round terrain of her umbilicus. He then reached up to cup her breast, touching her nipple with his thumb and forefinger, and pulled her snugly to him.

He could feel himself fully aroused now as he reached down to caress the firm outline of her athletic thighs. Elizabeth slowly began to rotate her body slightly away from Jake, extending her legs so that he could now find the moist area of her sex. Jake could hear Elizabeth taking long, deep breaths. He reached over to kiss her lips.

As she turned back completely towards Jake, the phone began ringing, but neither made any move to answer. She kissed his lips while reaching with both of her hands to cover his ears, to hold his head close to hers. Each seemed to freeze in position like a motion picture coming to an abrupt halt at the most beautiful scene of the story. After three annoying rings, Jake was chagrined that the party was so persistent. Why now? What if it was Deb? What would he say?

Jake reluctantly reached for the phone, imploring Elizabeth in a whisper, "Forgive me."

It was 4:30 a.m., and Jake had awakened to an empty hotel room. He turned off the alarm, briefly falling back into the bed. Nevertheless, he sat up and paused to look for any fallen clothes on the floor, any sounds of life in the bathroom, any scent of Elizabeth. He closed his eyes briefly, wondering, *What if?*

He rubbed both eyes with his hands as though to remove hallucinations and awaken reality. His throat was dry, probably the result of some snoring. He got up to get a drink of water, brush his teeth, shave, and shower. *Time to get ready, to prepare to meet Chris and later to join Elizabeth and her team at the Convention Centre. Enough of sweet dreams.* It was time to shed fantasy, to face the intensity and adventure that awaited him. He was anxious to see Elizabeth. He was sure he was in love with her.

XVII

A t 5:00 a.m. Elizabeth entered the Convention Centre with a team of four MI-5 inspectors. She was wearing a dark blue sweat suit with white leather running shoes. A black knapsack contained her weapon, a flashlight, cable ties, her cell phone, and a walkie -talkie. All four men wore dark blue or black suits, white shirts, and ties; they would blend in well with the delegates. Each also carried a lightweight, black canvas briefcase.

Elizabeth gave her team brief instructions. "Let's get these small, wireless surveillance cameras placed in ten different locations around the entrance and main hall right away. On the outside of the building, there should be teams of two inspectors dressed as ordinary citizens on each quadrant of the rectangular perimeter. All members of the teams have hidden microphones, and I expect updates at fifteen minute intervals. I'll be at the Command Centre on the second floor. There, I'll have four agents assigned to continual surveillance of ten video consoles. I'll have ten telephones as well. Report anything that seems unusual and anybody who does not seem to belong at the convention. The people we are dealing with are dangerous – full stop!"

Chris phoned to give Elizabeth an update from the hospital. He had arranged for additional surge capacity at King's; the hospital could now accommodate a hundred patients on regular wards, and thirty ICU patients. There were also thirty more respirators, giving them a total of sixty respirators for emergencies. He had obtained enough botulinum antitoxin for ten patients now and would have the capability to treat thirty more by noon. In a few days, he could acquire enough for up to a hundred if needed. Elizabeth listened with relief when he told her that the antibiotic stockpiles had already been increased to a level where he could manage several hundred patients. He had also quietly alerted the Communicable Disease Centre at Colindale and other area hospitals that there may be a need to transfer patients with serious infections, and plans were underway to involve other hospitals in London. He and Jake would arrive at the Convention Centre by 7:00 a.m.

Elizabeth relayed to her agents that a medical response team was in place. She also told them that the video monitors tracking the surveillance cameras needed to be located in a secure, second-floor room, which would be the control station. The Convention Centre's teams would be inspecting all visitors' bags, and each team member would be accompanied by one or two members of the local police force. She had made arrangements to have ten uniformed officers and would have eight female agents posing as ordinary convention guides.

"It's very important," said Elizabeth, "that we check the identification of all people delivering food and beverages. Specifically, I want photo ID's of all food delivery people checked. We don't know what to expect today. In addition to ID checks, I want a phone call to the supplier of each delivery and a local check here of each delivery against the manifest."

She told her agents that Professors Jake Evans and Chris Rose would arrive at 7:00 a.m. If Diana or Sasha Kontos got inside the building, Professor Rose would help by quickly identifying them, even if they were in disguise. The physicians' key roles, however, would be to coordinate all medical emergency and infection control operations at the Convention Centre and also at the Casualty Department at King's.

"I also want one of our agents to work early this morning with the engineer for the Convention Centre. Please check the ventilation system before the delegates arrive and be sure that only London bobbies and local staff have access to the system.

"All of our agents have photos of Diana Kontos," she continued, "but surely the twins have already shown a penchant for using clever

159

disguises. I think it likely that they plan to use some sort of cover to gain entrance to the convention, probably as foreign delegates. So I have a separate video camera just behind the desk of the on-site registrants. The camera will look directly into the face of each person. I've also checked to see if there are any underground entrances to the Centre, and I've been assured there are none."

She told her team that since she did not know what to expect, she was placing snipers on four rooftops across the street from the Convention Centre, and that she'd requested that a helicopter be on call. She wanted to be prepared; this was a dangerous couple. She warned the teams that the hard part was to wait patiently and yet to maintain a heightened awareness before the conventioneers began arriving.

At 6:45 a.m., Elizabeth left the ground floor and walked the perimeter of the Convention Centre herself, observing the positions taken up by her colleagues from MI-5. It was daylight, and the glint of early morning was reflected from scattered puddles on the sidewalks and streets, remnants of a brief overnight rain. The humidity was oppressively high, and a breeze was causing the rectangular green banners announcing the current meeting at the Convention Centre to flap on the street lamps from which they hung.

The agents outside had donned various disguises. One was wearing black suspenders over a maroon sweatshirt and holding a ten-liter plastic container of soapy water. The trousers of both legs were tucked into his green Wellington boots. He was carrying a tan rag, a separate white drying towel, and squeegees, which he would use to wash a pale blue Porsche two-door sedan. Across the street from him was a second agent sitting high in the cab of a softdrink delivery lorry. He wore a brown leather cap with a short brim, a blue denim work shirt, and a black leather jacket. He was reading a copy of one of the local tabloids.

At the next quadrant were two agents dressed as street cleaners, wearing blue overalls with fluorescent yellow stripes around the bottom of the pant legs. Each was holding a large push broom. They seemed in no hurry to finish the task at hand, pausing frequently between pushes to exchange conversation. Further around the Convention Centre were a man and woman team posing as a young couple, appearing very happy in each other's presence. Both were wearing black jeans and dark shoes. The young woman had a pale blue cotton sweater, and her male companion had on a black sweatshirt. They were holding hands while admiring each other, leaning against the brick wall of the building housing an antiques store.

Two more agents were on the street behind the Centre. Each looked somewhat unkempt and unshaven, one with closely cropped, auburn hair and the other with black hair standing on end, as if he had been struck by lightning. They could easily be taken for drug users, perhaps about to consummate a deal. Both wore dark jeans and dirty black sweatshirts. Intermittently, their discussions appeared to be intense, and each gesticulated wildly, suggesting that he had given more than the other could expect in a negotiation; the conversation was punctuated by raised eyebrows, feigned smiles, shrugged shoulders, and open-faced palms.

At 7:00 a.m. Chris and Jake arrived. Chris wore a tan sport coat over his blue shirt, his green bow tie squarely in place. In contrast, Jake was wearing a dark blue suit, white shirt, and gold colored tie. "Elizabeth," said Chris, "I have a triage team at King's in case we need to evaluate patients for microbiological exposures. Within an hour, they will have available a separate wing of the Emergency Department – Wing B – ready to conduct decontamination operations and place people in isolation if necessary."

"Thanks, Chris. I hope we won't need it, but it is comforting to have this in place. I've notified emergency crews to park six blocks away, and I'll instruct them to take any potential victims to Wing B at King's. As you both can see, we have ten video screens and as many telephones and walkie-talkies here in the control centre. My inspectors and I will continually observe the cameras, and we will maintain direct audio contact with our agents on the perimeter."

Elizabeth told them she was going to walk through the main hall and adjoining rooms to get a better sense of the building's layout. In truth, she was also restless and needed some physical activity to ward off a feeling of lethargy and regain a heightened awareness. She positioned Chris in front of the various monitors so he could identify anyone who might look like the Kontos women. She asked Jake to walk down with her to the ground floor and identify any activities that seemed unusual for a convention.

Just as they reached the last step, a man who was accompanying a woman with dark hair had apparently eluded check-in and was seen fleeing down the hallway away from the entrance. A policeman about twenty meters away was pointing to the man, yelling, "Stop!" Jake was only a few meters from the man and started to run with Elizabeth towards the pair, when Elizabeth exclaimed to him, "Stay right where you are – this is police business!"

Jake ignored her, running close to the man, whom he grabbed from behind with a leap and wrapped his arms around the man's chest, causing him to fall to the ground. The fleeing woman stopped and had started to swing a large leather handbag at Jake's head when Elizabeth intervened, giving the woman a sharp blow to her arm, following up quickly by placing her in a hammer lock and fixing plastic handcuffs behind her back. She then handcuffed the man on the floor, who was still short of breath after being tackled by Jake.

It was immediately apparent, though, that these were not people of interest. The woman was forty-five years old, and the man was her husband. They were eventually identified as professional pickpockets, not terrorists.

Elizabeth took Jake aside. "Jake, your spontaneity is foolish, and such misguided bravado could cost you your life. This isn't an athletic event, and it's not in your area of expertise."

Jake knew she was right and began to say how sorry he was, but Elizabeth continued, "Didn't you have enough of being in harm's way last night?"

They looked into each others eyes without saying anything. Then Elizabeth conceded they were both a little on edge, uncertain about what may lie ahead and how widespread the epidemic might become.

But after instructing Jake to return to the control room, she admonished him, "Please keep your focus on infectious diseases, and let us do the police work!"

By 11:30 a.m., over 200 delegates had arrived, creating an animated scene as the central hall began to fill up. The din of the conventioneers began to rise as the hall became more crowded, and one could hear the punctuated snippets of conversation in English, Hebrew, French, German, and Russian. There was a great deal of handshaking, hugging, pats on the back, kissing, and gestures of surprise as delegates encountered one another. Intermittently, groups of two or three gathered together for a photograph, some taken with cell phones for instant messaging to family and friends at home, others with flash cameras. It was clear that many had not seen each other for several years. At fifteen-minute intervals, Elizabeth began receiving audio reports from the four snipers and four teams at the perimeter. "Nothing new," each said in turn.

The excitement of the crowd was obvious as increasing numbers of delegates greeted each other. Several men were wearing yarmulkes. A few delegates were dressed in black suits with white shirts, black brimmed hats, with ringlets of hair extending down the sides of their faces.

Several women in the Convention Centre uniform – grey skirts, green sport coats, and matching knee socks – were serving tea and biscuits to the delegates who had completed the check-in process, periodically entering the kitchen to refill their supplies. No one seemed disturbed or preoccupied with the security at the front entrance. A few commented how much the world had changed on 9/11, that nothing was the same since, and that heightened security was a part of modern life. Others argued that in fact nothing had really changed; people had simply become more aware of terrorists.

By noon Elizabeth, still feeling anxious, was wondering if the two women had abandoned their quest to harm the delegates. Maybe the women were not in London at all, not even in the U.K., she considered. Perhaps they had continued to flee across the continent. Maybe this was all an overreaction, a huge expense of time and money for MI-5, that would undoubtedly result in some embarrassment or even an official inquiry if nothing happened. Taking a deep breath, she reminded herself cautiously that it was still early. This was not the time to second guess instincts that had been honed over years at MI-5.

At 12:15 p.m. she received the four reports from the perimeter of the Convention Centre: "Nothing new." In response, Elizabeth reiterated her warning: "Keep focused and be prepared." Meanwhile, four agents fixed their eyes on the ten video screens, including one at the onsite registration book focused on newly arrived delegates.

At 12:30 p.m., the same refrain came in from the teams: "Nothing new." At 12:35 p.m., however, one of the snipers said, "Just so you know and don't get distracted, I can see a building on fire about a kilometer away. I just noticed it through my binoculars, and the first fire brigade has arrived, ma'am. It appears to be an old warehouse, and I can't see any activity in or around the building"

"Wow, that's bad luck," said Jake. He was standing behind one of the seated agents who was carefully examining the video screens. He seemed to have recaptured his focus – and was hoping for an opportunity to see something important on the convention floor in order to redeem himself in Elizabeth's mind.

Elizabeth was behind Jake, in a position to examine the entire bank of video screens, hands on hips stiffly, as though ready to run in any direction if necessary. She didn't answer immediately. Instead, her face had that look of concerned intensity he had observed on the tarmac in Belgium. Jake could imagine the traffic of ideas in her brain and the efforts to synthesize the information.

Elizabeth was indeed attempting to make sense of these two events that could in fact be related: their efforts to locate the two terrorists and the sudden occurrence of an unexpected fire in a nearby building.

"It may or may not involve luck or chance," she responded. "Something may be surfacing. I need to warn all of my people to redouble their surveillance efforts. As you physicians both know, luck implies a coincidence, and I'm not ready to concede that strange events are not linked closely. You've both shown the greater likelihood of a single explanation for seemingly haphazard events in patients and organisms. I, too, have to question everything that happens from now on."

Perhaps it was in some way an accident, thought Elizabeth. But what if it was a planned distraction? If it was a distraction, what plan did the twins have? Why a kilometer away? She knew from a review of the London's fire brigade data that twenty-five percent of building fires were the result of malicious actions. Possibly she was overreacting, but with this investigation, nothing had been straightforward.

Elizabeth said, "I'll contact the supervisors of the fire brigade at the Command Centre in Lambeth as a precaution, to let them know there may be some link to what we're working on over here." She was counting on Chris to keep looking at every face he could and report on anyone who may resemble Diana Kontos.

She reminded Jake to let her know if he noticed anything unusual with the conference delegates, anything he thought may be different from the usual registration process for a conference, any bits of conversation that might be out of place at a medical symposium, any individual who looked especially uncomfortable.

Jake left the command centre to descend to the ground floor. He walked around the main hall of the Convention Centre, reminiscing about his own talk only days earlier. The London experience presented opportunities but also posed personal threats, destabilizing his sense of who he was and creating havoc here and at home. In his mind, he was trying to make sense of the fact that an outbreak of hospital-acquired infections was the initial event foreshadowing a bioterror act using a superbug never yet seen in the world. Suddenly, he felt anxious, lost, and he searched his mind for causes that might easily be dismissed.

Jake seemed to descend into the lower corridors of his mind to a depth not easily reachable. In that eerie darkness, he sensed his body quiver with the recognition that he was terribly uncomfortable, that he had lost his way. Too much had happened too quickly, and he couldn't identify all the signposts. He longed for the familiar, but the unforgiving tide of events had swept him away from light and warmth. He needed to find the morning.

Coming out of his reverie, Jake watched the delegates arrive, moving from one small circle of colleagues to another. He imagined that all conventions were really the same. The only thing that changed was the focus of conversation. Today it was a legal discussion, or one of medical-legal concepts, particularly involving the country of Israel. Otherwise everything – the queuing for registration and badges, the collection of handout materials with bold lettering inside the delegates' knapsacks, the name of the conference location – was exactly the same as every other day.

In one corner of a small conference room speakers were reviewing details of their presentations, rehearsing their talks, going over each Powerpoint slide. There were exchanges about the flights, the increased hassles at Immigration on landing, the pros and cons of the hotels. Jake had overheard and witnessed the same behaviors only a few days earlier.

Elizabeth picked up her cell phone to call her home office, still facing the video screens. "Sir, can you find out the precise location of a warehouse fire which has just been called in to the fire brigade, about one kilometer from the Convention Centre? Once you get the address can you quickly see if there is any connection – even trivial – between the warehouse and either of the Kontos twins, Ata Atuk, or an Elaina Raskin? I need to know if this incident might be part of a larger plan being executed even as we speak."

"I'll get back in five minutes, Elizabeth."

The blaring sound of a fire brigade passing the Convention Centre towards the warehouse caused Elizabeth to feel a chill of anxiety. Suddenly, she recalled the interview with Elaina Raskin where she had learned about the warehouse near the Convention Centre to which Ata Atuk had access. This fire had nothing to do with luck.

XVIII

O n the evening before, three kilometers outside of London, the two sisters stopped at the costume store and spent an hour reviewing the three options they had considered before making their purchases. Sheepishly, Sasha began the tongue-in-cheek banter, "You know, Diana, that there is probably no more respected person on the streets of London than the English bobby."

The owner of the store, a retired bank clerk who liked to recount the stories behind the costumes, reminded the two customers of the 175-year legacy of Sir Robert Peel's Metropolitan Police. The bobbies, he said, were named in Peel's honor. He held up several uniforms for inspection, pointing to a dressing room.

"This should be perfect," said Diana, pointing to the one held in her right hand. "Our friends at the party will just love the costume," she added thankfully. She tried it on and confirmed that it fit, then donned her street clothes.

"So I will be *honored* by the citizens of London, the delegates at the Conference Centre, and any security forces when I arrive tomorrow," Diana whispered to Sasha. She said she would take the outfit she was holding.

"And I will accompany you, since the Convention Centre guides have their own uniforms and are also well respected," said Sasha. "Surely, we will have little chance of any limitations to our travel, assuming that the authorities have any idea of our whereabouts."

They thanked the owner of the shop and paid the bill and deposit with cash, saying they would return the merchandise in three days. Collecting their purchases, they placed their bags in the back seat of the car and drove off. Ten minutes later, they pulled into a petrol station and filled up the tank of the Mercedes. Sasha asked for ten liters of petrol in a plastic can "for her husband's work at home." Subsequently, they stopped briefly at a hardware store to pick up a few additional items.

Sasha suggested that a small bed and breakfast on the southside of London would be an ideal place to spend the night. "When I spoke with the owner, he said that no credit cards would be required; we can pay cash, either pounds or euros."

The three-story brick house had only four bedrooms for guests. The owner had lived there for over thirty years and had raised his family there. He had renovated the home seven years ago, when all of the children had moved out, and now he had a large living room and dining room with a modern kitchen in the back.

The twins registered under different, false names; each wore a different colored wig to help further mask their identities.

They had supper that night at a Bengali restaurant, *The Chittagong Queen*. The conversation turned unusually serious. Diana expressed her worries to Sasha, running through her list of anxieties. "What if Palestine never gets its own free state and we never get a chance to return to our mother's home, to fulfill our dream of helping to restore the county and its people's pride?"

"When the Doctor was alive, he convinced us that peace is not a possibility," said Sasha, "and the extremists on both sides see no hope."

The two sisters held each other's hands while walking back over the rain-soaked sidewalks, the result of a short-lived downpour during dinner. "It hasn't been easy," said Diana. "We've been so isolated in life." She recalled the many times that their mother had said their destiny was prescribed in 1948, when Palestine fell and when all the Palestinian families became nomads in the world. "I would not have made it and persevered without you, without your constant love," said

Diana.

There is more, thought Diana. *Most people don't understand what it has meant to me to be a twin. Growing up I suffered much the same as Sasha. We would whisper our fears to each other night after night, sharing the same bed. We wondered if the Zionists knew where we lived, knew what we thought. Would they take away our home near Athens, and would we have to run away? Sasha has always been a part of me, an essential piece. I am not whole alone but only with my sister. Her cause is mine. When we are separated, even if only for several days, I become physically and emotionally uncomfortable.*

Sometimes when they were apart, Diana would get a sudden feeling that she needed to call Sasha, that something was wrong. And when she did call, she often found she was right, and they would work through the problem. Diana recalled the day when Sasha was raped. No one needed to call and say something was wrong or that her sister was in danger. She had a disturbing sensation almost to the hour of the event. She could not pinpoint the deep corridors of her mind from which these sensations arose, but she knew they occurred and had meaning for her.

"I love you too, Diana," Sasha said, almost as if responding to Diana's unspoken monologue. "This has been our fate. Inshala. I am sure that is why God willed that our single self be cloned in our mother's womb. He wanted the two of us to seek definitive justice in the world. The symmetry of our professions, medicine and pharmacology, has also been preordained, I am sure."

They continued to hold hands even inside the lobby of the bed and breakfast and as they ascended the stairs. Once inside the room, both fell down on the king-sized bed, exhausted from days of stress, days on the run.

Thinking of her aging mother and fleeting visits from a much-loved father, Sasha suddenly felt tiny droplets slipping down her cheeks. She didn't utter a word, but the few initial tears soon became a constant flow, the result of an overwhelming flood of sadness, later staining her cheeks black, her mascara washed away by the streams of emotion.

The dam that had held back the reservoir of her true feelings for years had been breached, possibly because she was so near to achieving her goal. Humans have a huge capacity to harness the energy required to keep unpleasant truths at bay. Sasha knew that this deep sadness was usually held intact by her profession, her routine, her goals, and her determination. But there was a stiff price to pay for hiding the darkness. "It's not easy keeping secrets," she sobbed.

"Let me tell you the story of the Minotaur," said Diana, giving her sister a tender kiss, her tongue tasting the salt of Sasha's warm tears. Sasha buried her head close to the breasts of her twin, closed her eyes, and listened to her favorite myth. Diana wrapped her arms around her sister's neck lovingly. They would fall asleep entwined and exhausted.

Eating breakfast at 7:30 a.m., the two women appeared to be average tourists having a comfortable morning meal, seemingly having no worries at all, even if few words were exchanged. There were four small tables in the dining room, each with lace placemats. The owner of the bed and breakfast, a widower in his early sixties, did all of the cooking. One could hear the bacon sizzling in the frying pan, detect the earthy smell of bangers and beans, fried tomatoes, and toast. Marmite, orange juice, and tea complemented the modest fare. The owner took pride in serving his guests himself, raising his eyebrows brightly as if asking if the breakfast were excellent.

Despite several overtures from two elderly American women at a far table, neither Diana nor Sasha engaged the other couple in conversation. Instead, they spoke quietly to each other. At the end of the meal, they retired slowly from the table, nodded politely to the Americans, and returned to their room.

At 9:00 a.m., the sisters dressed in their respective costumes, put on raincoats, which they buttoned up to the top to cover all of their clothes, and paid the bill to the pleased owner. Once inside the Mercedes, each donned a new wig. Sasha fetched the designer knapsack and placed the small aerosol generator at the bottom. "Plan B," she said.

Diana had placed some of the organisms into the dispersal apparatus in their dry form when they were in Cologne. All was airtight unless a simple lever were pushed, activating a microchip that instructed the battery-run motor to begin. It could be set off by a remote trigger, which could be prompted by a cell phone. They would make the call from the car during their departure from the Convention Centre. But first they would place the aerosol machine inside the Convention Centre. Their plan called for them to arrive about 1:00 p.m., when a maximum number of registrants would be assembled in the Convention Centre. After the distraction they would create, Plan A would be set in place. The opening lecture was scheduled to begin at 2:00 p.m., so a great deal of socializing would take place in the hour before.

At 12:15 p.m., they stopped by a brick, four-story building only ten blocks from the Convention Centre. It was one of several seemingly abandoned warehouses occupying space over a two-block area. Diana emerged from the driver's side with her raincoat covering the English bobby uniform she had donned, a whistle hanging from a chain in front, and a wooden night stick at her waist. In the automobile, she left behind the high, curving black helmet with the silver badge displaying the Queen's Crown design on the front. Sasha had a raincoat over her grey woolen skirt, white blouse, green knee socks, and forest green sport coat.

On the side of the warehouse was a latch with a padlock, keeping the two twelve-foot-high, wooden sliding doors from moving. Sasha had a key, which Ata had given her a year before, saying that the warehouse belonged to the owner of the store where he worked and might be a place to hide if necessary. Two years earlier, Ata had shown the twins where he kept approximately 500,000 euros in case of emergency. After opening the lock, she pushed the door aside, allowing the pair to enter quickly. Closing the door behind them, they went to the far side of the building, slowly dispensing liquid petrol on rows of old furniture throughout the ground floor. They then went to a point about halfway down a hall and pushed a fake panel to the right, revealing ten clear baggies, each one containing large denomination bills totaling 50,000 euros. They placed the baggies into a pocketbook Diana was carrying.

They then continued the task at hand. They doused several nearby couches, then some wooden tables that were piled on each other, then bundles of old paper used to pack lamps in boxes, then the cardboard boxes. They poured petrol over a row of fabrics, some rolled-up rugs, and several cabinets containing wood polish and cleaning fluids. They still had enough petrol to create a pathway for the fire from the far end of the first room to the side entrance of the building. Close to the sliding entrance doors, they lit a match that ignited a line of petrol racing towards the bundles of paper and cardboard. The wooden boxes and furniture ten meters away were old and dry, and lit up instantaneously. Within minutes, they could see flames reaching from floor to ceiling and hear the crackling sounds of burning wood.

At first there were just a few crackling sounds and white smoke. This gave way to a fog of black and brown haze and undulating waves of heat. Then suddenly a huge fireball erupted at the far end of the ground floor and seemed to roll slowly towards the entrance door gaining size as it approached. The sisters felt the heat wash over their faces, hands, and open eyes. As visibility in the building became reduced to almost nothing, both women began to cough and retreat towards the door. "It is time to leave, hurry!" said Sasha. The twins emerged unnoticed through the doorway and reengaged the padlock. They drove from the scene just as black smoke could be seen billowing upward toward the second floor or the four-level building. They rode in the car with the windows down, letting the air blow over them, clearing the smell of fire and smoke.

"Now to the major task," said Diana as they drove from the south side to the north side of the Convention Centre. Five blocks from the centre, they parked the car in a small mews just off a side street. They removed their raincoats and placed them on the floor of the back seat. They left the Mercedes unlocked. From the boot of the car they pulled out two official orange cones, which they had purchased at the hardware store, and placed them in front of the car so no one could park too close. "We may need to leave in a hurry," said Sasha.

Diana began walking next to Sasha, who had a designer knapsack hanging over one shoulder. Both smiled pleasantly and strode confidently as they approached the Convention Centre.

As Diana and Sasha reached Kipling Street, two blocks from the centre, nearby police officers were already responding to the fire, and many convention goers were milling about outside, trying to observe what was happening. The wailing sounds of approaching fire brigades could already be heard at the Convention Centre.

Within a block of the Convention Centre, a bobby and Convention Centre guide walked by a young man cleaning a 2004 pale blue Porsche, and they paused briefly to acknowledge the car's elegant lines. The man cleaning the windows of his Porsche took notice of these beautiful women and began some small talk. But both smiled and said that they had to return to the Convention Centre. The man by the Porsche said he understood and wished them a good day. Lost in the moment, he noticed that the rag he was carrying had markedly soaked the thigh area of his trousers as he watched the women walk away.

A man in a softdrink delivery lorry across the street also noticed the two women and paused to tip his hat out of respect. He then returned to reading the tabloid.

At the Convention Centre, the twins observed that all visitors' bags were being inspected, and a team of officers was walking around the site. Some officers had drifted from their post briefly to see if help was needed with the fire nearby. Two officers walked past the twins in the opposite direction, going away from the Convention Centre to get a better view.

As the female bobby approached the entrance to the main hall in the company of the Convention Centre guide, two male officers acknowledged them with a friendly smile and waved them in. Each male officer raised his eyebrows and smiled, acknowledging that he had noticed the two attractive women. Both twins smiled back as if flirting.

The male officers mused to each other, "Perhaps after the day's assignment I could locate that bobby and see if I can strike up a conversation – or something." His colleague responded with piqued interest. "Her companion would be fine company for me."

The attractive policewoman told them, "It appears that an electrical fire was at fault at the nearby factory, and as a precaution, I've been asked to inspect the wiring at the Convention Centre. Perhaps you can find an electrician on site while I take a first look." The two male officers seemed relieved and thanked them both for their help. The comely Convention Centre guide walking next to her agreed to lead the way, as did two other bobbies returning to the main hall of the Convention Centre.

The two male bobbies opened the door to a small room housing the electrical wires and agreed to give the two women time inside to look around for any defects while they sought the help of an electrician. "It should take only five minutes," said the female bobby.

In the command centre Chris had pulled up a chair to examine two of the monitors, one of which pointed directly at the registration area. Without breaking his concentration and not turning to look at Elizabeth, he told her, "The crowd is getting quite large now. I hope we can identify anything unusual, Elizabeth. Fortunately, many of the small groups of people are stopping to converse for several minutes at a time and aren't walking about."

The twins emerged from the small room after seven minutes and then asked to inspect the nearby room. Again, they were escorted graciously. When her cell phone rang, Elizabeth had turned away from the monitor just before the camera revealed a bobby and centre guide entering the ventilation room.

Once inside, the twins locked the door and unpacked the contents of the designer knapsack with the precision of an operating theatre team that had been through the procedure hundreds of times before. When they finished, they planned to exit the ventilation room and move back to the room housing the electrical equipment. But first they made a brief detour to the kitchen.

Elizabeth was on the phone with her Chief. "Elizabeth, the warehouse belongs to a Pakistani man who had employed Ata Atuk at his store. Apparently the owner stored old furniture for antique shows there, but Mr. Atuk had been given access to the place."

"That's all I need to know, Chief. I assumed this fire is no accident! Either it's a distraction to throw us off in our surveillance or in some way an integrated part of the plan. Either way, we now can be certain that the twins are in our neighborhood. They could be coming towards the building now!"

At that moment Chris saw someone he recognized.

"Elizabeth!" shouted Chris. "I just saw her, on the ground floor!"

XIX

At 12:45 p.m, two surveillance team members at the perimeter were eager to make Elizabeth aware that some of the bobbies had come out of the Convention Centre to see if they could assist the fire brigades nearby. "Thought you ought to know," said one, "since it may create an exposure for us. At least some seem to be returning," said the man standing by a green Porsche.

On the ground floor of the Convention Centre, a furious Elizabeth contacted the local commander of the police detachment on site and demanded that the officers return immediately to their assigned posts. With both hands squarely on her hips, she leaned her head into the face of the police commander. "This shows poor discipline on their parts, Commander," she said. "I'm positive now that the twins are in London and in the centre. They have a connection to the warehouse that's burning nearby. I need all of the police officials you can spare, and I don't need your colleagues to thin out our lines of security."

Flushed with embarrassment, the commander said he had to agree. He apologized briefly and went outside the centre to admonish those who had left their posts and direct them to return inside immediately. Lining up his four lieutenants on the steps to the centre, he raised his voice in anger. "Either you know what professional police do, or I will find replacements today who do!" echoed the commander to the men leading the task force. For good measure, he then got on his cell phone to ask for four additional bobbies to be on site within five minutes. "I prefer to have four female bobbies so as not to cause too much focus on security," he said.

Elizabeth raced down to the ground floor with Chris, hoping to identify either one of the twins. Chris said he saw the face of Diana Kontos, and he thought she was wearing an outfit similar to the guides. He scanned the area near the front entrance but saw no one he recognized.

Halfway down the large hallway, a delegate from the Centers for Disease Control and Prevention in Atlanta walked over to a bobby and the woman next to her, who was obviously a Convention Centre guide. Tapping her shoulder lightly, she addressed the guide, surprised that she was apparently a volunteer at the Centre. "Haven't we met before?" asked Dr. Marian Holloway, a blonde woman about five feet seven inches tall wearing a pale grey sports coat and black skirt. "Aren't you a microbiologist from the World Health Organization who visited us at CDC and requested some of our Detroit isolates of *Staphylococcus* that are totally resistant to vancomycin? I remember being struck by your beautiful dark complexion and brown eyes when you visited us in Atlanta."

"I'm so-sorry, but you must be mis-mistaken," said Sasha firmly. She was briefly alarmed by this distraction but continued quickly. "I've never been to your CDC o-or to Atlanta, for that matter. I know no-nothing of microbiology. In fact, I'm an his-historian, and I work fo-for the Convention Centre here."

"I find that so remarkable," replied an astonished Dr. Holloway. "You look so much like her. The reason I recognize you – or thought I did – is that I recall how striking she was. Why, you even have a dimple on your right cheek, just like the person I thought you were. That's incredible!"

"You're very ki-kind, and I thank you, but as I said, you're mi-mistaken," said Sasha. Trying to sound more credible, she added, "I am in fact a-a little envious, since the life of a microbiologist mu-must be very interesting."

Then, looking at the bobby, Dr. Holloway appeared even more puzzled. "I know it's a crazy thought, but you two look like sisters."

Diana responded quickly. "In fact, other people have said this, but we are cousins only, who, some people say, resemble one another. Others have said it is amazing. Now if you will forgive us, both of us need to return to work. I hope you enjoy the conference."

Sasha and Diana walked westward from the entrance hall towards the electrical utility room, leaving in their wake a musky odor that reminded Miriam of campfire smoke. A mystified Dr. Holloway moved excitedly to a group of colleagues, addressing two other epidemiologists from CDC. "You remember the WHO doctor who asked for our vancomycin-resistant isolates at CDC?" Second-guessing herself, she said, "I think I just saw her ghost. Actually *two* ghosts, since her cousin looks so much like her. Even the voice, the dimple on the cheek, the stunning beauty – they were all present in that Convention Centre guide!"

An MI-5 agent who had been milling around the registration desk serendipitously overheard this, introduced himself, and addressed the two physicians from CDC. "Did you recognize someone who had previously sought samples of bacteria from CDC, and did I hear you say that it was highly resistant?" he asked, showing his MI-5 badge.

When the answer was "Yes," he pulled out a photograph of Dr. Kontos. Dr. Holloway said, "That's her! That's the person I just saw!"

The agent motioned to the three to remain there and immediately phoned Elizabeth with the news. "Ma'am, our people of interest may be on site. One of the delegates, a medical doctor from the U.S., ran into a person who she swears had obtained organisms from the laboratory at CDC. She identified our suspect from a photograph."

Hearing this information and the description of a beautiful, olive-skilled woman with a prominent dimple on her right cheek, Elizabeth now knew that Diana or her twin was definitely on the premises and had somehow eluded detection. She asked if the officer would escort the CDC doctors to the front entrance immediately. "No one is to leave the premises," she ordered. "Seal off all entrances immediately!" She immediately asked the two agents on each quadrant of the perimeter to converge on either side of the entrance way. Elizabeth recounted the situation to Jake and Chris and asked them to stay with her.

When the officer and three physicians arrived, Jake immediately recognized Holloway and said, "Hi, Marian. I wasn't sure you would stay here for this meeting, since you just attended the Healthcare-Associated Infections Meeting."

"Yes, Jake. I tried to see you after your talk to congratulate you, but you left too quickly. As you may recall from my previous emails, two of us at CDC will be spending several months in Israel comparing the impact of medical-legal policies of the U.S. and Israel on public health. So I took advantage of this meeting being so close in time to the infection control meeting."

"Well, I have a lot to tell you, but most importantly, who did you recognize?"

"As you know," said Dr. Holloway, "I've been tracking all of the patients in the U.S. infected with fully vancomycin-resistant *Staphylococcus aureus*. We've had many requests for samples but have released our organisms quite selectively – and only to a few well-known U.S. investigators and a few labs at The World Health Organization. Jake, I swear that I just now saw the microbiologist who called herself Dr. Julia Avorn from WHO. She's had our isolates for over a year. But the person I stopped was a Convention Centre guide walking with her cousin, a police bobby."

"Was the bobby another woman?" asked Elizabeth.

"Yes, how did you know? In fact, I know this will sound like I'm seeing double, but except for the color of her hair, I'd have thought they were sisters."

"Marian, it's a long story, and I'll fill you in later," said Jake. "We need you to help Agent Elizabeth Foster from MI-5 to identify her."

Elizabeth again summoned all perimeter team members to secure the entrance area of the Convention Centre and asked for subsequent confirmation from each that they were in their new positions. Other members of the team would be in position throughout the centre.

"Affirmative," said each team in succession.

"They are here in the building and clearly started the fire at a nearby building to create confusion at the entrance to the Convention Centre. So far, they have succeeded," shouted Elizabeth.

As she turned to review the ten video monitors, the electricity was suddenly cut off. The lights went out, and the sound of air conditioning stopped.

Elizabeth didn't know what to make of the loss of power. Was it another diversion? A signal that a huge explosion would occur, unrelated to bioterror? Was she completely fooled, and would a nuclear bomb go off, making the entire saga of bioterrorism the real diversion? She gave out a broadcast call to her agents. "No one is to leave! Round up all bobbies and all guides along the edges of the wall on the ground floor. I'm on my way."

Seven members of the control team who had assembled in the control room – two women and five men – raced ahead of Elizabeth to begin carrying out her orders.

Chris looked at Jake, who was obviously confused. "I knew you hadn't banked on this bloody imbroglio, but we'll make it, my friend."

"Thanks," Jake replied. "Let's hope this all ends well, and no one else gets hurt." Both physicians raced down the stairs following Elizabeth, ready to provide medical assistance if their services were needed.

Within seconds, flashlights blinked on. Elizabeth felt her heart pounding as she ordered the team to fan out on the ground floor. The central command team near the video screen had run out of the stairwell to search for the two fugitives.

Delegates were anxiously moving about, most beginning to drift towards large windows near the main entrance. There was no panic, just some general confusion. Many joked about what can go wrong at conventions. The large ceiling windows let in light from the bright midday sun.

Elizabeth told the team, "We've got to find those twins and arrest them immediately. One is dressed as a bobby and the other as a centre guide." As she ran down the hallway, she could see over a dozen guides moving in all directions and an equal number of bobbies also moving about frantically. *It's impossible to get a clear view of faces with all the commotion and similarity in uniforms,* she thought. "My God," she said out loud. *What incredible misfortune,* she thought, *that we at MI-5 and the twins themselves both came disguised as bobbies and Convention Centre guides. How clever it was of the twins to choose costumes that would allow them to blend in with people at the centre.* "This will be utter confusion!"

Again Elizabeth felt some anxiety, sensing the prospect of failure. What if hundreds got killed and the bioterrorists got away? She ran up to one female bobbie and turned her around abruptly by her shoulder, only to find it was not one of the twins. Not taking time to apologize, she moved to the center of the hall and accosted a guide in the same manner, again discovering she was with the wrong person. In this case, it was a member of her own team.

Frantically pushing her way through the thick crowds and moving about erratically, Elizabeth was breathing heavily as she confronted still two more bobbies and three more centre guides. None of these was a person of interest. Showing her badge each time, she apologized with a single utterance, "Sorry!" Now beginning to sweat, she moved on, buffeted by the orderly but confused convention guests. She felt alone in a crowd of over five hundred, all on a single floor in an area about one-third the size of a football field.

Finding herself at the far end of the reception hall, away from the main entrance, she used her walkie-talkie to speak again with her agents. "Stop all women with any hint of olive-colored skin from leaving. Hold them until I can get there with Dr. Chris Rose or Dr. Marian Holloway, who can identify our suspects."

She zigzagged through the crowds like a rugby player looking for an opening in a scrum, pausing in front of a Convention Centre guide. She was increasingly aggressive, pushing people aside and constantly offering gruff apologies, occasionally getting rebuffed by an irritated convention guest.

Bumping into one of her team, she asked, "Any luck finding them?" Now she was in a full sweat, wiping her forehead with the sleeve of her right arm.

"None so far, ma'am."

"Well, they can't have disappeared into thin air, and we have the entrance blocked. Let's split up and go towards the front."

Almost in unison, four MI-5 agents met near the entrance of the Convention Centre, each one appearing a little winded, frustrated, and worried.

The door to the utility room was slightly ajar, but no camera had been placed inside to view any visitors there. "They're in the utility room and have just cut off the electric supply to the Convention Centre!" Elizabeth bellowed to her colleagues.

Elizabeth instructed all her agents to examine the faces of every person attempting to leave the building. She had six agents on the inside of the first floor looking for the twins. "Go to the utility room first and look for them. Begin to examine every delegate in a systematic and orderly way."

As quickly as it had gone out, the air conditioning and lights suddenly went on. An excited agent phoned Elizabeth. "I just arrived with the engineer, and it was only the main lever to the power that was pushed off. He pushed it back, and all is restored."

Elizabeth responded, "Then the whole idea was to create momentary confusion or in some way create more distractions for us."

Out of the corner of her eye she saw two beautiful women, a bobby and a Convention Centre guide, walking into the air handling room.

At that moment the crowd seemed more relaxed. Jokes about convention hall efficiency rose, and laughter was becoming more prevalent as an increasing number of small groups decided to enjoy the biscuits and tea that were being served. It didn't make Elizabeth feel any better, but now she knew her prey were cornered, and in a few moments, the two bioterrorists would be apprehended. Her confidence rose. But that nascent confidence was misplaced.

XX

Chris alerted the medical teams outside the Convention Centre and at King's to be ready to accept casualties. Full protection gear was available at both locations – gowns, gloves, boots, and enclosed face masks – each with its own oxygen supply and filters. Emergency wagons were poised to run back and forth to the hospital Casualty Department if needed.

Jake would direct any clinical activities in terms of assessment of needs, triage, and infection control. The vials of equine botulinum antitoxin were made available in Casualty, just in case, to neutralize the bacteria's poison quickly while still circulating in the blood and before attaching to their receptors and causing paralysis.

Both physicians moved toward the main entrance of the Convention Centre as Elizabeth and her agents closed in on the electrical utility area and ventilation rooms.

Chris decided to take up a position in the hallway between the entrance and registration areas to try to spot anyone who might look like Diana. Jake was standing next to him, still attempting to identify any delegates who looked out of place. He decided that, if he did see something suspicious, he would not take any action himself but instead would call Elizabeth on his cell. He still remembered all too vividly her admonition about acting impulsively.

Bobbies walked about randomly with quick and jerking turns around the same area, each observing the other in anticipation of finding a stranger. They carefully scrutinized the faces of all guides in the same hurried manner.

Jake, who was moving around on the ground floor to see where he could be of use, suddenly found himself near the refreshment table. A delegate was asking for milk to put in his tea. Suddenly an alarm went off in Jake's brain. *The twins could have poisoned the milk!*

Jake bluntly interrupted. "Not today, sir!" *Oh my God*, he thought. *The strange fire, then the lights out and our concern about aerosols – but we may be missing the key issue! We can't find the twins, we're worried about botulism. Meanwhile, everyone is lining up for refreshments for relaxation – and botulism has been known to be transmissible by milk products!*

He signaled for Chris to join him. "Chris, we should pull the milk off the tables, quickly, before anyone gets this. We're going to need to culture the milk."

"Don't let anyone near the milk!" Chris said to the people serving refreshments. "No one! In fact, to be safe, no tea or milk for anyone at all!"

Chris phoned an obviously out-of-breath Elizabeth with the news. She dispatched two agents to prevent the release of any milk or tea and to close the kitchen.

Two more agents went to the main hall and began to shout evacuation orders, creating some apprehension among the registrants, who found themselves being escorted to exits behind the stage. Each would be checked individually on the way out.

Running at full speed, Elizabeth and two senior agents reached the door to the air handling room only to find it locked. An agent was sent to fetch a sledge hammer; he returned quickly. "Knock the door down!" Elizabeth shouted. It took five blows to open the door, but they found no one inside.

Relieved at first, they then noticed something that heightened their worries. The screen to a large air vent leading to the duct going outside of the building was on the ground. "They didn't disappear into thin air. They must have found an opening to the outside."

Elizabeth used her walkie-talkie to alert agents outside to go back to their original perimeter sites and look for two women who were escaping from the centre. She had the nauseating realization that her original order to have them leave their post was wrong. "They must have crawled through the duct; find out where it goes on the outside," she commanded. "One is dressed as a bobby and the other as a centre guide. Arrest them on sight!"

On all the streets around the Convention Centre there were bobbies and Convention Centre guides who had been ordered to leave the premises. Elizabeth's agents were stopping each other, asking for formal identifications of any women. Each had a photograph of Diana Kontos in hand. The scene grew chaotic, with plain clothes agents chasing bobbies and guides. On occasion there were bobbies and guides chasing after other bobbies and guides.

Elizabeth scanned the room for any device that could be of use to a bioterrorist, although she was not sure what it would look like. She called Chris and Jake to see if anyone looked ill. "Nothing obvious," said Jake.

Elizabeth called back to Chris, "Please come to the air handling room, and bring a containment box in case we find anything." One of the agents had grabbed a flashlight and was already moving down the ventilation shaft, looking for a device and trying to track the two fugitives.

Glancing around the room, Elizabeth saw the vent of a second air duct, this one servicing the main sections of the Convention Centre. Peering inside with her flashlight, she saw something strange: a ten-by-ten centimeter box with a battery pack on its side and an attached microturbine. But there was nothing moving, no turning parts. "Thank, God," she sighed.

Chris arrived as Elizabeth, having donned gloves, was slowly moving the apparatus out of the duct. She passed it to Chris, and he put it in the containment box and closed the lid, taped the case shut, and placed the box inside two large, red latex bags. He carried the bag to the main entrance and placed it inside a larger, air-tight containment box, thirty-by-fifteen centimeters, to be transported to a Biosafety 4 lab, the facility with the highest safety level for examining microbes at King's. "Nothing's been activated," Chris said. "And even if it is activated remotely from now on, the two containers are airtight. I won't examine the contents until they are under a proper biosafety hood."

Elizabeth looked at the two air ducts and saw a pair of scissors, but these could not cut into the ducts. She was puzzled until she saw some dark hair on the floor below a metal closet door, inside of which was a large duct leading to the outside.

"They cut their hair!" she shouted over the walkie-talkie. "Look for two dark-haired men who appear feminine. They must be nearby!" In a closet she found a bobby's helmet and jacket, green sport jacket, two wigs, and an empty designer knapsack.

Now, three blocks from the Convention Centre, two young men in dark blue suits were walking purposefully towards the mews where earlier they had parked their Mercedes Benz. Each had five plastic containers with euros stuffed in their coat pockets. As they turned into the mews, they could hear some clamor two blocks away.

They ignored the shouting behind them coming from Elizabeth and four agents who hadn't picked up on the disguises initially. Elizabeth was leading the group that was now moving swiftly after the twins. She was invigorated now that she could see the two figures just ahead of her. However, as the voices from the law enforcement team grew closer, the two women dressed as men raced for their car, turning right into the mews.

"Fortunately, we left the keys in the car," Diana said. "We'll be able to get out of here quickly."

"Okay, Diana. As Go- God wills it. But we have to avoi-avoid any cars following us."

As the pair started the Mercedes, an MI-5 agent came by in an unmarked car for Elizabeth, who quickly slid into the front passenger seat. The Mercedes raced out of the mews and away from the Convention Centre. Again short of breath, Elizabeth just pointed toward the fugitives' car. It had begun to drizzle steadily.

Finding herself southbound on the wide Milbank Road, Sasha

pressed on the accelerator, passing a red double-decker bus and barely missing two exiting passengers. Accelerating past sixty kilometers an hour, she swerved to avoid a woman pushing a baby in a dark blue pram but was still able to make a skidding right hand turn to cross the Thames over the Vauxhall Bridge. A group of four inebriated young men almost became victims of the escaping Mercedes as Sasha negotiated a sharp turn away from them and the pub from which they just exited. She made another left on Embankment, but the pursuing car was still fifty meters behind, matching her speed.

Sasha exhaled loudly, then gasped that though she did not know the area, she vowed to escape the agents chasing her. She decided to make a pattern of hard right and left turns in sequence. However, finding herself back on The Embankment, she started crying, "I'm lo-lost, Diana, and can't fi-find my way out of this. It feels like we're going in cir-circles."

"Stay calm and keep going!" said Diana. "Go back across the Thames where you can reach the area we know. We're not in a maze. God is with us and our cause."

Now pushing up the speed, Sasha drove the car up the Embankment to the Lambeth Bridge, making a left hand turn. Horseferry Road had a detour sign, so she took a quick right on Bradley then on to Smith Square to Peter Street and a left again onto Milbank. She was able to accelerate on the wider road but had to take care to avoid the debris of ongoing construction work, even though her pursuers were now only thirty meters behind her.

Both sisters had tears welling in their eyes and felt increasingly anxious and fearful. "How can they be so clo-close to us, Diana? Those monsters are gain-gaining on us."

The Mercedes was now clocking over ninety kilometers an hour. Elizabeth's agents were still only thirty meters away.

"Go sharply right, Sasha, at the next crossroads," said Diana, beginning to feel queasy. "It looks like some new building going on ahead, and we may have to travel through the construction site. This car will outperform theirs, and it's our only hope. Remember: we have our ultimate plan if we get arrested."

"Hold tightly, Diana. It will be a difficult tur-turn," said Sasha, briefly looking into the rearview mirror. She then darted behind two buildings, obscuring her car from those in close pursuit.

But the car slid onto the wet dirt road, and Sasha was losing control. The rear end was skidding first right and then left as Sasha over-corrected. Now the Mercedes was aiming towards a huge opening in the ground – the four-story deep cavern that would become the building's basement.

Swerving to avoid plunging into the deep hole and sudden death, she missed the open area by only two meters, sliding tires sending gravel and debris into the hole below. Sasha found herself speeding along the edge of a four-block area of construction. There were only dirt and gravel roads at the site, which were separated by a maze of tractors, backhoes, piles of rocks for road bedding, and stacks of steel and lumber for building. Dust billowed in the air; clouds of dirt added to their disorientation.

"Oh, I don't know which wa-way to tur-turn," said Sasha. "I'm com-completely lost."

"Keep searching," said Diana, barely able to keep her seat. Looking back, she could see the pursuing car perhaps forty meters behind. "We're beginning to get away from them - just as I told you, Sasha! We'll be okay very soon. This Mercedes can outrace them."

Now the Mercedes was sliding to the left, and Sasha found herself skidding on light gravel and wet mud. She glanced to her left to be sure to avoid some foundation blocks for a building. Turning her gaze ahead, she experienced a horrific shock: the car was now aimed directly at the opening claws of a huge earthmoving machine, heading uncontrollably toward its claws at a hundred kilometers an hour. Instinctively she braked and swerved at the same time, making a 180-degree turn. But the car was moving backwards into the earthmoving machine just as the attendant operator pushed the button to close the claw.

Diana could see the teeth of the huge metal apparatus begin to clench down onto their car and could hear the grinding sound of metal crushing metal, the shattering of glass as the gears of the claw crunched through the windows first, then the windshield, before coming to a stop.

Seeing the fugitives crash, Elizabeth immediately phoned for rescue wagons and urged caution as she and her colleagues from MI-5 stopped near the earthmoving machine. Quickly exiting the car, she sprinted to the side of the Mercedes and could see the driver was crushed inside and unconscious, arms draped flaccidly around the wheel. She and her agents yelled to the construction worker to release the claw's death grip on the fugitives. The floor of the car was invisible beneath the mangled exterior.

Within minutes the rescue team arrived, and with a Jaws of Life machine removed the driver from the car, administered CPR to Diana, and inserted an IV line before carrying her via ambulance to the hospital at King's. Elizabeth had an agent escort the ambulance to the hospital's Casualty Department.

A CT scan of the chest, abdomen and pelvis revealed that Diana had a lacerated spleen and multiple rib fractures, and she was quickly wheeled to the operating theatre for a splenectomy. She was alert but weak and lethargic on the gurney as it passed a photograph of Professor Jeffrey Allen and a notice of a memorial service for him to be held the next day. Still in some pain despite the heavy dose of narcotics that she received in Casualty, Diana was overcome by a sense of sadness. *Maybe I did love him*, she thought. *He died from my love, and on my way to death I see him again. Maybe we will visit each other in a future life.*

Dressed in complete isolation gear with gown, gloves, mask, and plastic face guard, Dr. Jonathan White, who had managed several of the victims of *Staphylococcal* infection, was the physician on call at King's for the preoperative evaluation. He asked Diana a number of medical questions in a compassionate fashion, dealing with her pain by administering narcotics. Although she recognized him, Diana registered no emotions and uttered no words. He would have to monitor her closely for infection after her surgery, he assured his anxious patient.

After the operation, Diana's vital signs were stable, though she remained connected to a ventilator for twenty-four hours to control her breathing. Despite the blood loss and initial concussion, there were no neurological signs of brain dysfunction when the breathing tube was removed, and she could easily breathe on her own. Since there was initially uncertainty about the extent of her injuries, the surgeon subsequently made a large incision starting four inches above the umbilicus down to her pubic bone. It was very painful, but she was repeatedly told by the members of the medical team how lucky she was.

No one needed to tell her that Sasha was dead. Diana knew. Since they were children, she had always known when something happened to Sasha. She spoke to no one on the medical team. Elizabeth sat quietly by the bedside each day for a couple of minutes. She introduced herself each time. She tried to interview her, but Diana kept her eyes closed and responded to nothing. Elizabeth reassured her, "I'll return after you have had time to think about this and when you're not so confused."

Diana had asked the staff earlier if she could speak to an Orthodox Greek priest, and her request was granted. The MI-5 agent assigned to the watch nodded as Father Ignatius entered the private room, having had his identification checked and body scanned with a wand to rule out any hidden weapons.

"How are you, young lady?" he inquired in Greek, while examining the patient, whose grimace indicated that she was in some pain.

"The medications give me so much nausea and vomiting, Father, that I have some distress because I try not to take the narcotics," responded Diana in Greek.

He then introduced himself, and in an effort to put Diana at ease, he talked about himself and his personal history. He recounted his childhood growing up in the outskirts of Athens. Diana visibly relaxed and smiled briefly, saying she, too, had lived there after her mother had emigrated from Lebanon and before that from Palestine. They talked quite a while regarding what it was like for her and her sister as daughters of Palestinians.

"We Greeks have sympathy for the Palestinians," he said, "perhaps more than many other nationality. But I don't always agree with them."

Looking at this comforting man, perhaps sixty years old with curly grey hair, Diana merely said, "Thank you, Father."

Then she said, "Father, I am in some difficulty with the law, related to my sympathy with the Palestinians. I cannot contact my family. I haven't seen my own father in three years. Could we pray for guidance and courage? Would you contact them?"

As he nodded his head, Diana wrote a phone number on a small piece of paper and gave it to the priest, who folded his hands around it. A tear fell from her right eye. He removed a recently ironed handkerchief from his back pocket and blotted the tear from Diana's face, then gave her the handkerchief. Father Ignatius then placed the folded paper between his sock and his inside right ankle, and began reciting a prayer in Greek. When he was finished, he said, "God be with you, Christ be with you, and your prayers will be answered." He turned, left the room, nodded thankfully at the MI-5 agent, and walked down the hallway.

Forty-eight hours after she was removed from the respirator, Diana was breathing more easily on her own, and her blood pressure was stable. Two elderly Greek nuns arrived to give her their respects, stating that Farther Ignatius had suggested the visit. They were both walking stiffly, each perhaps in their mid-seventies, both hobbling with every step. The female agent guarding the door asked permission to screen them with a wand, and when no signal was heard, politely escorted them to the hospital room. At that point, they began to recite the Rosary, and thirty minutes later they left, bidding farewell to the MI-5 agent, proceeding to hobble down the hall.

Five minutes later, the agent walked into the room to check on her ward. She became horrified at the sight of an empty bed – the first floor window open to the outside and a cord – the nun's cord! – tied to the radiator and leading over the window sill.

Recognizing that the patient was too ill to scale even one floor, she knew then that one of the nuns entering the hospital was cleverly disguised as an elderly woman and was instead young and agile. Obviously, one of the nuns that had hobbled out past her was Diana Kontos.

XXI

T he late afternoon breeze was uncommonly soft and warm as Chris served Pimms and soda in narrow glasses to the guests strolling in his garden, all celebrating their role in helping to avert a bioterrorist attack. The brilliant-green grass was manicured with sharply demarcated, serpentine edging for a radius of fifteen meters, outlining the exterior plantings of golden lilies, lavender autumn crocuses, deep red chrysanthemums, and pale green hypericum berries. In a sunny corner were magnificent tea roses blooming in warm pastel colors, and under-plantings of delphiniums.

"Well, Jake, how do you like my garden? You haven't seen it in years," said a woman with a strong tone of affection in her voice. Her dark brown hair was swept back in wide curls over both ears, and fell just above the collar of her lavender dress. Her smile was relaxed and genuine, as one might expect from a person comfortable in her own skin.

"Mary, this place says 'you' all over! It might be the most colorful and best-kept garden I've ever seen."

"You don't have to exaggerate, Jake." Grasping his arm gently, Mary Rose walked the perimeter of the garden to review the plantings with him. "I'm glad you finally made it to our home, although I wish your entire family were here with us. I miss Deb and would love to have caught up with your children. However, Chris has promised me – and said that it was your idea – that our two families will meet next year somewhere in Southern Europe for a proper vacation."

Taking a deep breath, Mary continued, "You may have heard that my biopsy showed a benign breast mass, and now I want to celebrate with trusted friends." She placed both hands on Jake's shoulders and tiptoed up to kiss his cheek.

"Chris had told me the good news amid the action at the Convention Centre," Jake replied. "As for a vacation, I did agree, and it will be a way for me to apologize to my family for my delay in getting back to the U.S. from this visit."

"I know you were a great help to Chris in dealing with this infection outbreak. He is so grateful, and we're so very sorry about your abduction and robbery. It must have been terrifying."

Jake looked directly at Mary and then peered off into the distance. "Mary, I can't begin to tell you how frightened I was – still am, actually. In fact, I've been unable to sleep through the night in the last few days.

"The American Embassy staff were efficient in their assistance in getting a new passport for me, urged along, no doubt, by a grateful MI-5 agent. As for the infections, the irony, Mary, is that the outbreak at King's was an accident, one we eventually connected to the activities of the twins. Had they succeeded, it's possible the organism might have spread throughout Israel, and soon all hospitals would have run out of available respirators to support victims who needed breathing support. But there was no guarantee that the organisms would have stopped at the border of Israeli hospitals. It could have ignited a global pandemic; in fact, among the earliest victims might have been those Palestinians whose cause the twins espoused."

"And I understand from Chris that you may have saved his life and others by quickly figuring out that the twins planned to contaminate the milk at tea time."

"Well, that wasn't so clever of me. Some of my colleagues at Stanford a few years ago wrote a paper on the possibility of terrorists' contaminating the U.S. milk supply with botulism toxin. They created a model in which 400,000 would become ill and six percent would die. But they said the death rate could be as high as sixty percent, because the paralyzed victims would outstrip the supply of mechanical ventilators. It could have been a disaster! But the twins also sought to create great terror with an aerosol. Chris believes they had also hoped to have infected patients spread the staph – in the milk or aerosol – which was programmed with genes that would tell the cell to produce botulism toxin. It might have spread widely. It was Chris who was able to understand the molecular biology of the organism early and contain the aerosol device before it was to be detonated by the twins, apparently via cell phone from their car."

Chris and Elizabeth walked across the grass to greet Mary and Jake. Elizabeth extended her hand to Mary for the introductions, then kissed Jake on the cheek and thanked him for his partnership with Chris in the investigation. She apologized for her husband's not joining them. "He's been called to assist in a court case," she lamented, "and sends his deep regrets." In reality, he had made an urgent visit to his neurologist. On two recent occasions, he had forgotten how to drive home. After five or ten minutes, he had remembered the way.

"The sad news is that we still haven't caught Diana, and I have no idea where she is," said Elizabeth. "We – or rather, I – underestimated her in the end, an error I will regret for the rest of my career if she's never caught." In the meantime, she would have agents at all airports, seaports, rail stations, and bus depots. She had requested agents in unmarked cars at border towns in Belgium and France.

"Obviously, Interpol has mounted heightened surveillance in Greece and the Middle East. The best we can do is hope for the best. It will not be easy."

Elizabeth paused for a moment, then continued, "Perhaps the story may be even more complex, more deeply rooted, than we originally thought." She then reminded them all about the Christian Palestinian, Elias Chacour, author and lecturer. She recounted sections of his book about his family that described the plight of many families of Palestine.

"Chacour's father used to recite the story for the Chacour children. He told of the building of a fortified wall on the coastal town of Akko in the 1700s by the cruel Turkish sultan, Jezzar Pasha, who wanted a wall built to defend against attacks by foreign warships. The Sultan designed secret labyrinthine escape routes through the huge stones, and had them put in place by those who were enslaved to build it. One of the workers was a Chacour forbearer. After the wall was built, however, the Sultan killed all of the builders and buried them beneath the wall. Only the Sultan remained alive with the secret. In this way, an earlier relative of Chacour is literally a part of the 'foundation' of the Middle East.

"Can you imagine the sense of belonging, the sense of rightful citizenship that some might have?" added Elizabeth.

"Apparently the twins were programmed to hate the Israelis and their supporters," said Chris. "They were indoctrinated to believe they were to be agents to avenge the wrongs done to their ancestors, and they latched onto the idea of creating a superbug as their means of exacting vengeance."

"It happened to be part of a pattern of a warped sense of values shaped and reinforced over time," Elizabeth chimed in.

Elizabeth looked at Jake briefly, tapping his forearm as though seeking his attention. She told him she had spoken to Elaina Raskin again after she left the hospital in Cologne and was extradited to a prison hospital in Brussels. Elaina recalled Ata's telling her of the twins' obsession with the myth of the Minotaur and their unusual version of the story, involving the need for disguises to avoid danger. Elizabeth assumed that somehow their knowledge of mythology provided a rationale for their hatred, further warping their vision of the world. "In a real sense," she said, "their thinking was trapped in a self-constructed labyrinth of revenge, and despite the opportunities they had in life, they could not get beyond their need to seek retribution for the ills done to their mother and grandmother. Being twins simply made it easier for the sense of hatred to grow in each of them, because they constantly fed off each other."

"Were you able to speak openly with Diana?" asked Jake.

"Regrettably, Diana never spoke about her motives, so we're left to interpret her intentions based on limited information. However, I'm not sure we'd have gained any more insight, even after months of questioning." There was a note of resignation in her voice.

"There's great irony, too, in the fate suffered by Ata Atuk," continued Elizabeth, "who could not be weaned off the respirator in the hospital in Germany." She told her listeners that by the fourth day, both eyes were severely infected with a *Staphylococcus aureus* that was poorly controlled, eventually leading to permanent blindness and a bloodstream infection. Physicians were able to control his eye and bloodstream infections, but he remained on the ventilator because of botulism and would likely require breathing support for the rest of his life. She was sure this was what the twins intended.

"A sad footnote," said Chris, "is that I was visited yesterday by Phillip Allen, Jeffrey Allen's son. He mentioned his estrangement from his dad but said that he had a male partner whom he loved dearly." Chris added that Phillip lost the love and admiration of his father after he announced that he was gay. He was quite sad and lamented the fact that he would never have another conversation with his dad, a hope he tenaciously held onto with the expectation that surely there would be a time later in life for them to come together, to be reconciled. So he was mourning not only the death of a father but also the demise of a dream of some future rapprochement.

"But some good news has come from all this tragedy," Chris continued. "With some of his inheritance, he will fund a Chair in his father's name. It won't be a Chair of Surgery; it will be the Jeffrey Allen Chair of Medical Microbiology. Phillip's partner has HIV. Although Phillip is uninfected, he's naturally hoping for a breakthrough that might cure the love of his life."

"Elizabeth," asked Jake, "what will happen to Elaina Raskin?"

"We at MI-5 had expected her to be extradited to Belgium for a trial for conspiracy to kill the twins. The Germans also want to try her for her role in activities at the illegal terrorist laboratory in Cologne, but they yielded to authorities in Brussels. However, she apparently has ties to a global Russian mafia and is now talking incessantly, obviously in an attempt to curry favor with Interpol. Apparently, the Russian mafia is a clearing house for small terrorist organizations located primarily in the Middle East. It seems that somehow Ata Atuk and the Russians got into bed together, in all likelihood driven by greed rather than ideology. They financed much of his day to day activities in hopes of securing the superbug. However, the money was important to Ata because he could use it to fund his dream of returning to Kirkuk, perhaps securing an important governmental position where he could regain some of the respect he lost decades ago."

Hearing the word 'dream', Jake moved closer to Elizabeth. "I need to tell you that I had a dream about you, the night after you rescued me."

"Did I behave myself, Jake?"

"In fact, you were *perfect*, a perfect lady."

Overhearing this conversation, Chris raised his eyebrows and smiled, recalling the London school cohort's definition of *perfection* in a woman.

Sensing some irony in Jake's statement and noting the nonverbal communication from Chris, Elizabeth whispered softly into his ear, "So I was *that* bad." Then she smiled broadly and leaned over to give Jake an affectionate kiss on the cheek. She grasped his hand with both of hers, feeling a renewed romantic interest in him. They clasped hands while facing each other, oblivious to the presence of other people. Elizabeth was wondering if she and Jake would have time alone to pursue their passion before he left, or if perhaps their romance would have to wait until he could visit again.

A few feet away, Chris was holding two glasses containing a rose-colored liquid, which he passed to Jake and Elizabeth. "Jake, here is another British tradition for you to sample, our Pimm's Number 6 Cup based on vodka." It was, in his opinion, a perfect complement for the *al fresco* luncheon. "Of course, if you want a little more thrust, I can add some Cointreau."

When everyone had been served a drink, Chris raised his glass for a toast. "To my wife Mary, who has not seen much of me recently.

Thank you for your love and patience. To my friend and colleague, Jake Evans, who always makes a difference. I reiterate that I would hunt tigers with you any day. And to our mutual colleague, Elizabeth Foster, who introduced us to the world of criminal investigation and forensics – and on a few occasions frightened the bloody hell out of us!

"Jake leaves tomorrow for America, where we hope he'll find a new sense of peace, and be able to spend more time with his family, more odds ratios, multivariate analyses, and epidemiological influences. Elizabeth, I am sure, has a desk full of new challenges and an opportunity to revisit with her family also. And I return to King's, where I hope to enjoy a week or two at a slower pace before some new microbiological issue surfaces.

"However, there is always a distinct, if remote, possibility that sometime the three of us – with full permission of our spouses – will again convene to share our collective expertise on a new adventure! Cheers."

The next day, Chris walked into his laboratory, greeted his lab staff, and thanked them profusely for all of their efforts leading up to the time the twins were captured. He had brought in a large assortment of French pastries and invited everyone to join him in the conference room to celebrate jobs well done. "We couldn't have understood the importance of this outbreak without your diligent work, your skills, and your overtime efforts," he said. "Today, I'm suggesting that you do your routine work as soon as you can and take the remaining time off."

With a flourish, he pulled the tab of his green bow tie so that both ends now hung down, and he unbuttoned the neck of his blue shirt. What he did not tell his staff was his decision to consider seriously an invitation to apply for a post at Oxford. He finally had enough in his dealings with the administrator at King's.

Cecil Barnes was meeting a group of reporters in his office. "Thank you all for taking time to join me at King's. As you know, we successfully analyzed the cases of *Staphylococcal* infection here and helped in the capture of international terrorists. As soon as I heard about the cases, I notified MI-5 because I was immediately suspicious of foul play. I instructed the director of our laboratory to keep an open mind about the outbreak, and we pinpointed the problem. Regrettably, our clinicians were unable to save all of the victims, but the crisis is over. I for one am glad my instincts were so sharp, even if I initially appeared skeptical to my colleagues. Now, do you have any questions?"

Jake settled back in his aisle seat of a Boeing 777 heading for San Francisco, musing over the events that occurred during the visit to London. He took out his laptop and began the first draft of a manuscript that he and Chris would coauthor. He typed in a rough outline: Introduction, Methods, Results, and Discussion. Then he wrote down a simple title: *Outbreak of a Designer Strain of Staphylococcus in a London Hospital.* He closed the laptop and placed it in the overhead space. He thought of Elizabeth and his dream of a sexual encounter with her. In their parting conversation they had embraced and made allusions to his 'next visit'. He then thought of Deb and his two children. Life was confusing. Peering out of the window at 10,000 meters he noted the early day's sun. Looking over the optional movies on the airline schedule, he found a title that interested him: *Lost in Translation*, starring Bill Murray.

In Palo Alto, Deborah Evans, who had planned a five-day second honeymoon with Jake at a small inn in Sausalito, was packing her clothes. Her parents had taken the children for a week, and she decided that she would go by herself since her husband had missed their wedding anniversary a few days earlier. Jake called, said he loved her, but would not plan a flight home for a few more days. She stopped on the way out of the house at the small maple table with inlaid mother of pearl on which Jake always kept his car keys. She removed her wedding rings, placing them on the table, so as to be unencumbered as she went off to contemplate the value of her marriage.

In a small village south of Athens, two men knocked on the door of a white stucco house in a cul-de-sac. A woman about sixty-five years old answered as her elderly mother in her mid-nineties looked on from a chair across the room. The two men showed their Interpol badges and asked to be allowed inside for some questioning. The agents could not help but notice a family photograph of a robust man with his wife and two stunningly beautiful women, each about twenty years old, obviously twins.

A few days after the garden party, at a public cemetery south of London, two men lowered the body of a toxicologist who had recently died at King's Hospital into a deep grave. The only visitor was an elderly Greek Orthodox priest, who, with bowed head, was reading a prayer from a small bible. He had marked the location of the prayer with a small piece of paper on which a foreign phone number was written by hand.

Parked in an unmarked car nearby with binoculars in her hands, Elizabeth Foster was watching, curious about anyone who might show up, since the story of the outbreak had been headline news over the last three days. On the cemetery road was a black limousine driven by a hired chauffeur and a man in the back seat. Both were speaking in an Arabic dialect, sometimes switching to Greek. The man in the back seat, who appeared to be about seventy years old, said he had been pleased to receive a call from a priest regarding Diana's hospitalization. He had followed the story in the international press and had taken a private plane to be here this morning, he said. He asked the driver to stop just briefly, looked over the graves, and bowed his head. He wiped the tears from his eyes with his hands, asking God to take care of his little girl. He lifted his head and summoned the driver to return to the private airport. "Let's leave here by a back entrance."

Elizabeth turned to notice the limo, lifted her camera with its telephoto lens, and began taking pictures of the man, the car, and its license plates. She picked up a walkie-talkie and announced, "He's here, gentlemen."

In a small, thirty-bed hospital in the heart of Palestine, a beautiful woman was saying that almost all of her pain was gone. Pressing on her swollen lower abdomen, Diana was smiling, happy to be pregnant. "I wonder what he'll look like," she said out loud, recalling the handsome Jeffrey Allen. *We were worlds apart,* she thought, *each relentlessly pursuing different goals in life, but we came together for a brief period to share our love. And now a magical new life emerges.*

The elderly male physician kissed her on the forehead. "What will you do when you completely recover?"

"I am not sure. Perhaps work here for a while, helping my people. Then, after a few years, maybe my son and I will travel."

ABOUT THE AUTHOR

Photo credit James A. Stygar

Richard Wenzel is a physician and former chairman of the Department of Internal Medicine at the Medical College of Virginia (VCU) in Richmond, Virginia, and like his character, Chris Evans, is an authority on infectious diseases. Dr. Wenzel draws on his medical knowledge and worldwide experience to tell a story that takes us into the ailing heart of today's political and social realities. This is his first novel.